THE
DAUGHTERS'
STORY

MURIELLE CYR

THE DAUGHTERS' STORY

A NOVEL

Baraka
Books

MONTRÉAL

© Baraka Books

ISBN 978-1-77186-182-3 pbk; 978-1-77186-186-1 epub; 978-1-77186-187-8 pdf; 978-1-77186-188-5 mobi pocket

Cover Illustration by Bruce Roberts
Book Design by Folio Infographie
Editing and proofreading: Robin Philpot, Brian Redekop

Legal Deposit, 2nd quarter 2019
Bibliothèque et Archives nationales du Québec
Library and Archives Canada

Published by Baraka Books of Montreal
6977, rue Lacroix
Montréal, Québec H4E 2V4
Telephone: 514 808-8504
info@barakabooks.com

Printed and bound in Quebec

Trade Distribution & Returns
Canada and the United States
Independent Publishers Group
1-800-888-4741 (IPG1);
orders@ipgbook.com

We acknowledge the support from the Société de développement des entreprises culturelles (SODEC) and the Government of Quebec tax credit for book publishing administered by SODEC.

Société
de développement
des entreprises
culturelles
Québec

Financé par le gouvernement du Canada
Funded by the Government of Canada   Canada

à Marie-Jeanne

CHAPTER 1

Montreal, Quebec
October 1970

Nadine quickened her step crossing Victoria Square. Everyday rush hour didn't bother her. The swarm of workers scampering to get home gave her a sense of being part of a larger movement—of being a tiny ripple in a vast ocean.

This morning was different.

A swarm of soldiers patrolled the sidewalks, long rifles slung over their shoulders. Each step she took intensified that cold feeling in her belly. The presence of the military challenged her right to walk Montreal streets. She felt like a tiny mouse scurrying across a room full of people—someone was bound to stamp on it. The morning papers advised erring on the side of caution. Arrests were imminent for anybody suspected of sympathizing with FLQ terrorists. No warrants needed. Rights and freedoms were on hold.

Her stomach clenched at the sight of three army jeeps parading down McGill Street. Armed, menacing-looking soldiers peered at the sidewalk crowd from their moving vehicles. The benches surrounding the statue of Queen Victoria in the square were empty. No one taking advantage of the late afternoon sunshine. No one flinging leftover sandwich crusts at the usual swarm of plump grey and white pigeons. She stepped off the sidewalk heading for Craig Street, stopping in her tracks to avoid colliding with a tall soldier.

Bulky and imposing in full khaki uniform, he waved her on. "No loitering, lady. Keep on moving."

He resumed his robotic policing, not bothering to glance at her as she forged her way through the heavy traffic. His job was to catch terrorists, not to ensure her safety.

She tightened her grip on her handbag. Why didn't these intruders go back to their military base? Quebec didn't need Ottawa to solve its problems. Then again… the Quebec police hadn't been doing a great job of bringing calm back in the streets. The army presence wasn't welcomed by everyone, but neither were the terrorists. To fight fear with fear seemed pointless to her.

Soldiers patrolling both sides of Beaver Hall Street scanned the cars parked along the sidewalk. An army helicopter soared above the buildings with a deafening sound. A red federal mailbox spray-painted with FLQ OUI in large white letters stood cordoned off on the corner. She hesitated before hurrying past it.

Last year's string of mailbox bombings by terrorists had put everyone on edge. People avoided using the mailboxes or crossed the street when they approached one. And now two high-profile political people had been kidnapped. First James Cross, the British trade commissioner, and five days later, Pierre Laporte, the Quebec deputy premier.

She didn't approve of the violence, yet she quite understood why the FLQ existed. Her mother, from a tightly knit Gaspé family, raised many eyebrows in the staunch Irish-Catholic family she had married into. The worst fault Nadine had been guilty of while growing up was letting her French blood surface too often.

Prime Minister Trudeau had invoked the War Measures Act in the middle of the night. City-wide arrests of FLQ sympathizers were already in full force before she headed for work. Soldiers were posted in front of government buildings. Others patrolled the streets with semi-automatic rifles. The eyes of people she crossed on the sidewalk reflected alarm at seeing Canadian soldiers circulating among them.

She passed by the statue of King Edward VII in Phillips Square and crossed Ste-Catherine Street in front of Morgan's department store. The shoppers and tourists seemed oblivious to the disturbing signs of violence a few blocks away. Streams of people scurried about their business. That's when she felt most comfortable—as a face among a sea of countless others. No one to ogle at her narrow hips, nor at the horizontal scar on her lower right thigh. The other deeper scar that slanted down from her right shoulder was well hidden beneath her turtleneck sweater. She made sure to avoid wearing anything revealing. The Grey Nuns with their dome-like garments back in her school days had drilled them well. A modest dress and a well-baked pie were the way to a man's respect. Maybe that rule worked for nuns. But she still got the occasional lewd look or suggestive comment from men passing by no matter what she wore.

Talk of the FLQ bombings often came up at Nadine's work, on the subway, and even in line-ups at the grocery store. Now the War Measures Act was about to become the main conversation piece. An invasion by their own people. Arrests of hundreds of innocent people—even the average Joe who hung the green, white and red Patriote flag on his front balcony.

She sped up. The army intrusion promised to be on everyone's mind this morning. Her notes needed to be reviewed to make sure all the important points were on the agenda, and that no one went off topic during the meeting.

The garment workers' union Nadine worked for had invited representatives from a few other Quebec trade unions in hope of getting their support in negotiating their new collective agreement. "Strength in numbers" had been her director's rallying cry at yesterday's office pep talk. If they banded together they stood a better chance of obtaining their demands. They expected a large group of like-minded people to back them up.

The director had called minutes before she left for work to inform her of a change of plans. Five of the invited representatives had been detained during this morning's mass arrests. A couple of unions had been able to send a replacement, but she'd have to contact those who could not and brief them on the proceedings. More work for her, but she had no choice if she wanted them on board.

She pulled out a chair from the conference table and settled in for a long meeting. The garment employers had refused all past negotiations. Discussions were at a standstill. A one-day strike wasn't the ideal solution, but the workers were ready to go ahead. This meant docked pay with no guarantee of compromise from the employer.

A day's wages less on the paycheques of the garment workers she represented only spelled bad news. For most of them—single mothers or one-salary families—it meant cutting the food budget or being late with the rent. All the bosses had to worry about was having a little less profit at the end of the year.

She jotted a few notes in her agenda and slipped out of her shoes. It had taken many years of attending these kinds of meetings before she could allow herself to relax like this. A far cry from that scared sixteen-year-old who had started in the garment industry twenty years earlier. She had lost touch with the shy girl she used to be. Memories of her past self still surfaced now and then, only to be pushed back to an era she had buried, if not forgotten.

The conference participants started to file in and take their places at the table. She glanced up and saw quite a few newcomers besides the familiar faces from previous meetings. The last one to walk in made her heart skip a beat. For a brief moment, she thought it was Aunt Jan's father—Papi, she used to call him, so as not to confuse him with her other Grandpa. In her little girl's heart, Papi had been her real grandfather. The one whose stories of flying canoes and the scary *loup-garou* kept her clinging to his side each time he came down from the lumber camps. The one she ran to with a scraped knee or a bleeding nose. A brown paper bag of pink Canada Mints always waited for her in the inside pocket of his jacket.

Another glance at him. If this man wasn't Papi, the resemblance was uncanny. He'd be around the same age as this man by now. His presence at the union meeting was unlikely, but not impossible. She remembered his frequent conversations with Aunt Jan at the kitchen table. They spoke often about the harsh working conditions at the logging camps. He vowed one day to help change all that. She lowered her head and pretended to read her agenda again. A few moments later, she lifted her gaze in his direction.

One sure clue will tell me if it's him.

Her eyes darted down to his hands. Her stomach tensed up.

There. It's him.

His ring finger, cut off at the knuckle.

A chainsaw accident had forced him to stay home to recuperate that winter, allowing him to visit often and to take care of personal matters. One day he had appeared with his late wife Rose's diamond wedding ring, handing it down to Janette, their only child.

She kept it with the faded photos of her mother in a rusted red and yellow tin of Vogue tobacco beneath the extra blankets in her closet. Nadine sometimes waited for the odd times her aunt was out of the house to sneak Rose's ring out of the tin. She'd press it to her chest and imagine the love Papi felt for his late wife surging straight to her own heart.

She gripped her pen and lowered her eyes. Apart from the creases around his eyes and mouth, and his thick hair now almost completely white, he was still as handsome as he was twenty years ago. Those long years of manual labour in the bush had kept him trim and robust-looking.

Why is he here? Does he recognize me?

She scanned the list of participants. Her stomach contracted.

There: Paul Brault, representative of the Forestry Workers' Cooperative.

That makes sense.

He was well past the age to fell trees. If he was attending the union meeting today, it was clear he was following his dream of improving the lot of his fellow workers—just as she was. Her beginnings in the sweatshops of Montreal's east-end garment factories hadn't been easy. She had persisted, determined to learn enough of the business to help make life a little easier for the women there.

Thinking back, heartbreak had linked her life journey to Papi. The sudden loss of his young wife to the ravages of the Spanish flu at the end of the first war had pushed him further into the isolated forests of northern Quebec. For her part, it had been the mindless piecework on the industrial sewing machines of the garment factory that had been the escape. It had taken many years to detach herself from the broken person she used to be. Papi had been a big part of who she was back then. Meeting up with him now was sure to jar her back to a place she didn't want to be. Her decision to break all ties to her past had been her lifeline and she wasn't about to let that go. It just wasn't negotiable.

Her gut reaction was to slip out of the room before he even noticed her. She'd ask the receptionist to tell her director she had taken ill. She never took time off. No one would question her. This meeting was the first of three touching on issues she was already aware of. She closed her agenda and was about to slide her chair back when Papi sat down across the table from her, three seats away.

Too late. The meeting's about to begin.

All eyes will be on me if I stand up.

If he recognized her, he was sure to go after her. A tall, broad-shouldered elderly man sat in the chair beside her. She slid her chair back far enough to block Papi's view and placed her agenda on her lap. His presence made it difficult to focus on the discussions, but when the meeting ended in an hour, she'd be able to slip out without any fanfare.

Her neighbour leaned towards the table to reach for his pen. Nadine observed Papi from the corner of her eye. He was scanning the list of participants on the sheet in front of him.

My name won't give me away.

She had stopped using her family name years back when she first applied for work at the garment factory. She didn't know what had taken hold of her. She had written her mother's maiden name instead of 'Pritchart' on her application form. At the time, she gasped when she realized what she had just done. The manager looked up at her, a puzzled look on his face. It was critical that she land a job right away before searching for a place to stay. Crossing out her own name would make her look foolish, or worse, that she was hiding something. She bit her lip and continued filling out the form. She felt no guilt in dropping the Pritchart name. They had never accepted her as their own. Too much like her mother's people—too French to live up to their standards.

Papi lifted his head and glanced around the table just as she leaned back out of view.

No problem. He only remembers me at sixteen.

Her hair was short and tapered now, a few shades lighter than the mousy brunette she had been then.

He can't know who I am.

Yet she had recognized him almost right away. She took a long breath and looked down at her agenda. If she listened to the burning pain in her heart, she'd run and embrace him. His visits with her and Aunt Jan had made her feel special, like she belonged to a real family. It was always only the three of them. Uncle Denis didn't speak a word of French. So whenever Papi showed up, he'd remember, out of the blue, a person he'd promised to look up, and off he'd go. Aunt Jan was always more relaxed and laughed more often once Uncle Denis had closed the door behind him.

Now wasn't the time to let her guard down. Cutting all contact with the Pritchart family had been her only way to protect herself from the pain. But that decision also meant hurting the only two people in that family who had ever shown her any love. Aunt Jan, who had brought her home from the hospital after the incident, and Denis' mother, Grandma Stella. The others were as good as dead to her and she had no intention of reviving them.

She had buried the link to her past a long time ago.

I can't let it resurface. Not without reliving old wounds.

Not even for Papi.

Nobody had ever mentioned the incident—at least, not in front of her. Nor had they acknowledged the sadness in Papi's eyes, or his long lapses gazing out the window while everyone went about their business. Nadine would lean against him and together they'd stare up at the clouds. He never once told her to leave him alone.

CHAPTER 2

Lisette edged her chair back from the screen of the microfilm reader, closed her eyes, and massaged her round belly. Her back ached and flashes of pain shot from her temple to the back of her neck.

Time to stop.

She pulled her glasses off and rubbed her eyes. She had spent a little over two hours this morning scouring microfilms of Catholic Church birth records at the university library. A complete waste of time. Meanwhile, her term paper for her political science class needed work.

Her date of birth and gender were all she had to work with. The name her adopted family had given her was no help. The moment her new parents scooped her out of her hospital crib, all her biological background vanished. Did she even have an identity at that age? Newborns must come into the world with some kind of foetal memory.

What did I expect to find?

An obscure reference to a red-faced infant screaming for her mother? Father unknown. Girl child given to the highest bidder. The link to that primal self had been broken long ago.

Why am I even bothering with this?

Scrutinizing old church records appeared futile. Yet an urge tugging at her heart pushed her to continue. Somewhere in that cellophane world was a clue to her origins. It wasn't a mother she was looking for. There had been plenty of those in her life, both adopted and foster. Megaflops, each one of them. The black void part of her existence, that underexposed negative of her birth, kept her searching.

Her adopted identity hadn't lasted long. At five years old her parents divorced and placed her in foster care. She had limited her search to the Montreal area, but that was another shot in the dark. She had no memory of ever leaving the city to visit other members of her adopted family. Too many unknowns for her to zero in on any reliable sources.

She let out a long breath, placing her hand on her belly. Her research had made one thing clear: unwed mothers didn't have much going for them twenty years back. Either they went to live out their pregnancy with a distant relative, or were banished to a group home away from their own family and the scrutiny of neighbours and friends. If that was her birth mother's case, the home had most likely forwarded the details of her birth to Social Services. But that they were ready to disclose any information was another matter. Quebec adoption files were harder to crack than police files. The birth mother and the child were denied any information about each other, even when the child reached adulthood.

She sensed a presence behind her and glanced back, recognizing his usual attire—tight jeans and a black T-shirt. Serge stared at the screen, and by the sound of his short, quick breathing, she assumed he must've raced up the six escalators to the reading lab again. The slow-moving stairs spooked him. Makes me feel like a sitting duck on a conveyor belt, he'd said to her. His shoulder-length black hair, sweaty and clinging to his neck and forehead, made his dark eyes appear more intense than usual.

"You're all out of breath. Are those big bad soldiers chasing you down with their guns?" She switched off the reader and smiled up at him. He was the most categorical person she knew—he liked you or completely ignored you. No grey area with him, even when it came to his clothes. If he liked a certain T-shirt, he bought six of them and wore one for every occasion.

"Not funny, Lise. It's like a damn war zone. Army tanks and trucks all over the damn place." He stood rigid beside her, fists clenched. "I'd love to throw a stick of dynamite right smack into one of them stupid jeeps and wipe the smug look off the faces of those frigging assholes."

"You sound like a comic book guerrilla fighter. Not a good model for your child. My womb might be safe and warm, but it isn't sound proof."

He fixed his eyes on her a moment and shrugged. "You might think it's crazy talk. But it still pisses me off to have them push us around like that." He flung his head back to remove the strands of hair from his face. "Let's forget all that bullshit for now." He leaned down—"Nice to see you, Lise"—and patted her belly, "and whoever you're hiding in there."

He didn't crack a smile too often, but when he did, his whole face beamed. His ability to switch in a heartbeat from one mood to another still fascinated Lisette. He always kept her on her toes. Nothing predictable about him except in the way he dressed. Moving in with him and his roomies at the end of spring break last year hadn't turned out too badly—if it wasn't for politics. Whether it was Quebec's independence, the war in Vietnam, or the shootings at Kent State University, the three of them ranted till all hours. Serge was so much sweeter to her when they were alone. Sylvie and Pierre had been good enough to allow her to stay rent-free, but it was time to move on. She and Serge were a family now and needed a place of their own.

"You're right on time, Serge. I was about to put my foot through that stupid screen."

"Find anything?"

She reached for her bag. "No trace of me anywhere. I don't know why I'm even doing this. If I do find her, I don't know if I even want to see her. I've hated her all my life, so nothing is going to change that."

"Your hormones, Lise. Guess it's like craving pickles with ice cream. Those urges will disappear once the baby comes. You won't have the luxury of goofing around in stuffy archives after that."

She looked straight at him. "Goofing around? This is authentic boring research. I suppose you've been spending your time on more worthy things."

He grinned. "Only kidding you. You have extra time on your hands, so why not? I just don't see how knowing the name of a woman who pawned you off with a complete stranger is going to make your life any easier."

She placed her hands on her hips and stretched her back. He was usually right about things. "I know my term papers are due, but I've got this neurotic urge to know. Call me obsessive all you want but I guess I just want to put a face on someone I've always hated. I did manage to get an appointment with Social Services, though. I'm glad you're here. Now I don't have to take the bus."

"Social Services? That'll put a damper on things. They're as tight-lipped as a nun's twat."

"I still want to go in case something turns up."

"No problem. I'll go with you. Just leave everything to me." He smiled and helped her up.

"No funny business, Serge."

"Don't worry. I won't do anything to embarrass you. But I promise you'll have the name you're looking for by the time we leave the office."

His eyes swept the room. "Looks like you have the reading section to yourself. Is there a back exit out of here?"

Lisette swung her bag over her shoulder. "Classes will be finished soon. The other students will be storming in here." She took a step forward, turned back and fumbled for her glasses on the tabletop to her right. "What's wrong with the front door?"

"Nothing." He pointed to the left side of the microfilm machine. "Your glasses are on the other side of that machine. I swear your eyesight is getting worse. You should get that checked."

"It's only eye strain. And I did get my eyes checked, remember?" She bit her lip and groped on the left tabletop till she found her glasses. "If I get contact lenses, I won't have to hunt for my glasses all the time." Her loss of night vision had increased after the third month of pregnancy. The eye specialist, concerned about her occasional flashes and blurred vision, had suggested corrective surgery, but not if her medical history revealed that a genetic disorder was the cause of her problem. Any medication affecting her child in any way was out of the question. She hadn't mentioned the surgery to

Serge. He'd only obsess about it if she told him. Things just might go back to normal after the baby was born.

"Contact lenses won't change things. You'd lose those too."

She turned to him. "So what's with the back exit?" He wasn't making eye contact. Something was up for sure.

The door to the microfilm room swung open and Serge jerked his head back. A student plopped down in front of one of the readers. Serge turned back, a look of relief on his face.

She stared at him, her arms crossed. "What's going on, Serge? Does it have something to do with what we talked about?"

"Talked? Is that what you call it? More like being sent to the office in grade school." He shook his head. "I'm parked out back. Saves time waiting for the elevator. Is that a crime?"

"Only if you park your car where no one can see it." She knew he still hadn't gotten over the discussion they'd had the night before. He was right. It had been more arguing than talking. He had ended up crashing on the living room couch for the first time since they started living together. But still, things had to be out in the open. The baby was due soon and she wanted everything settled before that.

He cocked his head to one side. "What's with the raised eyebrows?"

"You normally park in front of the café, so why in the back alley this time? I know that look of yours by now. You're hiding something. Tell me what's happening."

He turned on his heels and beckoned her to follow. "Let's get out of here before the crowd comes piling in here."

"Hey. We haven't—"

I hate it when he turns his back on me when we're talking.

One day he'll walk away and never come back.

He wouldn't be the first. But she wanted this one to stick around. He was her baby's father and she intended to do whatever it took to give her child a real family.

He pushed the door to the microfilm room open and was almost at the emergency exit when she caught up to him.

"So where's the logic, Serge? You've got seven flights of stairs before you hit the ground floor. Wouldn't the elevator be a better time saver?"

The doors to the elevator at the end of the hall swooshed open and Serge quickened his stride. "Let's go. We'll talk in the car." He darted down the first stairway, straddled the landing with a wide step, and dashed down the next set of stairs.

Lisette held on to the banister and took another careful step down, intent on taking the longest time possible to descend. She needed to gather her thoughts before this turned into another argument.

"Where's the damn fire?" Her voice echoed through the stairwell. He had promised her. No more banks. No more depanneurs. He was going to be a father soon. He had to find a better way. Let Sylvie and Pierre take care of getting funds. Sylvie's father was a big-shot lawyer, so she'd have no problem getting help if they got caught by the cops.

"What's keeping you, Lise? Didn't you say you had an appointment?"

She paused to look down from the side of the banister. He stood three floors below, leaning back against the outside exit with his arms crossed. She continued her slow descent. "Go on ahead if I'm too slow for you. I can take the bus."

"The bus? Don't be silly. I came all the way here to pick you up." A short silence and she heard his voice again. "Shit, Lise. Sorry about that. Take your time. It still hasn't sunk in that you're pregnant. You hardly showed the first few months and now you burst out like a watermelon. Taking all them stairs can't be good for you."

"No kidding, Einstein." How was it possible he forgot about the baby when it's all she thought about these days? "Write 'I'm going to be a daddy' on the back of your hand as a reminder. You'll just have to wait for me to drag my watermelon belly down the stairs. I'm sure in no hurry."

Going down stairs wasn't that big of a problem for her. Her doctor had told her she was in great shape for a woman going into her eighth month. Yet she sometimes caught herself exaggerating her effort to tie her shoes or get into the car, just so Serge would pay her a bit more attention. Pregnancy brought out a needy side of her. Maybe she just wanted to be sure he'd be there for her and the baby. Not like her birth mother who'd abandoned her at birth, and her unknown father who probably didn't know she even existed. It was vital to her that Serge stick around. No way was she going to allow her baby to experience what she had. A baby was a package deal, complete with a mother and a father.

She crossed the third-floor landing and stepped down. The sound of his shallow breathing reached her from below. Something was bothering him. Whatever it was, she wished he'd come clean. The message from last night's argument was clear.

Stop playing Robin Hood or I'm gone.

She had only wanted to shake him up a bit. Hard to imagine living without him. They had a baby to think about. She and Serge weren't hitched, but they were a family just the same. The baby had a right to that, and she was going to do her damn best to provide it.

She didn't see herself living on her own. She'd miss waking up nestled under his arm. And tea. He made the best cup of tea—served on a saucer too, although it rarely if ever matched the cup. They got on well enough. He was the first guy who let her be. No pressure about anything. Not even about sex. The bedroom side of things was pretty good. She had never reached orgasm, but she didn't miss something she had never experienced before. He didn't much care either. That belongs to you, he told her. I can't control any part of you, and I sure don't want to either.

Her part-time job at the depanneur didn't cover rent and food. Applying for student loans wasn't what she had planned, but she'd have to reconsider if she wanted to continue her studies. Not that she lived free at the apartment. Sylvie and Pierre had agreed to her sharing Serge's room if she took care of all the housework, including everyone's laundry. Sylvie insisted her clothes be washed and folded a certain way, but Pierre and Serge never complained.

She stepped onto the ground floor. He was still leaning back on the emergency exit door, eyes closed and arms crossed. The urge to kiss his thick black eyelashes stopped her from probing further. Had she overreacted again? Did she expect too much of him? She didn't want to fall into the same pattern as in her previous relationships. The guys had all been deadbeats. This one sure wasn't. He was kind and tender, and he'd make a great father. She was sure he'd have a good explanation. She touched his cheek and his eyes flew open.

"Sorry... I didn't think about them stairs, Lise. I'll get used to this father thing one of these days. Going out the back just seemed a safer way out."

Her chest tightened. She went to put her arms around him but sat down on the step instead. "Safer? Why? Did something happen?"

He lowered his head and stared at the floor

"You're in some kind of trouble. I just knew it."

"I told you I'd try not to do anything stupid." He rubbed the back of his neck. "Sylvie and Pit heard us arguing last night. They came to me after you left this morning and asked me to help out one last—"

"Sylvie, again. She always has to have things her way. And Pit backs up every stupid thing she says." Why did she even bother? Sylvie and Pit could do no wrong, in his eyes.

"A bit harsh, don't you think? Pit might be a little different, but—"

"Strutting around in front of people with his hand in his undies isn't normal behaviour for a grown man. And why is he always trying on her clothes?"

He laughed. "It's part of his brand. Last time I went to one of his gigs he came on stage wearing a pair of Sylvie's silk panties and a huge plastic crucifix hanging from his neck."

"How do you know they were hers? Does she parade them for you while I'm not around? Reminds me of a foster home of mine. The husband used to strip and walk around naked when his wife left. They shipped me off to another family when I snitched on him."

He sucked his breath in. "Please. Don't get clingy. Nothing kinky is going on. I've known those two since high school." He stretched his back and gazed down at her. "I know you didn't have it easy growing up, but you're a big girl now. Ease up and give people a break once in a while. Pit and Sylvie might be hard to take at times, but those kidnappings have put us all on edge. And then there's the damn army breathing down our necks. We can't just give in because Ottawa set their dogs on us. This isn't all about you, you know."

"Don't tell me." She pushed herself up and crossed her arms. "Sylvie convinced you guys to do another bank while she stayed home to polish her nails."

"No, Lise." He frowned. "Nobody is making me do anything. But the FLQ needs ammunition. Pit figures he can do one last bank, but not for a while yet. It's too risky with all those cops on our tail. I can't see him trying this with someone else. We're a good team, him and me. Don't worry, we'll come up with a safer way. Sylvie's not as shallow as you make her out to be. She gets it… about your condition… they both do."

"What gets me most about her is that she'll land on her feet no matter what. Her daddy will make sure she gets a happy ending." Her shoulders relaxed. "You're right, I have no right to judge her. I just got worried when I saw how jumpy you were."

"I promised you, didn't I?" He pressed his lips together. "To be honest, we did have something planned for today. I told them it was out of the question. Pit was a bit ticked off but he'll get over it. With armed soldiers and tanks all over the place, it makes our job a bit more difficult. Not impossible—just riskier. Stop stressing, Lise. Nobody's blaming you for the change of plans. They get where you're coming from."

She lowered herself down on the steps to tighten the laces on her running shoes. "I just want us to be a family. That doesn't seem possible right now. I can't see myself bringing our child to visit you in jail."

"Neither do I. Believe me. It's just not going to happen."

"So what's bugging you?"

He hesitated. "You're going to think I'm paranoid."

"Maybe. You can't know unless you tell me?"

"I think someone's following me."

"What do you mean?"

He stiffened and motioned her to be quiet, relaxing after a few moments. "I thought I heard someone on the stairs. You can't trust anybody."

She frowned. "I hope that doesn't include me."

"Should it?"

"Don't be stupid. What makes you think someone is tailing you?"

"The other day when I was driving the cab I noticed this black car in my rearview mirror. It followed me till I got to the client's home and it disappeared. But it showed up again a few cars behind me. The same thing happened with my next three fares. The car vanished once I dropped my fare off, and reappeared again. I thought maybe I was imagining things. The car had a tinted windshield, so I didn't get a look at the driver." He fell silent and combed his fingers through his hair. "And today on my way here—the same damn car. When I saw it in the rear-view mirror, I swerved and took a few shortcuts through the back alleys. I'm pretty sure I lost him, but I didn't want to risk parking in front of the building."

It took a while before Lisette found her words. "What did you expect, Serge? You can't go around planting bombs in mailboxes and government buildings without someone catching on to you. The big guys always get you in the end. They love it when you do something violent, that's when they can control you by arresting you."

Serge leaned back on the door and slid down, squatting on the floor in front of her. "Come on, Lise. You know I don't do any of that. My job is to help with the financing. I don't even know who picks up the money. We're just giving back to the people of Quebec what the capitalists took from them." He stared at her, a pained look in his eyes. "You knew what I was doing when you moved in with me. I thought you were with me on this."

"You might not be planting the bombs, but you're giving them the cash to do it. How is that giving back? The little guy isn't getting a cut of what you steal. All you're doing is investing in dynamite that has the potential to blow off the head of any innocent bystander. That might not be your intent, but it makes you just as guilty as the one who plants the bomb. I believe in what's behind your actions, but not the way you're going about it. I want the same thing as you for Quebec. But I can't see how bombing mailboxes and robbing banks will help anything."

"Think for a moment. We have to get the English where it hurts—in their greedy capitalist pockets like the big banks and businesses." He brushed his hair back with his fingers. "We've been trying to get them to listen for a hundred years. Nothing gets through to them. What do you want us do, Lise?"

"Demonstrations, protests—become political bulldogs. Focus on our language. That's how they got the upper hand in the first place. They forced everybody to speak English and made us second-class citizens. Only the Church, the farmers, and the poor speak French. When you don't speak the language of your ancestors, you lose your soul. That's how they win. You lose all connection to your past and end up wanting to be like them."

"Yes Prof... This sounds like a political science class. We don't have another hundred years. If we don't act right now, our great grandchildren will be singing the same song as you are today. Einstein even said it—nothing happens if nothing moves."

"At least my way doesn't involve blowing up the ordinary Joe."

"Hey, hold on there. I had nothing to do with that." He pulled himself up and looked her in the eye. "Accidents happen all the time. Nobody planned for anyone to die. I hope you believe at least that."

Lisette reached up for his hand. "I know they were accidents, Serge. But when terrorist acts happen, people get hurt. You weren't at the crime scene, but it doesn't mean you have no responsibility in all this. You're a facilitator, and that's more than enough reason for them to arrest you. I'm sure you're under surveillance. The city is crawling with cops and soldiers with their noses to the ground. You don't have to be a *bona fide* member of the FLQ for the cops to go after you."

"No way. We're careful." He paused. "Unless somebody ratted on me."

Lisette bit her lip and fell silent. A recurrent worry had taken over her after the James Cross kidnapping. Pierre Laporte's abduction followed shortly after. Her unease now turned to alarm each time she saw Serge go out with Pit. She asked no questions and they kept her in the dark about their activities.

"You've got to keep a low profile, Serge. They've only just slammed us with the War Measures Act and over two hundred people have already been arrested. They'll pick up anyone that speaks up for the FLQ. Even members of the Parti Québécois are being picked up. You have to think of our child."

"Bloody fascists." His jaw clenched. "I'd love to sneak up on them while they're sleeping and put a stick of dynamite up their ass."

She grabbed the metal railing and pulled herself up. "Talking like that will get you thrown in jail. Each time you leave the apartment I figure you'll never come back. You've got to lay low. I don't want to lose you over this. When this is all over, nobody's going to call you a hero."

"Get serious, Lise. I'm not trying out for a stupid medal." He pushed the door open a crack. "Time to get out of here. We'll talk in the car. Let's pick up hot dogs on the way home from your appointment."

Lisette stepped forward but he reached back to stop her. "Wait here. It's better they don't see us together. If there's no sign of that car, I'll honk for you to come out."

CHAPTER 3

Nadine bolted the door to her second-floor apartment, kicked off her pumps, and dropped her purse and briefcase on the floor. Her brief stay at this morning's meeting had been a complete waste of time. She had taken zero notes and had no recommendations to bring back to the workers. She'd have to shape up for tomorrow's wrap-up meeting. The workers depended on her advice on how to proceed. She couldn't let them down, especially when their livelihood was on the line.

Papi's presence occupied her thoughts the whole time she sat at the meeting. Each time the person beside her leaned forward, Papi came into full view across the table and she'd steal a glance in his direction. If Papi was aware of this, he never let on, jotting down copious notes the entire time. Instead of following his example, she spent her time decorating her agenda with sad faces and stick figures. Her doodling had triggered a happy memory of her eighth birthday, sitting on the linoleum floor with the new crayons and colouring book he had just brought her. A steady eye on her colouring and attentive to every word coming from Aunt Jan and Papi at the kitchen table.

She had jammed her agenda into her briefcase as soon as the director closed the meeting. Most of the participants had gotten up from the table before she slid her chair back and weaved her way through the group. Glad to see the elevator door was still open, she squeezed into the already crowded space. Papi hadn't approached her, which must mean he hadn't recognized her.

Tomorrow's all-day meeting was an important one, ending with a final vote to decide on the strike. Negotiations promised to drag on. It was a tug of war between poor workers and rich bosses. If the workers gained anything, it would be minimal. Big bosses came out winning no matter what concessions they made. That might involve a lot more meetings to come. If Papi was still on tomorrow's list of participants, she'd better prepare herself to come face to face with him. The workers were counting on her report. Disappointing them wasn't going to happen.

Years of experience slaving on the shop floor of women's clothing factories had made her sensitive to the pressing needs and issues of the garment workers. Fluent in both French and English, she stood her ground in the male-dominated meetings, and conceded that her English upbringing with the Pritcharts had allowed her some benefits. She spoke French with the workers, making it possible for them to follow the bargaining process. Sending a representative that spoke only English was useless to them.

Her work wasn't limited to attending union meetings. Studying the employer's policies and settling grievances took up a good part of her time. If she missed the important meeting tomorrow, she'd be letting the workers down. She'd have to be there whether Papi attended or not. If the representatives who were arrested this morning were released right away, he might not have to come back. If he did, she'd have to sit as far away from him as possible. It'd be hard not to listen to her heart and walk up to him for news of Aunt Jan and Grandma Stella. Just thinking of them brought back her old self and the wounds that came with it. Did she even have the right to ask about them after neglecting them all this time? Papi just might decide to ignore her if she ever decided to approach him.

She flopped down into her armchair, leaned her head back, and waited for the onslaught. It wasn't long in coming. A short meow. A loud crash on the wooden floor and her orange tabby plumped down into her lap.

"Bad cat. What did you do this time?" She stroked him as she surveyed the floor. "Ah, Peaches. Look at the mess you've made. Bad, bad cat. Try to stay out of trouble while I clean up."

Peaches had knocked down the wooden document box from the top shelf of the pine hutch beside the couch. The lid had broken off, scattering all her important papers on the floor around her: lease, insurance policy, birth certificate, tax forms. She gathered them up and was about to reach for the broken lid when she spotted a man's black leather wallet sticking out from beneath the skirt of her armchair. Maman's old wallet, tucked and forgotten years ago in the bottom of her wooden box.

Her mother, Claire, smiling, tall and blond, had tossed her the wallet while she was playing with her dolls under the cover of the kitchen table. This old man's wallet, she'd said, squatting down to tousle Nadine's tight curls, was my ticket to the big city lights.

She reached under the armchair and pulled the wallet towards her. The cool smoothness of the soft leather dredged up another memory. Painful, even now. How determined she had been as a child to discover any hidden flaps or secret pockets in the silk lining of the square flat wallet. Anything that might hold clues to her mother's life before 'the incident,' as everyone called it. The muscles of her throat contracted and she swallowed hard. No one ever mentioned Claire's name after that. In her little girl's mind, her mother had taken cover somewhere in a mysterious crevice of the wallet.

She had kept it all these years, enclosing under the inner folds all that she held sacred. She opened it and pulled out the two black and white pictures Aunt Jan had given her when she was old enough. One was a high school picture of herself, shoulder-length wavy curls that Aunt Jan had put in tight rollers the night before. Unsmiling. Round-collared white blouse and navy blue cardigan imposed by the Nuns. A fragile look of not belonging.

The other picture, folded in half, showed Claire on one side. Glamorous with her long blond hair flowing from a soft turban hat, staring straight at the camera, sensuous mouth open as if to speak. Or was she singing? She loved loud cabarets and knew the words of all the popular jazz songs she heard on the radio.

On the reverse side was a picture of John, her father, a handsome boyish look with pensive eyes and hair slicked back from his forehead. Looking away from the camera. Was it Claire he was staring at? Aunt Jan claimed he had eyes only for her. Nadine had always kept his face hidden from view in the dark folds of the wallet.

She snapped open the coin pocket and pulled out a small plastic ID bracelet. She had discovered it on the bureau beside her bed alongside her towel and glass of water. The nurse had no doubt been in a hurry to fill out the hospital documents and forgotten all about it. Pritchart. The first name left blank. The date of birth and the hospital ID number. She pressed the tiny bracelet to her heart and placed it back into the coin pocket, slipping the wallet under the papers in the wooden box.

Peaches came into view batting a small object across the floor and pouncing after it. Nadine stretched her arm out. "What do you have there, my pesky cat?" A twinge of sadness darted through her chest at the sight of the gold wedding ring. It must've dropped out when the box crashed to the floor. She scooped it up and stuffed it back in with the documents.

She got up, slumped down on the couch and pulled her knees to her chest. Adherence to her daily routines of work and home kept her sane, saving her from dwelling on the past and feeling guilty about things. Peaches jumped onto her shoulder and she pulled him down on her lap. The day had turned out to be a series of intrusions. First, the army took over the streets. Papi appeared from nowhere. And a reminder of her past came crashing down on the floor by her feet. Was this a sign? Ottawa sending the army was a major disturbance, yet it was the War Measures Act that had brought Papi back to her.

As far as she knew, Papi still lived a good distance downstream in Saint-Roch, just below Quebec City. Maybe he had driven back home after the meeting. The pit of her stomach felt empty. Not much chance of ever seeing him again. So what if she had eased up a bit on her stubborn resolve? Papi had nothing to do with the Pritchart family. Talking to him wouldn't have caused anybody harm. But he was Aunt Jan's father, so he was bound to tell her he had run into her. Chances were Aunt Jan had forgotten about her by now. Better she leave things as they were and not open old wounds.

The Pritchart family lived on the opposite side of Montreal from her. They rarely ventured outside their Verdun neighbourhood, so running into them wasn't likely to happen. She had only met up with Uncle Peter once in the twenty years since she had left home. The encounter had left a bad taste in her mouth, erasing any idea she had entertained of ever contacting Aunt Jan and Grandma Stella again.

She glanced down at the broken box on the floor and got up to place it back on the shelf. It seemed strange that on the same day Papi had appeared, the only connection to her past would burst open in front of her like that. What did this all mean? A sign that she give up her dream? The agent from Social Services had warned her not to get her hopes up too high.

She sat back down on the couch and Peaches pounced on her lap again, digging his claws into her thighs. Nadine pulled the cat closer, leaned back and closed her eyes. It was quite possible that Papi had recognized her and hadn't wanted to let on. She'd sure deserve the snub. The Pritcharts must've been happy to see her gone back then. But not Aunt Jan. She must've been worried sick when she never went back.

She was nudging the cat off her lap when there she heard a knock at the door.

CHAPTER 4

Lisette and Serge climbed the stairs to the second floor of the Social Services building about an hour before lunch time. He took hold of her arm before entering the reception of the archives department.

"Keep a Kleenex in your hand so they'll think you have a cold or something." He lowered his voice. "You know they're not about to give you the information you need, but there isn't only one way to skin a cat. Trust me, we'll get what we're looking for in the end. So keep it simple. Ask a few basic questions to get things rolling and watch for my cue. When I nudge your foot, start coughing. We'll be out of here in no time." He tossed his hair back. "Right, I almost forgot—" He reached into the inside pocket of his jacket and pulled out a wedding band. "Put this on your ring finger."

She smiled and slipped it on. "Is this from a box of Cracker Jack?"

"It comes in handy when I go watch Pit sing at bars. Keeps the girls away."

Her eyes narrowed. "I don't imagine you flash it very often."

He tugged the door open and followed her into the office.

A grey-haired woman with dark-rimmed glasses sat behind a wooden desk leafing through the pages of a file. Tall metal cabinets lined both sides of the tiny windowless office. An IBM electric type-writer and a black rotary telephone sat on a narrow table running perpendicular to her desk. An open door on the far wall led to a hallway where more office doors could be seen. She raised her head and nodded at them when they entered.

"Lisette Laflamme?" She gave Serge a puzzled look.

"Husband." Serge gave her his best grin.

The woman motioned for them to sit down on the two black vinyl chairs in front of her desk.

"My name is Mme Beaubien. I'll do my best to help you, but as I explained on the phone, we have strict rules about the information we can give out. Quebec keeps adoption records sealed for the full duration of the biological mother's life. Only general unidentifying details of the birth are available when requested by a mature adoptee. We are under a legal obligation to protect the privacy of the biological mother at all times. However, if she agrees to release information to the adoptee, we follow a different approach." She turned to Lisette. "I'm going to need a picture ID to proceed." She pulled a form from the file in front of her. "You also have to sign this Request for Information form."

Lisette pulled out the Kleenex from her purse and pretended to blow her nose while she groped for her university ID card. "So what happens after the mother agrees to release her information?

"She has to drop by to sign another form before we contact the person making the request. Are you taking anything for that cold?" The woman folded her hands on top of her desk and waited.

"Allergies." Serge patted Lisette's knee. "Plus she can't medicate in her condition. That's one of the reasons why it's so important for us to have Lisette's medical history. We might need it if our baby has any health problems. So how long does it normally take before you contact us after the form is signed?"

Lisette placed her ID card on the desk, scribbled her name on the form and forced a sneeze. She glanced at Serge. Noticing how sharp he was at coming up with answers, a slight tenseness settled on her shoulders. They hadn't discussed any of this beforehand. He was making it all up as he went along, as if they were playing some kind of game. This was a side of him she hadn't seen before. He sat straight in his chair, his eyes blazing. Challenged, waiting to deflect Mme Beaubien's next words.

"We get back to you as soon as the birth mother gives us permission. If the mother's permission to disclose is already in her file, it happens fast enough. If we can't contact the mother, we don't proceed with the request." The woman checked Lisette's ID card, pushed her chair back and brought the file she had on her desk onto her lap. "Is there anything specific you want to know?" She smiled at Lisette. "While we're limited with what we can disclose, we still do our best to help."

My mother's name for a start, and how I can contact her, Lisette almost blurted out, but settled for, "Any complications with the birth?"

"You must be getting a little nervous about the baby coming." Mme Beaubien studied Lisette, a thoughtful look on her face. "Things were different when your mother gave birth. Doctors didn't want women to suffer the actual birthing, so they used gas to sedate them. It was easier on everybody if the mother remained calm. Of course, that meant the mothers didn't take an active part in the birth. Sometimes"—she paused to read something in the file—"the baby was already given up for adoption by the time the mother woke up." She fell silent for a moment as she read, then lifted her eyes. "No complications noted here. Normal delivery. You were a healthy eight-pound girl. There's no mention of the mother having any health problems at the time."

"You mean my mother went to sleep and woke up when everything was all over. Like waking from a bad dream. Did she spend any time with me at all... or was I handed over to a stranger as soon as I came into the world?"

Mme Beaubien hesitated before answering. "I'm afraid unwed mothers didn't have much say in the matter twenty years ago. The women entering maternity homes understood they'd be giving up their child. The homes run by religious groups made them feel almost like criminals for being pregnant outside of wedlock. Their families wanted them hidden from view until the baby was born."

"Still... didn't they have to consent to the adoption?"

The woman nodded. "If the mother was past eighteen years of age." She flipped a page in the file, stopped to read and looked up. "In your case, your biological mother was sixteen. A guardian or a member of her immediate family had to sign the consent form."

Lisette wrapped her arms around her stomach and fidgeted in her seat. "Or she signed it herself."

"It's possible, but—"

"They didn't throw that form out, did they?" Lisette straightened, grasping the sides of her chair. "It'd be kept in the file?" For some reason that detail seemed important to her.

Serge nudged her with his foot.

"I'm sorry." Mme Beaubien folded her hands together on her lap. "Again, that's privileged information. Please try to understand our position. Our mission is to make any possible reunion favourable for both parties. If we disclose a decision made by the mother that the adoptee later disagrees with, this could jeopardize their relationship. Is there something more specific you'd like to know?"

"Well then... " A knot formed in Lisette's throat. The meeting seemed to be getting nowhere. "How about visitors? Did anybody visit her while she was at the home?"

"That wasn't noted. Most of the homes discouraged visitors. The girls had no contact with the outside world. They entered the home three months prior to their due date and were more or less treated like servants. Homes like the *Miséricorde* here in Montreal forced the mothers to stay and work six months after the baby was born. It was a way for the women to pay off their medical bills and adoption fees before they left." She checked in the file again. "I believe that's where you were born." She paused. "The nuns had good intentions, but they didn't believe in giving unwed mothers an easy time."

"But what happened to them after they—"

Serge slid his foot over and nudged her a little harder this time. She hesitated a moment on whether to follow his cue, then coughed, pretending to blow her nose again.

"I know you can't tell me much, Mme Beaubien. But can you at least say where she was from?"

Serge squirmed in his seat.

Mme Beaubien gave a quick glance down to the front of the file. "She gave a Verdun address, but whether she went back there after the birth isn't indicated. Most families refused to take them back and the girls had to fend for themselves."

"Did she give me a name?"

"I can't disclose that information. In any case, the adoptive parents always rename the child."

"I know it's a minor detail—" Lisette dug her fingers into the side of her purse—"but it's important for me to know." She paused. "What did she look like? Or is that information classified too?"

Mme Beaubien closed the file, removed her glasses, and gave Lisette a sympathetic look. "These meetings are never easy, dear. There's nothing I'd like better than to see you reunited with your biological mother. People think the reunion will be a joyful occasion and that bonding is automatic. But it doesn't always happen that way. My job is to protect the mother's privacy as well as protect the adoptee from a possible negative reunion."

"I understand what your job is, and that there's certain things you're not allowed to tell me." She swallowed hard and drew in a long breath. "But I still have a right to know what my mother looked like. It's not like I'll recognize her on the street because you've told me she used to have red hair, green eyes and was tall and skinny. The description you have is twenty years old. She's had plenty of time to dye her hair and gain forty pounds. Don't worry about me being rejected. Believe me. I can deal with it. I don't need all this bureaucratic protection."

A wave of heat surged through her body. She tugged at her shirt, dampened with sweat and clinging to the roundness of her belly. Why was she being so emotional? Were all those details necessary? Not that this information belonged to her. Her mother had mortgaged her right to know with the adoption papers.

Serge started fidgeting again. She was aware of his intention to cut the interview short, but the questions she was asking had troubled her most of her life. This visit might not give her all the answers she hoped for, but she'd leave with some kind of image of where she came from.

A short tense pause. No one spoke. Mme Beaubien stared down at her file. Sounds of the distant whir of typewriters, telephones ringing and subdued voices floated from offices down the hallway.

The burning twinge in Lisette's chest and the mad thumping in her heart didn't belong here. This was a place of paper memories and recorded facts—not emotions. They only told her what her mother did, not how she felt. There were no answers for her here. She was about to push herself up when the woman glanced up.

"Your mother belonged to an Irish-Catholic family. She was five months shy of completing high school when she entered *Miséricorde*. She measured 5'10, which was considered tall for a woman. Weighed 150 lbs. Don't forget she was six months pregnant at the time. Brown eyes and light brown hair—"

Serge laughed. "Sounds a lot like you, Lise."

The woman continued. "She had a scar on her upper right thigh and another one near her left shoulder." She slapped the file closed.

"That's about all the information I can disclose. Anything else will have to be obtained from the biological mother."

"Scars. From what?"

Mme Beaubien adjusted her glasses. "No details noted."

Serge pressed down on Lisette's foot and she broke out in a coughing fit, bending forward and grasping her neck. He reached over to slap her back. "Water, please. She's having one of her allergy attacks. She needs water, now."

The woman got up and turned on her heels. As soon as she disappeared through the doorway, Serge sprang to her desk, flipped the file open and scanned it.

They heard the sharp clicking of Mme Beaubien's heels on the ceramic tiles soon after.

He slammed the file closed and dropped back down in his seat just as the woman appeared with a glass of water. Lisette continued coughing. He grabbed the glass, handing it to Lisette, who gulped most of it down before straightening herself up. She handed the glass back, thanked the woman and headed towards the exit with Serge.

"Take care of yourself, young lady." Mme Beaubien picked up the documents and went to the filing cabinets.

Serge closed the door behind him and led Lisette towards the elevators. "I thought you were going to go on forever with your damn questions."

"And you were being a real ass." She gave him a hard look. "I came here wanting answers and all you wanted to do was leave right away. At one point I almost asked you to wait outside. The woman was doing her best to be helpful."

"But she didn't give you what you wanted, did she?"

"I still came out with a clearer picture of my mother. I didn't get the medical history, but she wasn't obliged to give me all those details. It's a good thing I didn't know about your plan beforehand. I figured the coughing thing was to cut the interview short. Now I feel like we tricked the poor woman."

He grinned and guided her towards the stairs. "I'm pretty sure if we had placed a few bucks on the desk in front of her, she would've spilled."

"Don't bet on that. You're so damn cynical at times." She looked at him. "So, did you manage to catch my mother's name?"

"Not a problem. I was about to get your father's name but the old bag came back too fast. In any case, it probably said he was unknown."

"So? What's my mother called?"

"Nadine Pritchart." He grinned at her. "An English name. Looks like your colours are starting to show. Funny how you don't approve of the trickery, but you're not against taking advantage of the spoils. I'm giving you something you want and you want me to hand it over for free. You're a real capitalist."

They walked down the two flights of stairs. "Don't be an idiot, Serge. You're starting to sound like Sylvie and Pierre. I'll start phoning the Pritcharts in the Montreal phone book when we get home. There can't be that many of them."

"If that doesn't help, I can do a bit of digging myself."

"What do you mean?"

"Remember I told you about my asshole uncle who runs that investigative agency. He fired me when he recognized my picture in the papers. A few of us were pushing a cop car over during a protest."

"Yeah, so?"

"Guess what? I still have the access codes to his data banks." He grinned. "Two years working for him gave me a lot of experience on how to find people. Just give me a name and I'll locate them within 24 hours. Maybe I can help you out with your research. If she's on the radar, I have a good chance of finding her. An address and a date of birth would've helped. So far we know she was born sometime in 1934—that's if she was sixteen when she gave birth like that woman said. But if no social insurance number is attached to that name, it'll be a bitch. First things first, let's stop at that hot dog place near the apartment."

Lisette hung up the phone just as Serge walked back in.

He had scooped up their greasy lunch wrappers earlier after listening to Sylvie complain about the nauseous smell of hot dogs and French fries and dumped them in the outside garbage bin before driving to the depanneur for bread and milk.

He locked the door, kicked off his runners and went to place the groceries in the fridge before dropping down on the sofa beside Lisette.

"That'll clear the air." He winked. "Who was on the phone?"

She beamed at him. "You won't believe—"

"Don't tell me the line is finally free?" Sylvie flicked her long brown hair back and strutted into the living room, a coffee mug in one hand and a magazine in the other. "Pit must be real pissed he can't get through. What if he's in trouble and can't reach me?"

She placed her coffee mug and the magazine, open at the page she'd been reading, on the coffee table. She leaned down to yank the phone line from the wall jack behind the sofa. "I'll plug this in my room. That'll free the line until I hear from him." She stomped back down the hallway to her bedroom, phone in one hand and coffee mug in the other.

Serge and Lisette exchanged glances.

She inhaled and held it a moment before letting it out. "She's been real bitchy for the last couple of days. If I don't get some fresh air soon I'll clock her one."

"She's just feeling the pressure." He grimaced. "The party's about to make a big move but there's no funds to get things off the ground. If they sit around too long, they'll lose momentum." He reached over and took her hand. "It's got nothing to do with you, Lise. That last kidnapping has got everyone freaked out."

"So why don't they just let the guy go? It's not as if anybody is getting any points for that one. Isn't one hostage enough?"

"You don't know what you're talking about. Negotiations are going on as we speak. Letting him go would defeat the purpose. They'd look like they didn't know what they were doing."

She cocked her head at him. "And you figure they do?"

"Each FLQ cell might look like they're working on their own, but don't let that fool you. They operate from different locations with their own group of guys, but they still coordinate. That's what gives them the advantage. Nobody from the outside can figure out where they're going to strike next."

"But where's the coherence? Each cell is doing its own thing. One kidnaps a British diplomat and asks for safe conduct to Cuba." She pulled her glasses down and peered over the rims at him. "And another group kidnaps one of our own Quebec ministers, threatens to finish him off, but keeps on extending the date. Is that group going to ask for safe conduct to another militant country too? How is all this advancing anything? Hiding out on a sunny island beach isn't going to help fight for an independent Quebec."

He raised a finger to his lip. "Keep it down. Sylvie gets mad when you talk like that. Her and Pierre already think you're not involved enough. They're pretty paranoid about moles. The fascist police already know too much as it is."

She raised her middle finger towards Sylvie's door. "Screw the two of them. I do enough. I go to all the damn demonstrations and I put up as many posters as she does."

"Time to change the subject, Lise. Your hormones must be pushing too many buttons." He leaned forward with his elbows on his knees. "Hey, check this out." He picked up the open magazine Sylvie had left on the coffee table.

"What now?" She edged closer to him and scanned the title of the article: "Unclaimed Accounts Waiting to be Discovered." She glanced back up at him. "What's the big deal?"

"I know this might be a bit far-fetched, but what if we discover someone's left us a huge amount of dough? All we have to do is look for our name on the lists." He cracked a smile. "It won't hurt to try it out."

"Maybe you have a chance." She gave him a slight shove with her shoulder. "There still might be an old aunt or uncle who might leave you something. You've got a proper family. That rules me out."

"You'll have to keep searching. Something will pop up." He continued reading the article.

Lisette sat up straight. "Wait. That's what I was about to tell you before. I had time to call all the Pritcharts listed in the phone book while you were out. There wasn't that many, so it didn't take long. I got someone on the sixth call. Stella Pritchart. And she said she'd like to see me." She checked her watch. "It's only two o'clock, and I'm working this weekend, so this afternoon is a perfect time to visit." She beamed up at him. "Could you give me a lift? I promise it won't take long."

"Sure. Why not?" He slapped the magazine down. "Nothing else is happening. Let's get going."

"Thanks, Serge. I didn't have the energy for a long bus ride." She stood up and reached for her purse.

"That list idea of yours might be a good way to get the funding we need." Sylvie leaned against her bedroom door jamb, staring at them. "Check my name out, and Pit's too while you're at it."

Serge laughed. "It's just a thought, Sylvie. Less risky than what we're doing."

Lisette took his arm. "Let's get going. I need some fresh air. And I don't want that woman to forget about me. She sounded a little confused on the phone."

He nodded at Sylvie before closing the door. She raised her eyebrows at him and turned back to her bedroom.

CHAPTER 5

Nadine eased the door open without unlocking the chain. Her heart skipped a beat when she saw who was standing there.

They stared at each other in silence. Besides the lines around his eyes and mouth, he still stood tall like a mountain in front of her, just as he always had. Her stomach cramped and her fingers tightened around the doorknob. She held in her breath, trying to hold back the tears.

How did he find her? The office didn't usually give out personal information. She tried to speak but the words stuck in her throat. She had often fantasized about one day meeting up with him or Aunt Jan. Along with Grandma Stella, they were the chink in her resolve to obliterate her past. Only the flimsy chain of the lock separated them now. She couldn't pretend she didn't know him and shut the door in his face—the Pritcharts maybe, but not Papi, not Aunt Jan, and never Grandma Stella. Linked to the past she wanted to forget, they were still too close to her heart to cast away.

Here he stood. Papi. Alive in front of her. Smelling of the pine woods he had lived in a good part of his life.

"Nadine?" His voice shook, his hand in a fist by his side.

She needed to say something—anything to help push down the burning in her throat. But no words came to her.

"I... asked the receptionist. I told her I was... family... your grandfather. Hope you're not offended. But she only agreed to take my business card to give to you in the morning. A pleasant girl—only doing her job. From that window beside her desk we can see everybody walking out of the building from the ground floor. I spotted which direction you took and grabbed the next elevator down. A tall

44

slim woman in a bright red sweater isn't too hard to follow. Especially when she stops to inspect the displays of all the shoe stores along the way." He lowered his gaze. "If you want me to go I—"

She unlatched the chain. "No... please... come in Papi."

His eyes lit up. "It's been a long time since someone's called me that."

It was out of her hands now. He had come to her. She hadn't been courageous enough to approach him. To deny him was to also deny the emptiness in her heart. She motioned him to follow and headed towards the kitchen area.

He pulled a chair out from the kitchen table, sat down and looked at her, hesitant. "Excuse my barging in like this. I tried to control myself. It was like a dream. I had to know. I was sitting in that small lounge beside the elevators just before the meeting started. Then I saw you. The way your shoulders slump a little. That walk of yours—short quick steps like you want to pass by unnoticed. But I wanted to be sure before I approached you. It wouldn't be the first time I made a mistake like that. I felt you looking at me at the conference, but I didn't want to look back in case I was just imagining things. At my age, the mind sometimes plays tricks and the memories push reality aside."

Nadine made for the stove. Words spilled out of him without effort while the burning lump in her throat blocked all hers from escaping.

"I'll be driving back as soon as I leave here. I've got to check out a couple of bush camps in the morning. I needed to know for sure it was you. I might never see you again and I'd always wonder. It took me a while standing in front of the building before I got the courage to check for your apartment number in the vestibule. When I checked the list of participants at the meeting, I figured you were using your married name." He paused, as if waiting for her to say something. "I had to take a chance. If I was wrong, all you had to do was sic the cops on me for stalking you. Not that I haven't had my own dealings with them over the years. The guys can get pretty rowdy in the bars up north near the logging camps."

She reached for the kettle and brought it to the sink. Her heart was pushing through her chest. A deep sense of sadness had erupted within her. She had kept Papi locked away in her album of safe memories, thinking it was the only way to move on with her life. A chance meeting had just blown open the door to her shelter. All the love she had for him, for Aunt Jan, and for Grandma Stella came surging through her, leaving her unable to find the right words or move her legs. Looking him in the eye only reminded her of the pain she had caused. If she spoke, tears were sure to fall.

"You've done us proud, Nadine." He smiled at her. "Nice apartment, good job."

She knew he meant to lighten the tension between them. Life had altered them both, making them almost strangers. So many unknowns separated them. She tried to force a smile and come out with some small talk to help him out. But the tears were too close to spilling. A barrier of pain and heartache had kept them apart too long for this reunion to be easy.

"How about you, Papi?" Her words tumbled out, gasping for air.

"My home base is still back in Saint-Roch. Rose is buried there and the union office is within walking distance. Janette wants me to move closer to Montreal. Maybe when I retire full-time. I put in two days a week at the office and I go check up on the bush camps every couple of weeks. I got the call to come here and replace one of our guys early this morning. The cops must've started their raids the minute Ottawa hauled out the War Measures Act. They sure didn't waste any time."

She placed the kettle on the burner and leaned against the counter, waiting for the water to boil. "You didn't find the soldiers downtown too... disruptive?" The words she forced out managed not to sound too awkward. Keeping the conversation away from what was causing the upheaval in her chest might help pull off this reunion without too many tears.

He leaned back in his chair and crossed his arms. "I've seen all this before. It's not the first time Ottawa has sent its army to bully

46

the Quebec people. When the war started in 1914, a lot of us refused to join up. After treating us like dirt for over 150 years, they expected us to die for them too. It wasn't our fight. During the Easter holiday of 1918 trains full of soldiers came to Quebec City to force us to enlist." He fell silent a moment, his eyes far away. "I guess the soldiers downtown make me feel more threatened than anything else. It's like I have no right to be walking down my own streets."

She reached in the cupboard for two mugs. "Those bombings make people scared of going out. These days all we hear about are the kidnappings. And then there's all those manifestos being broadcast." She braced herself and brought down the sugar bowl. Politics wasn't what she wanted to talk about, but it was stopping her from coming apart. She'd have to face him across the table any second now. "Things will go back to normal soon. The army might not stay too long."

"I agree it's been pretty tense here for a while." He unbuttoned the top of his shirt and relaxed his shoulders. "But sending the Canadian army to stop a small group of Quebec radicals is just putting more wood on the fire. It's only going to back what the terrorists are shouting loud and clear—that Quebecers are living under the thumb of the English. The FLQ are only expressing the frustration of every French worker slaving for the English bosses. The thing is, violence might get them the attention they need, but Quebecers will end up wanting a more peaceful way."

The kettle started to boil. She bit her lip and stared at the bursts of steam escaping. Talking about politics only went so far in containing the emotions whirling inside her.

"Enough of all that—" He shifted in his chair and cleared his throat. "It's been so long… you were just a girl of sixteen last we saw each other. Life has been good to you, I hope."

She switched the burner off and let out a long breath. "It hasn't always been smooth." She placed the tea bags in the teapot and turned to face him. "I've made mistakes, some of them I never figured out how to fix. Time can sometimes bury these for a while, but they find a way to surface when you're not looking."

"Everyone has the right to mess things up once in a while. It's the only way to grow." He looked down at the floor a moment and lifted his gaze with a smile. "Believe me when I say this. I've always taken full advantage of that right. I have to confess I had to repeat some mistakes over and over again before I got it right."

"You, Papi?" She didn't imagine him ever doing anything wrong.

"Well, I don't deny it. " He frowned. "After Rose died, I left baby Janette with my mother in Saint-Roch and only came back to visit on holidays and special occasions. Working in the bush was my escape from the loss of my wife. I became that faraway father who paid the bills and appeared at the kitchen table at Christmas and Easter. I only realized how distant my daughter and I had become when she announced her intention to marry Denis. She didn't ask my permission and didn't care what I thought. I guess when I lost Rose, I also lost my daughter."

"But I remember how happy she always was to see you. It wasn't Christmas and Easter until you arrived—for me too."

He shook his head. "I wanted to make up for lost time. The closeness I had lost with Janette, I thought I had found with you. You were such a sad little girl."

She slumped back against the counter, one arm holding the other at the elbow. "I can't begin, Papi… to say how sorry I am. Aunt Jan was always a good mother to me. I just… wanted to put everything behind me when I left… build myself up again. But while I was doing that… I hurt people along the way—people that were kind to me. The longer I stayed away, the more I convinced myself I wasn't welcome back, and that Aunt Jan was better off without me."

"Please… don't apologize. Not to me. You were still a child when you left. That was the worst part of it for Janette. She waited on you hand and foot from the moment she brought you into her home. She felt responsible for what happened to you. She figured she hadn't prepared you enough for what was out there. But you did what you had to do. Our decisions always come from what we happen to know at a certain point in our life. But people hardly ever get to the same place at the same time and end up disagreeing with each other's choices. Whatever decision you took in the past was the best one for you at the time. I'm just glad to find you alive and well."

She turned to stare out the window over the sink. "If you only knew how much I longed to see Aunt Jan and Grandma Stella when I was first on my own. But that meant also seeing Uncle Denis. I didn't want him or the other Pritcharts knowing anything about me. I was just an embarrassment to them. They were glad to see the back of me and I wanted no part of them. If they thought I was dead that was OK with me—just like they were dead in my mind."

"Love them or hate them, they're still part of who you are. Ignoring them is sticking your head in the sand. You've got to deal with what you hate about them before you can make them disappear. Hating them gives them more space in your life." He paused to glance around her orderly kitchen, taking in the ample oak cupboards, the ceramic flooring, and the modern fridge and stove. "Let's put them aside now and talk about you. You've done OK from the looks of things."

She took her time before turning to face him. "I moved around a lot the first few years. My first place was in an old rooming house in the east end. I got a job as a baster in a garment factory near there. I'd stitch the different parts of the garment by hand and the sewers assembled them on the machines. Long hours with slave wages. After my day's work, I had blisters on my fingers, and my back ached from bending over the cloth. Coming up with the rent money was tough and there wasn't always enough food in my cupboard."

"I would've been more than happy to—"

"Yes, Papi... I know that. I almost called you a few times." She tucked her hair back behind her ears and gave him a weak smile. "I'd stand inside the telephone booth with my eyes closed trying to find the courage. But work got better after a while. The women at the factory looked out for me. They took turns sharing their lunch with me. A few of them took work home to make a bit of extra cash. A kind Italian woman invited me to her home and showed me how to do piecework on her sewing machine. That meant I was allowed on the machines at work and able get a pay raise. I owe those women a lot. It's because of their help I was able to survive."

"Janette had so wanted to go see you while you were at the home. But Denis told us visitors weren't allowed. We knew you had to stay and work there six months after the birth to pay off your debt to the nuns. She crossed the days off on the calendar waiting for you to come back. It took her awhile to move on with her life." He looked down, his eyes pained. "And all this time you were living on the opposite side of town."

"I wasn't worried about running into anyone in the family. Especially not in the area where I was living."

"The police were no help, and Denis' family didn't insist on the search."

She pressed her lips together. "The cops searched for Nadine Pritchart, so they weren't able to find me. I used my mother's maiden name on my first job application. All the other paperwork followed suit. We didn't need supporting documents then—not for my type of work. The name stuck with me. Dropping the Pritchart name helped me make a clean break."

"The pieces are starting to fall into place." He paused. "If only we had known."

"Black, right?" She placed the teapot and cups on the table and sat down across from him. She had so loved pouring his tea as a little girl.

He reached over to pat her hand. "This will be the best cup of tea in the world."

"You always said that to me no matter how weak it was." She poured his tea, an empty feeling compressing the walls of her chest. "I wanted to keep her, you know." She swallowed hard. "I was going to find a way no matter what. The government gave a five dollar monthly baby bonus. Not much, but it was better than nothing. A few women's groups were helping girls like me. I was ready to face anything to keep my baby. I lay awake at night trying to figure out how it was going to work. But when I woke up after the birth... she was gone. It was like I had just woken up from a bad dream. The nuns used to guilt us girls to sign that adoption consent form, but I always refused."

She sipped her tea, trying to come up with the right words before placing her cup down. "After I learned that the nuns had a signed consent form on file, I demanded to see it. That's when I saw Uncle Denis' signature. I cried for days. I hated him so much for giving my baby away. He had only ever agreed to adopt me because Aunt Jan wanted him too. He never once referred to me as his own—I was always his brother's daughter. I never wanted to see him or anybody from that family ever again."

Papi leaned back in his chair, letting out a slow breath. "You were underage. They needed his signature no matter what." He straightened back up. "I'm sure Janette didn't know about Denis signing that form. She had fixed up a corner in your room with a crib. She continued knitting baby outfits till Denis told her you had given the baby up. I visited her often in those days. She needed someone to confide in. The rest of the family refused to even mention your name."

"There's lots Aunt Jan didn't know."

Papi drank his tea in silence. She fiddled with the sugar bowl and the milk jug, adjusting their positions beside the teapot and switching them again a few seconds later.

After a short silence, he put his cup down. "Sometimes, things are better left unsaid until you're free of them. It took me years before I even mentioned Rose's death. I didn't think my heart was capable of ever breaking again. But it shattered into a million pieces when Janette's little Philip died. Then… you disappeared. I wondered if I was being punished."

She averted her eyes, willing her hot tea to wash down the burning sensation in her throat.

"Having a child taken away from you attacks your very soul." His voice wavered. "Janette lived through it twice. First with young Philip's death and again when you didn't come back. There's nothing I'd like more than to see a bit of light in my daughter's eyes. I'd hate to keep this visit hidden from her, but... if you don't want me to, I won't say a thing about it. I'm just so happy to have this moment with you."

She turned to him, tears in her eyes. "Papi, I didn't mean to hurt anybody. I never saw myself as anybody's child. I needed time to put my pieces back together. All I did was work. And eat and rest. And work again. No time to feel the pain and loneliness. One day I woke up and a large period of my life had flown by."

"Stop blaming yourself—it will eat up all that's good inside of you. What's done is done. Beating yourself over the head won't erase the past."

She swallowed hard and straightened in her chair. "If she ever finds out you kept this visit secret, it'll hurt her even more. Tell her you've seen me, but don't tell her what we talked about. I owe it to her to tell her myself one day. I don't want the Pritcharts to know. I can't go back right now. I don't have the courage to face Uncle Denis. Not now... maybe never."

He pressed his palm to his chest. "What you're giving me is going straight to my heart. To know you're well will make my Janette very happy. Don't worry. She doesn't visit much with his family. She won't say anything, but—" He hesitated. "I don't suppose you knew. About a year after you left, your grandfather Pritchart died. They found him dead beside the railway tracks near his home."

Her eyes widened and her shoulders dropped. "Grandpa Pritchart? I thought he'd always be around to rule over everybody." She had imagined his death a thousand times when he was alive. He was the raging monster in her nightmares as a child. The evil one staring at her from her dark closet at night. Grandma Stella would always be there when she woke, sitting beside her on the bed, waiting for her screams to stop.

"I'm sorry to bring you such sad news. He'd lost his hearing bit by bit over the years, and his eyesight had deteriorated quite a lot at the end, leaving him almost deaf and blind. The CPR forced him to retire ten years early—before he caused an accident, that is. He never got over losing his job. He spent his days walking along the tracks with the help of a cane. Stella lived in fear that he'd get hit by a train one day."

"He always bragged about never taking a sick day off work. What did he die of?" Her vision clouded thinking about Grandma Stella. She must've felt so disoriented without him. Grandpa Pritchard had been in her life since she was a young girl of thirteen. "I remember the pink stains he left in the snow when he went to pee beside his back porch. In my kid's mind, I thought he had dragon's blood."

"It's a good thing he only had sons. He had a rare kidney disorder and never told anyone. Stella only found out at the very end. It's a disease that's only passed on to female children." He paused when he saw the look of shock on her face. "Don't worry, male children can only get it if the mother is a carrier. So no danger of your father having it. The sad part is there's no cure. He was lucky to have lived as long as he did."

Papi had assumed the news of the death had shocked her, but nothing was further from the truth. It was her daughter she was thinking of. She'd be old enough to start a family by now. Knowing the danger, she might not be willing to risk having children. Didn't she have the right to know her family's medical background? A pain throbbed in the back of her throat. She pushed herself up and leaned against the counter, facing away from Papi. Not only had she given her child away to perfect strangers, but she had also passed on a crippling disease.

"Nadine?" He slid his chair back and went to get up, but she waved him down.

"I'm alright, Papi. This was just so... unexpected. I might've... for Grandma's sake... gone to the funeral. She was always so good to me." She walked back to the table and sat down.

He stared at her a moment. "That's all water under the bridge. It might not have been a good time for you to show up then, at least not with his sons being so upset about the will. You see, your grandfather left Stella the house and enough to live on, but he also left you a nice sum of money, and—"

"Me. Why me?" She sat back in her chair, her stomach rock hard. "I don't want his money."

"Maybe not." He smiled. "But Peter and Denis sure do. When you disappeared without a word, they went to court to contest the will. After seven years they tried to have you declared legally dead. But Janette blocked it by claiming she received a postcard from you about a year after you left. She keeps it in her safe deposit box. As long as there's a possibility you might still be alive—and Janette refuses to back down—the courts won't grant them what they want."

She recalled how desperate she had felt when she scribbled those quick words—Don't worry. Everything's fine. Love, Nadine—on a postcard of New York City she had found on a park bench. There had been nothing fine about her life at the time. She had even cut back on her milk budget for the week to afford a postage stamp. She had hoped to help reassure Aunt Jan, but also to get closure on her struggle to go back. If they thought she was doing well, nobody would insist on trying to locate her. Her heart rose to her throat at the thought of Aunt Jan holding on to that card after all that time.

She raised both palms up in front of her. "I don't want Aunt Jan to fight over this. Tell her they can keep it all. I don't want any of it." Any connection to Timothy Pritchart left her with a knot in her gut. It was his way of keeping a hold on her even after death. She wouldn't be able to spend a penny of it without thinking of him. She had managed well enough without help for this long and didn't need his money to carry on. Accepting the money also meant having to deal with Uncle Denis again, and that was out of the question.

"You won't have to worry about any of this after December of this year. Your grandfather didn't want his money rotting in trust for a hundred years in case you never showed up. He added a condition in his will that your inheritance go to his two sons if it wasn't claimed by twenty years after his death."

She shook her head. "I don't care about all that. Seeing you today sure makes me want to see Aunt Jan and Grandma again, but the timing isn't right. If I go back now, Denis and Uncle Peter will say I went back just for the money. I'll only go after they've gotten what they want. Maybe they'll hate me a little less and I won't get the door slammed in my face."

He finished off his tea and slid his chair back. "You might be right, but Janette isn't well. It'd do her good to finally see you. Stella is living in a seniors home now. Janette visits her when she can. I had planned on a quick stop to see Janette after the meeting today, but I came here instead. It's a three-hour drive back to Saint-Roch so I'll be driving back home as soon as I leave here. I hear those arrested in the raids today will stay locked up for a while before they even see a lawyer. So I'll probably be filling in again at another meeting. We'll visit Janette together when I get back. Denis usually finds some place to go when I go there, so we'll have her to ourselves." He grinned at her and headed for the door.

She managed a weak nod and swallowed hard. If Uncle Denis was still home when they got there, she didn't know how he'd react. He might refuse to let her in and tell her never to come back. Maybe Aunt Jan didn't even want to see her after all. She closed her eyes, thanking all the forces in the universe for sending Papi her way. If things went wrong at Aunt Jan's, at least she had Papi back.

CHAPTER 6

Lisette and Serge entered the glass vestibule and pressed the information button on the wall panel. She pulled out a jagged piece of paper from her jacket pocket and looked at it. "I'm pretty sure this is the place." She studied the small metal sign posted beside the door. "Looks like some kind of retirement home. The woman I spoke to never mentioned anything about that. If she answered the phone, she must have a direct line to her room."

A middle-aged woman came from the reception desk and headed down the marble-floored hallway towards the vestibule. She unlocked the door and smiled. "May I help you?"

Lisette noticed the name tag pinned on the woman's sweater and smiled back. "I see you're the manager, Mrs. White. We're here to see Mrs. Stella Pritchart."

"I see." The woman's gaze shifted from Serge's shoulder-length hair down to the lit cigarette in his hand. "Is she expecting you?"

"Yes. I spoke to her earlier."

"She must've forgotten to inform the office. Please give me your name. I need to check with her first. We're never too careful these days."

"Tell her it's Lisette and—"

"Sorry for interrupting, dear." She stared at Serge's cigarette. "We do our best to provide a safe and healthy environment for our residents. You'll have to finish that outdoors, young man, or if you prefer, in the glassed-in room beside the office. Safety regulations, you know. Some of our tenants tend to be forgetful. So we keep the smokers in one spot to keep our eye on them. I'll be right back." She pulled the door closed and trotted down the hall.

Serge blew out a cloud of smoke from the corner of his mouth. "Stuck up English cow. Bet everyone here is a bloody squarehead."

"Get real, Serge." She gave him a sharp look. "This is NDG. Not Westmount. Names have nothing to do with the language you speak. Lots of families all over Quebec with names like McDuff or McGregor don't speak a word of English. Try to keep your politics on ice for a bit. The building might have an English name, but it doesn't mean none of the residents speak French. This place looks posh to us, but that's because we're used to crappy student apartments. Stub out—the manager's coming back."

"This place stinks of lavender. English lavender." He looked back at his car. "I might take a snooze while I wait for you." They watched Mrs. White approach. "I better get out of here before the old bag notices the torn seam on my fly, and here's me not wearing underwear. Her blood pressure will explode." He patted Lisette's backside and strutted towards the road just as the woman unlocked the vestibule.

"Will the young man join you later?" The woman stretched her neck out the door and glanced in Serge's direction.

"He'll wait for me in the car. Did you manage to find her?"

"She's not hard to locate, that one. Sitting beside her favourite window in the lounge. She likes to view the garden while she drinks her afternoon tea. Follow me." She swung the glass door open, let Lisette in and locked up again.

The spacious lounge had a variety of stuffed armchairs, a leather sofa along one wall and a large TV set on the higher shelf of a wooden wall unit. A bright kitchen section equipped with modern electrical appliances filled the far end, with a long oak table surrounded by twelve matching chairs.

Mrs. White headed to a partitioned corner of the room, greeting everyone she met along the way. A tall bookcase beside an array of potted plants on pedestals separated this corner from the rest of the room. A delicate-looking woman, her white hair tied in a loose bun at the nape of her neck, sat gazing at the tree-lined backyard through a large picture window.

Mrs. White leaned down to touch her arm. "Here's the visitor I told you about, dear."

Stella Pritchart stared at Lisette and remained silent a long while. "Claire? It can't—" Her eyes darted between Lisette and Mrs. White. "Is this a dream?"

The woman patted Stella's shoulder. "You're not dreaming, dear." She looked towards Lisette. "The longer they stay with us, the harder it is for them to distinguish what's real and what's not. It's worse for those who never get visitors."

A clog shifted into place within Lisette's heart. The older woman had seen a resemblance in her with someone she knew. This meant she was linked to a family chain. She was connected somewhere— she belonged.

"We're serving your favourite—shepherd's pie—for supper later. I'll come and get you when we're ready to serve." Mrs. White gave the elderly woman a quick wave and walked away.

Lisette hesitated before speaking. The woman had seemed to understand why Lisette wanted to see her when they spoke on the phone, but right now, she seemed pretty muddled. If she proved to be unreliable, this visit was a complete waste of time.

Stella stared at her, her hands clasped together on her lap.

Lisette felt a slight twinge in her left eyelid. Two things were possible: she had an actual family somewhere, or the woman was senile. The questions she had prepared were useless if the second possibility was correct. But still... any clue she offered might be helpful. She dragged a metal chair in front of the woman's armchair and lowered herself down. "I'm not Claire, Mrs. Pritchart. My name is Lisette."

Stella flashed her a weak smile. "How foolish of me. Of course, you're not Claire. That's why I thought I was dreaming. The poor girl... such a tragic end." She paused to stare down at her lap and after a moment, lifted her gaze. "You're just as beautiful as she was, though. Her hair was lighter, but there's no denying you."

Lisette forced back a smile, her heartbeat increasing. "I don't know who Claire was, Mrs. Pritchart." This woman had just confirmed she had a family. "I'm here to find out about Nadine Pritchart. I think she might be my mother."

The woman blinked and reached out to touch Lisette's knee. "Nadine's child? Can this be true? No one knew what happened to her." She tilted her head and studied Lisette. "Yes, I remember now… it must've been you who called before." She paused, her eyes far away. "Our Nadine was pregnant when we last saw her. I hope life has been kind to her." She leaned back and closed her eyes. "When you're alone with your memories so much… it's hard to know what's real after a while."

"Believe me, Mrs. Pritchart, I'm as real as it gets. I'm looking for the woman who gave me away for adoption twenty years ago. I'm not expecting a joyous reunion, but I do have some questions about my medical history she can help clear up for me."

Stella remained silent a short time before speaking. "What choice did that poor girl have?" She bit down on her lip, a look of sadness in her eyes. "What about you, dear? Was your adopted family good to you?"

Lisette stiffened in her chair. "The less said about that, the better. My adoptive parents divorced when I was five and decided they didn't want me anymore. I moved in and out of eight different foster homes until the day I wrote my last high school exam. I packed my bag and left without a word. Does this answer your question?"

"I'm… so sorry to hear that, dear." She lowered her gaze and fidgeted with the blanket on her lap.

Lisette shifted in her seat. Why was she talking so rough to this woman? She had nothing to do with anything. "Don't be sorry, Mrs. Pritchart. I didn't mean to sound so harsh. Where I grew up, talking tough was a girl's only defence, besides knowing how to throw a punch or place a kick in the right place." A sharp pain shot across her forehead. She tore her glasses off and massaged her temples. If she was lucky, a couple of deep breaths and she'd be OK again.

"Are you alright, dear?"

Lisette tilted her head forward and inhaled. "This happens sometimes… it comes and goes." She straightened and pushed her hair away from her face. "If Nadine Pritchart is my mother, that makes you my great-grandmother." She patted her stomach. "And here is—" She stopped to think about it, then grinned. "Your great-great grandchild. So, can you help me find my mother?"

Stella looked at the roundness of Lisette's belly and smiled. "My heart stopped when I first saw you before. I thought it was Claire come back to us. It's been so long since I heard her name mentioned. The same thing with Nadine. I stopped asking Janette about her. It pained her too much to talk about it." She paused a moment. "I don't know if I can help you find her, dear. She was just a young girl last time I saw her. But I'll tell you whatever I can remember about her."

"That works. I don't want to keep you too long. I've got someone waiting for me outside."

Stella pulled her sweater closer, a pleased look on her face. "It's a joy to have a visitor. And someone as young and beautiful as you. It doesn't happen often here. You feel like you've fallen out of circulation. People forget about you. Not that the boys ever came often to see me when I was at home. My youngest son, John, used to drop off little Nadine with me. I was so happy for the company with Timothy being away on the trains so much." She broke her story to smile at Lisette. "Please excuse me... you must think I'm babbling. I thought age blanked out a few memories. But they crowd together instead, some cut into each other and I have to figure out what goes where."

"It's OK Mrs. Pritchart. If you don't mind, I'll be taking notes to help me figure things out." Lisette pulled a pen and notebook out of her bag.

"Please. Call me Grandma Stella... our Nadine always called me that. She never saw her mother's side of the family. Claire came from a little fishing village back east. She never did get around to bringing Nadine back there to visit." Her eyes grew pensive. "I'm not sure John encouraged that. He liked to have her close by."

Lisette glanced up from her writing. "A control thing?"

"Perhaps—" She halted for a brief moment, her look pensive. "John needed more attention than my other two. Good-looking child, and bright too. Didn't have to work as hard as my other two, but the awards kept coming. He was shorter than the other boys he grew up with on the block and got pushed around a lot. Timothy said it was me coddling him too much. He'd say the boy got all his nervousness from me." She leaned her head against the back of her armchair and closed her eyes.

Lisette hesitated a moment, not sure if the woman had dozed off. She was about to put her notebook back in her bag when Stella opened her eyes. "You seem so young, dear. When is the baby coming?"

"Mid-November, but my doctor said it might be sooner."

Stella turned towards the window, a wistful look in her eyes. "I never wanted a girl. I would've loved her, but I didn't want to bring another girl into this world."

CHAPTER 7

Griffintown
September 1939

Stella woke up with a start and strained to listen. Footfalls from the cellar. At times they'd pause for a while and, just as she was falling asleep, start over again. Some nights they climbed higher up the steps and hovered at the cellar door to the hallway a few feet away from their bedroom. She'd pull her quilt over her head and curl up tight, praying they'd think her dead—willing them to disappear. But the acrid smell of panic lured them back—where there's fear, there's life. If she were lucky, she'd fall asleep from sheer exhaustion.

Her bedside lamp was still on and the bedroom door left open as usual. Even when Timothy was in bed beside her, she never fell asleep with the door closed. She stretched her neck to check down the hallway. The two bolts on the cellar door were in the locked position. Timothy had relented and agreed to install the first lock when they moved in years ago. And a second one after she insisted it wasn't enough. Waste of my hard-earned money, he'd told her. There's only a tiny window beside the alleyway and that's blocked with metal bars. What you're hearing is all between your two bloody ears.

The footfalls stopped. Sometimes they never came and she'd have the rare good night's sleep. She sighed and closed her eyes, knowing she'd stay awake now till the sunlight filtered through the drapes. Her time would be better spent keeping busy in the kitchen. Turning on the radio in the darkest hours of the night helped drown out those footfalls creeping up the basement steps. She'd haul out the pots and pans and scrub them till her reflection shone from every angle—from her mother's way of holding her own. Resigned to staying awake while Timothy worked the night shifts, she juggled time to nap during the day.

Her three boys and their wives were invited for dinner along with little Nadine. She wanted to prepare all the vegetables ahead of time to be able to sit with them while the meal finished cooking. If the conversation got too heated between Timothy and John, she'd be ready to intervene. Peter and Denis never contradicted their father, preferring to change the subject rather than argue. This was their last chance to have a meal together before Peter and Denis sailed overseas.

She lifted her head off the pillow and listened. Silence, except for the soft rhythm of her breathing. A couple of hours of sleep before Timothy came home would've done her good. But those footfalls would be sure to start again as soon as her head touched the pillow. So many things to do before everybody arrived.

She swung her legs off the bed and reached for the heavy tartan housecoat on her bedside table. Handed down to her from her late mother, it was a comfort to her on those cold sleepless nights when the footfalls came. The hem reached down to her ankles and the wide collar served as a hood. The deep pockets hid the tiny flat rocks—amulets, soft and comforting in her palm—she sometimes found on her way to and from church. Timothy, claiming the housecoat made her look ghoulish, had bought her an elegant pink satin one which she kept in its original wrapping in the bottom drawer of her dresser.

She got up and was heading towards the bedroom doorway when a wave of cold sweat mushroomed from the back of her neck down to her knees. Her breathing slowed and she sat back on the edge of the bed. The walls pressed in on her. Something was wrong. Not footfalls this time. Her head shot around. Everything was in place. Nobody lurking. She sucked in her breath and let it out—slow and rhythmic like a summer breeze. Again, a few times. This would pass. It always did.

Breathe in again, Stella.
Don't let him see you like this.
Get yourself together before he gets home.

63

She never mentioned her fears to him anymore. She had realized long ago that he had no control over them. The dark of night kept them alive. They had come with her on the day of her birth, brought over on the famine ships of Ireland by her maternal grandmother. Passed on in greater force by her own mother who used to hide out in the root cellar for days on end. Stella's father, fed up with taking care of the kids, would pry her out kicking and screaming. Stella had long ago accepted that these fears, rooted in the lining of her womb and the tender pulses of womanhood, would never leave her. As a young girl, they came in the form of horrific nightmares that disappeared when she woke. They mutated later to ghostlike footfalls marching straight to her in the night. She thanked all the patron saints available to her that she had never given birth to a girl.

Timothy Pritchart was Stella's first and only lover. Their fathers were first cousins who lived ten blocks away from each other in Montreal's Irish district of Griffintown. Her father, Michael, was a mechanic for the CPR at Windsor Station, and Timothy had started training to be a train conductor after fourteen years working as an apprentice car man. Her mother died of an epileptic seizure seven months after her younger brother, David, came into the world. Stella stopped school at eleven years old to take care of the household chores and to be with the baby, who howled each time she stepped out of his sight.

Timothy was a tall brawny bachelor sixteen years older than her. Michael appreciated having a male presence at home while he was on the evening shift. Timothy, being family, was expected to check on Stella and David when Michael was at work. He stepped in and out of Michael's flat so often that the neighbours thought him a permanent lodger. He took his family obligations to heart and always had a bag of hard candy ready for his young cousins in his jacket pocket.

Stella was a nervous girl plagued with nightmares of wild and formidable creatures pursuing her. She'd toss and turn with such abandon that she'd often tumble off her narrow cot and wake her young brother sleeping in his wooden cradle beside her. Michael recalled his late wife's nightmares and worried Stella had inherited her mother's sickness. He nailed shut the trap door going down to the old root cellar populated by the monsters that had tormented his wife every day. He left spoons in strategic spots in the flat in case Stella might have also inherited her mother's seizures. By the age of two, David grabbed any spoon he found lying around, ran to his sister, and tried shoving it between her teeth.

Timothy made sure Stella was sound asleep before slipping off to meet his mates. He'd wait on the wooden bench by her bed until her breathing was slow and regular. Sometimes he dozed off and only came to when her nightmare had taken over. He'd reach over to massage her back, as Michael had advised him to, till the monsters left her for the night.

Stella loved that faint burnt smell that clung to Timothy's skin and hair. The same odour of motor oil that permeated the air in the flat when her father came home. It lingered even after hours of soaking Michael's work clothes in an old metal basin on the back porch. Scrubbing them till her knuckles turned blood red didn't help it go away. The smell of the men in her life gave her a secure feeling of being part of their world.

Baby powder, she had heard, helped remove the stubborn grease on his shirts and pants. A few trials with the smooth velvety powder and the skin of her hands regained the pale ivory shade of her Irish ancestors. She emptied David's leftover orange and white tin of Johnson's Baby Powder into the cracks of the floorboards to stop them from creaking at night. And along the door frames and window sills to stop the army of black ants from invading the flat in hot weather.

When Michael saw how excited she was about this magical white powder, he asked Timothy to pick up a case on his next run to Toronto. With the arrival of the cold season, she'd hang her father's work clothes to dry on the clothesline beside the stove in the kitchen. The heat rose from the stove, spreading the faint odour of oil and grease from his clothes throughout the whole flat. She felt safe and protected then, knowing no harm would come to her and little David.

Timothy watched her grow from a skinny blond girl too shy to look him straight in the eye into a beautiful young woman. She had sprouted tight round breasts which dug into his chest when he hugged her goodnight. Gone were the girlish blond braids. She now kept her thick curls shoulder length like the models in the fashion magazines he brought her. He had completed his conductor training for the CPR at the time, and when passengers left their magazines behind, he saved them for Stella. They'd leaf through them together and he'd choose the dresses he imagined she'd look best in. His choices made her giggle. She'd never dare go out in such skimpy outfits. Her father would go to an early grave if he ever saw her step out wearing so little. And then there was Father Murphy—he'd excommunicate her before she got halfway up the church steps.

Timothy was strong and virile with thick dark hair brushed back from his forehead and a thin moustache outlining his full mouth. He always had a smile with a ready compliment for her. His visits left her with a feeling of giddiness, bringing back the Irish love songs her mother always used to sing. On her fourteenth birthday, he kissed her on the lips and held her close. She stepped back and lowered her head. He stared at her, his arms limp by his side. After a long moment, he spun round and reached for his coat.

She snapped her head up. "You're going—"

"It's best—you tell your father everything."

She didn't answer so he rushed out the front door.

He waited for a confrontation with her father. Two weeks later, Michael's behaviour towards him at work still wasn't any different than usual. Timothy figured Stella hadn't said anything and decided it was safe to see her again. That night, he sat by her bed as he always did and waited for her to fall asleep. He was meeting a friend later in the Red Light district in the east end of the city. But Stella's demons invaded her sleep again. She tossed and turned, throwing her blanket off. He reached out to massage her back.

Her breathing calmed right away and she let out a low moan. His pulse quickened at the sound and he continued massaging lower down her back. Before he knew it, his hand glided to the warm region between her legs. She mumbled his name, and still asleep, nudged his hand away. He sat back on his bench, all his senses alive, and waited for the blood surging through him to slow down before he left. The full moon filtered through the narrow window above her bed, outlining her firm nipples pushing through the thin cotton nightdress. He knew she'd never tell and wondered if she had really been asleep while his hand wandered to the sacred warmth of her young body.

He stayed away close to a month. The sweet smell of the baby powder she sprinkled on her sheets every night to ward off bad dreams followed him everywhere. When he thought of the silkiness of her skin, a deep ache took over his lower body that kept him awake even with the double shifts he was doing to avoid seeing her. He lost his appetite for his mother's cooking and dark black rings formed under his eyes. She made a last-ditch effort to figure out what evil had befallen her son, who had never before refused her shepherd's pie.

"Why is there a pile of women's fashion magazines by your bed?" She pointed to his cot beside the coal stove. He leaned down to swoop the pile up and marched down the street, lured by the girl whose magical talcum powder had cast a spell on him.

Stella hadn't told her father about the kiss but had confessed to Father Murphy after Sunday Mass. Michael waited for her with young David in the crowd of locals catching up on gossip in front of St. Ann's Church.

"Don't let it happen again." The priest slammed down the window of the confessional. "Not before your father consents to have the marriage banns read on three consecutive Sundays during Mass."

Timothy assured her that he'd respect the priest's advice and they didn't kiss again. He continued to look after her when the nightmares assaulted her body at night. She got used to the roughness of his hand on her skin. She'd sometimes lay awake listening to the different staccato bursts of his breath as he explored the intimate parts of her body.

One night she woke spread-eagled and gasping from another horrific nightmare. She had just escaped the claws of a headless zombie with swarms of green worms spurting out of its festering neck. Timothy's body stretched over hers like a long covered bridge, balancing his weight inches above her on his elbows and knees. He looked so big and strong—the hero come to protect her from all her monsters.

The heat from his body was so intense her loins rose like a magnet to meet his. His moist breath transformed into mist in her hair. His hardness rubbed against her, probing her upper thighs and the soft area between her legs until he fumbled his way inside her. A cry of panic escaped from her. He pressed his hand over her mouth so as not to wake young David and pushed deeper. His frantic thrusts felt like sandpaper scraping against the tender walls within her. Burning spasms of pain shot up from her loins straight to her heart. His body shook and he collapsed, gasping and sweating on top of her. He promised her it would be better next time.

The pain became more tolerable after he brought her back a jar of Vaseline Wonder Jelly. He made sure she kept it hidden in her socks and underwear drawer. His hardness was still too large for the taut entrance to her young girl's body. But she needed him to always come back to her. She squinted her eyes and bit her lip each time he reached inside her underwear drawer for the jar of petroleum jelly. They had followed Father Murphy's orders about the kissing, but Stella would've preferred to disobey that rule and not take part in the rest.

Two months after her sixteenth birthday she told him she heard the swishing of water inside of her. At times she felt a distant thud as little feet danced beneath her rib cage. He stopped visiting as often, needing to figure out what to do next. He had noticed the change in that angular girlish body he loved so much. Her breasts had swollen, her hips had widened, and her concave belly had started to inch outwards. Marriage seemed the only option if he didn't want his whole family, as well as the relatives back in Ireland, to turn their backs on him. Stella's father was a well-respected mechanic at work, and Timothy had worked hard to get to the position of conductor. His job required he abide by high moral standards of conduct. One negative word from Michael was all that was needed for his co-workers to have nothing to do with him.

He loved stepping onto the platform of the train station each day. His energy level soared knowing he was the one in control.

His duties kept him scurrying back and forth through the series of railway cars from the time he slammed the door closed when the train took off till the moment he pulled it open again when they arrived at their destination. His job was to make sure the train ran on schedule. Check that the proper signals were on the train and that employees followed safety rules. Complete all paperwork as well as the train travel log. Board the passengers on time and punch their tickets. Make sure the passengers were comfortable. Check for items left behind and report unnecessary delays and cancellations. He was on call twenty-four hours a day, seven days a week. He never refused a double shift, nor the Montreal-Vancouver run, which kept him away from home almost two weeks at a time.

He loved the grease and hot oil smells. The chuffing sounds of the engine. The lonely moan of the whistle as the train trailed its cloud of steam into the approaching station. He most enjoyed strolling through the cars looking out for any young girl clutching the ticket her parents had warned her not to lose. She was, in most cases, travelling alone to visit an aunt who needed help with the housework, or maybe to join another member of her family. He checked her ticket and offered to show her the caboose—the only place on the train with great views of the countryside, he'd tell her. Spurred by the tall, handsome man in the dark blue uniform, she always followed. The girl was happy to see something of interest on this boring, uncomfortable ride.

The caboose car consisted of the conductor's desk, a tiny cooking area, and sleeping bunks for the crew. Metal steps led to an elevated platform with a windowed cupola and a fixed seat used by the crew to supervise the back of the train. Timothy guided the young girl up the rickety steps and held her down on his lap with a tight grip. He didn't want her tumbling off the bench if the train happened to go down a steep hill. He pointed to the various points of interest that flashed by them, his voice rasping with excitement. Vibrations from the engine's rods and pistons, as well as the unexplained bumping beneath her, sometimes caused her to bolt down the steps.

A conductor's job was secure and sought-after. Any smear on Timothy's reputation as a reputable employee and a devoted family man might affect his position. They married the first Saturday in May after the reading of the wedding banns. She clutched a large bouquet of flowers close to her belly. Her father marched her up the church aisle, and with a look of anguished resignation, handed her over to the man he had once trusted with his own life.

The old neighbourhood of Griffintown—where the sweet-sounding Gaelic language had once been spoken on the streets—wasn't the best place to start a new family. It had become a manufacturing slum.

Timothy's generation now had electric tramways and weren't obliged to live within walking distance of their work. The poor and the elderly still clung to their decrepit wooden housing, reluctant to stray too far from the protection of St. Ann's Catholic Church. Some dwellings near the waterfront still had outdoor toilets, and basement or ground-floor flats continued to be flooded each spring by the St. Lawrence River.

Irish and French-Canadian children—whose parents shared the same religion and held on to the same distrust of anything British— fought daily for a spot to play in alleys between factories, breweries and machine shops. Toxic coal fumes from the huge chimneys spewing black smoke day and night added tuberculosis to Stella's growing list of worries for their unborn child. Timothy left behind what had once been a refuge for his Irish ancestors fleeing the disastrous Great Famine and moved to a healthier and cleaner place to live.

Timothy's steady employment with the CPR allowed him to rent a spacious flat with a small backyard in Verdun, away from the railways and factories. He moved Stella's few belongings, including her large pile of fashion magazines. Often called to do double shifts, including the Montreal-Vancouver runs, he no longer had time to leaf through magazines with her. She started using the older editions to light her stove in the morning. The latest fashions inspired her to create her own designs on the back of the brown paper used to wrap the meat and cheese she bought at the market. She cut out the shapes of the fashion models she liked in the magazines and pinned them up, at first on the kitchen wall and later on the inside wall of the pantry. Timothy had objected to paper bodies staring at him while he ate. She'd open the pantry door as soon as he left for work and sip her tea, imagining herself wearing the same outfits as her models. They became her loyal confidantes.

Peter was born five months after the wedding, in October 1912. Denis followed on Christmas Eve of the next year, and John came eleven months after that. Back-to-back pregnancies had drained Stella. A pungent smell of urine-soaked diapers overpowered the familiar odour of motor oil. Timothy stayed away often, signing up for all available overtime.

Three months before John was born, England declared war on Germany, and Canada was pulled into the fray. Shiploads of Canadian soldiers were sent to England's defence. Married men with a family weren't expected to enlist yet, but Timothy packed his duffle bag and whistled a happy tune. A few complaints had been circulating at work about him inviting female passengers to the caboose while on duty. Volunteering to fight overseas was a sure way of sprucing up his reputation. A well-deserved break from the constant holler of babies and the smell of curdled milk and urine was much needed. His mother agreed to give his wife a hand when he sailed off to England with the First Canadian Contingent in October. His two younger brothers followed him overseas with the 199th Regiment of Irish Canadian Rangers.

Timothy hopped on the train heading east to the new Valcartier training camp north of Quebec City—his first time travelling as a passenger. Stella sprinkled more baby powder on the floorboards in the flat and hung a large crucifix on the door leading down to the cellar. She braced herself for more footfalls and swore never to open that door till Timothy came back. She vowed to do her household chores during the dark hours of the night and sleep when the boys napped in the afternoons.

She remembered how her father had tried without success to fend off her fears when she was a child by keeping her hair short and dressing her up as a boy. For a while after, Timothy's caresses had kept them at bay during the years her girl's body transformed into womanhood.

Timothy needed complete darkness for him to sleep. But darkness beckoned the footfalls, approaching even when he was snoring beside her. She'd inch over in the bed till she was close enough for her body heat to blend with his. His energy infused hers and, like an aura of protection, surrounded every inch of her. The footfalls stopped then. Unless her heart was about to burst through her chest, she tried not to sap too much of his energy. He'd notice his loss in the morning and accuse her of being selfish by hogging the bed, putting his job at risk.

"A man needs all his energy to be in charge of the train. I'm responsible for the lives of my passengers. Not like you, staying home and napping any old time, even at Sunday Mass."

He hated when she woke up screaming during the night. "Keep it down. The neighbours will think I'm beating you."

During their three years of marriage before the war, he assumed that carnal desires drove her to touch him during the night. He'd clamber on top of her, even with an unborn baby kicking the walls of her swollen belly. Half asleep and disoriented, he'd pry her legs open and blunder his way inside her before collapsing on his side. But it was only the warmth she craved. She learned after a while that touching him wasn't necessary to ease her fears. Edging as close as possible till she felt that aura of heat radiating from his body was enough.

If the children cried in the night while Timothy was overseas, she'd tuck them in beside her in bed. All three boys sometimes ended up nestled against her skin, their body warmth circulating around her like a protective stream. Her motherhood awakened a courage that allowed her to, if not conquer, at least face her nightly fears. The footfalls never approached the basement door when the babies slept beside her. They became her talismans. She'd never leave the house without them nor ever let them out of her sight.

That all stopped when Timothy came home in 1919. He was strict about the boys sleeping in their own beds no matter how loudly they wailed. After the war, touching Timothy while he slept didn't trigger the same reaction from him as in the early days. Three consecutive

72

pregnancies had left her with swollen breasts and stretch marks on her hips and stomach. A rounded figure hid that girlish body he had once hungered for.

Another pregnancy could be the end of her, the doctor warned Timothy. He advised him to disregard Father Murphy's insistence that she give birth every year as prescribed by the church. Timothy heeded the doctor's advice. Stella was now a woman and didn't need the attention he used to give her when she was only a girl. He had given her and the Church three healthy sons.

"If you consider the wife I have to deal with," he confessed to Father Murphy, "I've fulfilled my duty as a good Catholic family man."

The priest agreed with Timothy, who was, after all, a good bread-winner and a generous contributor to the collection plate. But he forbade Stella from receiving the holy sacraments. By not seeing to her husband's matrimonial rights, she wasn't living up to her Catholic faith. She avoided Sunday Mass after that, only sitting in the family pew on the rare times Timothy wasn't called into work.

The mustard and chlorine gases used during the war had clung to and weakened the soft, moist areas of Timothy's eyes, groin, lungs, and nose. He came back wearing dark-rimmed glasses. His snoring was so loud on the pillow beside her that sleep didn't come to her even with the aid of the strongest sleeping potions. Sunlight allowed her a few short naps between chores, but it wasn't enough. The doctor refused to renew her prescription when he discovered her heart condition.

The bolt to the front door clicked. Timothy was home. She pushed herself up and smoothed her hair back. He'd want his breakfast before taking a nap. A quick glance at her dresser and her eyes paused on the Minnie Mouse design on the sweater she had knitted. The last row of stitches was finished in time for Nadine's fifth birthday. She imagined the child jumping for joy when she brought out the Minnie Mouse cake she had taken such pains to decorate. She had asked Timothy to look for a black food-colouring and liquorice extract for the icing on the mouse ears. He had grumbled about it at first, but Stella knew he'd go out of his way to please their only grandchild. Timothy doted on her, often insisting she stay with them on the weekends he was off. Their two eldest, Peter and Denis, were both sailing to England with the 1st Canadian Infantry Division in October. Any grandchildren from them would have to wait until they were back from the war.

Timothy stepped into the bedroom and unbuttoned his work shirt. "Don't bother with breakfast. I ate something at the station. Will all the boys be coming over?" He threw his shirt on the chair and started undoing his belt.

She noticed how thin his hair was when he leaned down to pull off his trousers. He had come back from the Great War with a full head of white hair. That dark curly mat that had made him look so debonair as a younger man had disappeared. This didn't make him any less attractive; women still looked back over their shoulders at him on the street, even at church.

His enthusiasm for his job on the railway hadn't faltered. His return from the war as a decorated veteran, as well as the protective arm of the union, had cemented his position with the CPR. The many layoffs over the years had never affected him. Stella wasn't forced to find work in factories and restaurants to make ends meet like a lot of women in the neighbourhood. His diminishing eyesight now required him to squint when he filled out his train log. He found no reason to retire despite the occasional tremors he had while punching his customers' tickets. His dark eyes still had that stern, piercing look that made Stella hesitate before contradicting him.

"I'm not sure when Denis and Janette will get here, but the others will be here around eleven. I have time to finish icing the cake and prepare the vegetables before they get here." She leaned down to pick up the work pants he had just dumped on the floor. "That leaves you plenty of time to rest before they get here."

He slid under the blankets. "Claire told you they were coming... or was it John?"

"She called me yesterday to say John wanted to stop at the recruitment office before going to work, but they should be here on time. Does it matter who said it?"

"Humph... well if she said it, I can sleep longer. She's too dizzy to remember."

Stella folded his trousers and placed them on the dresser. "Try to be a bit more patient with her, Timothy. She's a little excitable about things, but she does have a good heart. It's Nadine's fifth birthday... no arguments... please, for the sake of that poor child."

Timothy had taken an instant dislike to the flamboyant blond girl their youngest son had married five years ago. John had been in awe of her easy laughter, her French accent, her thick red lipstick, and the sharp way men swerved to look at her when she passed by. He was shorter than she was and had always been prone to depression, but her smile made him feel ten feet tall. They became inseparable. After two months of cabarets and wild parties, they used Timothy's family train pass and eloped to Niagara Falls.

"That girl is holding him back." He glared at her. "That promotion to chief engineer was supposed to go to him. He's got the brains for it. I warned him to keep her away from the office. She waltzes in there any old time she feels like it. I met up with John's secretary at the station last week. She says Claire sprawls herself on his desk with her cheap perfume, her plastic bracelets, and whips out her powder compact every five minutes to look at herself. What do you think that does to his image? They're not going to want him heading their engineering firm with a wife like that. But he won't listen. None of them do."

Stella walked to the window and pulled the drapes closed. "Claire makes him laugh. They might argue a lot, but at least she can still get a smile out of him. You forget how depressed he was before he started with her—even as a boy." She pulled her housecoat closer. "It always warms a mother's heart to see her child smile."

"Humph... you've always kept that boy hidden under your skirt."

"He was a sickly child."

Timothy turned on his side. "Didn't stop him from getting his engineering degree at nineteen. Showed all those dumb friends of his."

"Friends?" She headed towards the door. "John never had any friends. Unless you count those bums who kicked him around in the schoolyard. You were never here when he came home from school bruised and bleeding almost every week."

"Someone had to put food on the table. You snitching to the teacher never helped him either. He's always been your favourite."

She paused beside the door and stared at him. "Not that again. I've told you. I have no favourites. I love them all. Get some sleep and try to wake up in a better—"

"Did you say recruitment office?" He lifted his head from the pillow. "He's finally decided to enlist, has he? I suppose he doesn't want to be outdone by his two brothers sailing off next month. The air force will grab him right away, you know. They don't take just anybody off the street."

Stella took a long breath, a faraway look in her eyes. "I wish to God none of my boys were going. Not one of them has the heart to kill anyone. It's not as if they had to enlist—three of them married with a wife to support. I just hope John doesn't pass that recruitment test. Besides Claire, he has a young daughter to think of."

"Momma's boys, all three of them. Let them have a go at crawling in muddy trenches with bullets whizzing past their ears for weeks on end. They'll soon toughen up and shoot at anything that moves. Mackenzie King better stop tiptoeing around and have parliament bring in conscription. A prime minister is supposed to bring out the big guns when it comes to the safety of his people. No damn reason why married men can't go out and fight for their country like everybody else."

She shook her head at him before stepping out, clenching the doorknob a moment after closing the door.

The wall clock had just struck two when Stella checked it again. She tucked the half-completed wool scarf in her knitting basket by the rocking chair. Not one of them had called to cancel. She reached for the Minnie Mouse cake on the table and put it away in the pantry. Timothy was about to wake up and was sure to rant about all the trouble she had gone to baking that cake for nothing. The angry words she'd be forced to listen to would only confirm her fear that something was wrong.

76

She had so looked forward to seeing Nadine's eyes light up when she saw the cake. John and Claire's no-show had spoiled all the joy she had preparing for their visit. A feeling of dread had taken over her, making her hands tremble and her pulse quicken. Claire had planned to buy Nadine a Minnie Mouse doll when Stella told her about the sweater she had knitted. The woman wasn't going to forget her own daughter's birthday surprise. She might be a little flighty at times, but she always jumped through hoops for the girl. John was another story—he had never taken well to being a father. Something was definitely wrong.

John had always been the sensitive one of the three boys. Short and frail, he preferred to stay home and read while his older brothers went out gallivanting with the local boys. Any insult or rejection John experienced stirred up long periods of melancholy. Stella spent days trying to boost him up. His brilliance had allowed him to skip three grades in primary school. Yet he had neither the physical nor the mental maturity to fit in with the bigger boys.

He'd won a scholarship to McGill University when he was fifteen and Stella had let out a sigh of relief. He'd at last get the encouragement and approval he needed to feel better about himself. When he landed a job as executive assistant for a major engineering firm after graduation, Timothy crowed about him. But John's depressed moods resurfaced soon after. The employees working under him resented having to take orders from him, a short upstart fresh off the benches of Sunday school. Then he started seeing Claire. He became his normal self again. Claire was loud and fun-loving. She kept him moving and smiling—until Nadine was born.

John resented all the attention Claire gave the baby and became moody again. She'd often leave the baby with Stella to have more time alone with her husband. They quarrelled often and Nadine grew more and more withdrawn.

The bedroom door opened. Stella hurried to put the extra place settings away. She'd tell him that Claire had phoned—no, better to say John had called. Timothy was right about Claire being absent-minded about these things. The long years working with trains had made him unbending about being on time and following schedules. The boys had missed many a meal for being a minute late at the dinner table. Or had had the back of their heads slapped for not running to him the exact moment he called them.

She knew without a doubt that John's absence had nothing to do with Claire's forgetfulness. Stella had lived with fear all her life. The terror that had compelled her to hide Nadine's cake was surging through her now, leaving her sluggish and bewildered.

"Didn't show up? I knew it." He stood rigid in the kitchen archway squinting up at the clock. "I told you she'd forget. Marrying a Frenchie was the worst move he ever made—and from a hick town too. Does she even know how to use a phone?"

Stella jumped at the sound of his voice. The plates slipped from her grasp and crashed to the floor. Ceramic shards scattered in a wide circle around her feet. He glared at her while she stood frozen, unsure of where to step.

"That's what happens when you go out of your way for them. Two days preparing John's favourite meal and slaving on that stupid cake, and for what? You've got yourself all worked up for nothing. Now don't move till I clean this up... my mother's best china, no less. Don't go trying to pick this up and cut yourself. That's all I need." He reached inside the hall closet for the broom and started sweeping. "Now sit down, woman. Let's have a normal meal and I don't want to hear nothing about John and that ditsy wife of his."

The front door swung open. Footsteps clacked on the wooden floor of the hallway towards the kitchen. Timothy looked up from his broom, ready to give anybody walking in a piece of his mind. Stella held her breath. She hadn't heard the patter of Nadine's little shoes.

Their eldest son Peter and his wife Helen appeared, both looking serious. Peter glanced at Timothy and waved him towards a chair. "Leave that broom, Father. There's something I need to tell you." He turned to Stella. "I think you'd better sit down too, Mother. Something terrible has happened."

CHAPTER 8

Lisette paused to study the fragile, handsome woman with blond streaks poking through her thick white hair. She sat clutching her hands in her lap, staring out the window. Her shoulders relaxed as her eyes followed a cardinal fly by and land in the cedars beside the building. Lisette waited, not sure whether Stella had finished her story or was just taking a break.

She had sensed the woman's desperate quest for love from her father, her husband, and then her boys. There had been no mention of interaction with friends or other family members. Lisette understood this—whatever friends she had made growing up never went further than the schoolyard. She never brought them home to meet her foster parents—that was only for normal kids who had an actual family. Her home had been an address, a place to stay until she had to move again.

Stella had somehow managed to keep her fears at bay with her padlocked basement door, her crucifixes and her refusal to sleep after dark. But Lisette didn't have such protection. There had been no locks on the bedroom doors of her foster homes. While Stella's footfalls might have been in her head, Lisette's had been real. The footfalls in her life hadn't halted at a locked door but had advanced without hesitation to where she cowered under her blankets. Screaming had made the touching stop, but it had also triggered a move to another foster home after Social Services got involved. Not all the homes had been the same. When the father figure hadn't been a threat, her own attitude had been the problem—too moody or bad-tempered to be a good fit. She'd stay awake long after all the lights went off, listening for any creaking on the stairs or footfalls heading her way. When she got older and stronger, she took to pushing her dresser against her bedroom door at nights—in case.

"Grandma Stella. Are you alright?" She felt a slight twinge in her chest when she said that name, like she somehow belonged. This visit had given her a slew of family members. Still no closer to her own parents, but a breakthrough was sure to happen soon. "If this is too much for you, we don't have to continue. I work weekends, but I can come back Monday before classes."

Stella came to with a weak smile. "Sorry, dear. Even after all this time, it still hurts to think about it. That poor girl didn't deserve to—"

"Supper time." Mrs. White stood in front of them. "Better get you to the table while it's still hot."

Lisette shoved her notebook into her bag and got up. "I better be off too. I have someone waiting outside."

"Hope I haven't chased you away with all this talk." Stella reached for Mrs. White's arm to pull herself up. "I think I'll pass on supper… if you don't mind. I'm too exhausted to even lift a fork. Maybe after a short rest."

Mrs. White glanced at Lisette. "Talking about upsetting things, were we?" She smiled at Stella. "Come along, dear. We can warm your plate up when you're ready to eat." She led her away. "Now let's get you settled in your room."

Lisette followed them out and stopped at the reception. Stella hadn't mentioned whether her husband was still alive. Her staying in this senior's home didn't imply he wasn't living on his own. She had wanted to ask for her sons' telephone numbers, but Mrs. White had whisked her off.

The receptionist behind the desk dropped her pen and looked up at Lisette. "May I help you?"

"I'm hoping you can. I need you to please check something for me in Mrs. Pritchart's file."

The woman cocked her head. "And you are?"

Lisette pushed her shoulders back. "I'm her granddaughter—her great granddaughter, that is."

"I see." She checked her watch. "Do you have legal access to her file?"

"Legal access? No. Listen, I don't want to see her file. I only want my uncle's phone number. I was going to ask her myself but Mrs. White walked her back to her room before I had a chance to."

"Mrs. Pritchart?" The receptionist pulled her glasses off and pinched the bridge of her nose. "She wouldn't remember anybody's phone numbers. She'd have to go up to her room to search for them. And she never makes a call. She picks up the odd call when she's in her room, but that's about it. Giving her a phone message is useless—she forgets to call back. Her son insisted on having a line put in her room so she doesn't feel so isolated. A lot of them do that. Calling saves them a visit." She gave Lisette a quick smirk. "But we all know their isolation starts way before they end up here."

"I guess I lucked out today." Lisette recalled how difficult it had been for Stella to figure out who she was speaking to. "She answered on the third ring."

"Must've been right after lunch, during nap time. Any later, she would've been out of her room." She straightened in her chair and pulled her shoulders back. "Unless they need to nap, we don't encourage our residents to stay all alone in their rooms during the day. They need to mingle or they'll disconnect with the outside world—although most do after a while. We make sure everyone gets the proper sleep aid to get them through the night. Nothing worse than having them roam the building at all hours." She checked her watch again. "I'll be closing up now. My lunch break started five minutes ago."

"What about the phone number?"

She let out a long breath. "Listen, this can get me into big trouble. I'm not supposed to give out information about the residents without their permission." She wheeled her chair around, slid open the drawer of the cabinet behind her and pulled out a file.

"I'm just asking for a simple phone number, not to see her medical file. Although I wouldn't mind taking a look at that."

The woman scanned the file and then slapped it closed. "Sorry, can't help you." She slammed the drawer shut. "I've got two phone numbers on file and both of them are private." She reached for her purse and walked towards Lisette. "Please step back. I have to lock the office during lunch hour."

Lisette marched towards the exit. Another dead end. Social Services hadn't helped her much. Serge might come up with something on his uncle's database, but it didn't look promising. Grandma Stella hadn't seen Nadine in twenty years, so she wasn't much help either. The conversation with the receptionist had made her blood boil. Not because she had refused to give her the phone numbers—she was only doing her job. It was all these stupid roadblocks stopping her from meeting up with her own mother. Having that phone number might've made her search a little easier. Her uncles had more information than Grandma Stella had to offer.

Her best bet was to forget about the whole situation and get on with her life. She had managed to survive without a mother all these years and would be able to continue her journey without one. But meeting with her own great-grandmother had awakened a burning need to attach herself to some clan—to be part of a cluster in the universe. She might end up not liking any of them, but at least now she knew she was attached to some family link, and not floating debris nobody wanted to associate with.

Serge was fast asleep in the back seat of the car. He jumped up when Lisette slammed the passenger door closed.

"Sorry it took so long. The woman had a lot to say."

He climbed back into the driver's seat. "No problem. I needed that nap before I start my shift. So, did you learn anything?"

"The woman turned out to be OK. But nothing she told me will help me find my mother. It doesn't look like the family has had any contact with her in years. I tried to get my uncle's phone number from the receptionist, but she wouldn't budge."

He started the car. "A phone number—piece of cake. Why didn't you let me ask her?"

She frowned. "Your charms don't always work. This girl was a hard nut to crack."

He grinned. "Even with the seam of my fly ripped open?"

"Naw. No dice with this one. She was too much in a hurry to go eat her lunch. Even a hunky flasher like you"—she smiled—"didn't have a chance of tearing her away from her sandwich."

"You underestimate my male charms, missy. I'll drop you off at home and I'm heading to work. Friday evening gets pretty busy. You'll probably be asleep by the time I get back."

"Maybe, but I'll probably be up late. I've got to hit the books. My term papers are due soon. I still need to come back here again. I told the woman I'd come visit on Monday. She had started telling me about something bad that happened and the manager broke us up."

"Did she mention any other names?"

She pulled her notebook out. "Timothy, that's my great grandfather. But he might've kicked the bucket by now. My grandparents, Claire and John. She was about to tell me about them, so I don't know whether they're still alive or not. And Grandma Stella's two other sons, Peter and Denis. The receptionist said she had two phone numbers on file, both of them private—most likely belong to the ones in charge of her welfare." She shrugged. "So that's where the trail ends."

"Not so fast." He stopped at a red light. "We have the names, don't we? They might have private phone numbers, but they've got to be on some kind of list. If they worked, owned a business, or were part of some criminal activity, they'll show up somewhere. That database will at least give me an address to start with."

"Thanks, Serge. That might be helpful. Maybe you can do your research—it won't take you long—before I go back to visit the wom—" She paused before finishing her sentence. "Before I go back to visit Grandma Stella."

Serge laughed. "Looks like she's gotten to you."

She gazed out the passenger window. "She is… my great-grandmother, you know. That's big enough for me to go back and see her."

CHAPTER 9

Lisette woke to the clanging of church bells a few blocks away. She reached for her glasses on the small table beside her and squinted at the round face of the alarm clock. Eight fifteen. Too early for Sunday mass—unless somebody big like a hockey player or a politician died. She stretched her arm out under the blanket. The sheet on Serge's side of the bed was cold. His next taxi shift didn't start till mid-afternoon. He'd most likely gone to the depanneur to pick up the *Journal de Montréal*.

The sound of voices from the kitchen told her Sylvie and Pit were up. They never got out of bed before noon on a Sunday. Something must be going on. The ache in her lower back that had kept her awake most of the night had gone away. Any sharp, quick movement on her part might trigger the pain to come back. The urge to burrow under the wool blanket and snooze a couple more hours was tempting, but she wanted to proofread the term paper that was due on Tuesday before going to work at the depanneur. She planned to finish up her other two term papers within the next three weeks, leaving her a bit of time to relax before the baby was due.

She rolled herself to a sitting position on the edge of the bed. Her round belly was making it more and more awkward for her to move around. Tying her shoes, slipping her boots on, or even cutting her toenails were now almost impossible tasks. But damn if she was going to rely on someone else to do things for her. Especially when having a baby hadn't been part of Serge's plans. Nor hers. She had figured on completing her studies and for him to find steady work before starting a family. But there you have it. These things happen. She'd find a way to deal with it without losing Serge in the process. *I don't do cling,* he'd told her when they first started together. *And I'm not made of Velcro,* she'd answered back. It was something she had learned fast and early: *until the end of time is for dreamers.*

Her mountainous belly was a problem—and it was getting bigger by the day. Using Serge's footstool to sit on allowed her to bypass her belly and to manage to reach her feet without asking for help. The cramped bedroom made it easier for her to grab onto something and pull herself up. Serge had moved his boxes of books from the far corner of the room to the basement locker to make room for the small wooden crib. But by the looks of things, they'd only be in their own place after the baby arrived.

Driving a taxi part-time might cover the rent, but not much else. She'd have to work more hours at the depanneur once the baby was born. Serge's boss had promised him more cabbie hours. The living arrangement with Pit and Sylvie wasn't ideal, but at least they had a roof over their heads. That FLQ craze was on the verge of petering out soon, giving Serge more time to focus on their little family.

She felt a quick movement beneath her ribs and she reached down to massage her belly. The voices in the kitchen were getting louder. She pulled herself up and headed for the door. Serge's dirty jeans, shirts, and socks littered the narrow walking space available to her. Damn if she was going to pick up after him. She had agreed to keep the apartment clean instead of paying rent. Laundry duty was part of the deal, but not picking up after everybody. If clothes didn't make it to the laundry basket, they didn't get washed. She'd have to bring this up again with Serge before he left for work. Why did things always get so complicated? She reached up and jerked her housecoat off the hook behind the door.

The bedroom opened out into the hallway that led to the kitchen. All three of them hovered around the table staring down at an open *Journal de Montréal.* Serge stood shoulders hunched between Pit and Sylvie. His long hair grazed the newspaper in front of him, his black leather jacket unzipped and glistening with morning rain. Sylvie held on to Serge's arm as they read, her quilted, pink nylon housecoat unbuttoned to just above her nipples.

Pit wore one of Sylvie's silk camisoles, his dark chest hair poking out from the edge of the lace neckline. He puffed on his cigarette, one hand stuffed inside the front of his tight red Jockey shorts. "The idiots thought we were bluffing, eh? Screw the bastards." He swung a clenched fist up in the air. "*Vive le Québec libre!*"

"What's up?" None of them had noticed Lisette standing in the doorway. "By the way, do any of you know where our polling station is? I know voting day is only next week, but I was just wondering where people have to go."

All three turned in her direction.

"Polling station?" Pit fixed his eyes on her. "Is she for real?"

Sylvie pushed her shoulders back and smirked. "Get serious, girl. Voting at a capitalist rigged election? No damn way. Drapeau is scaring people to get their votes. He accused the opposition of having ties to terrorists. So of course people will vote him in again. Why play the sheep game? Any idiot knows it's a waste of time."

Lisette bit her lip and sucked in her breath. If she let loose she'd crack Sylvie's face in. "Well, I prefer placing my sheep vote rather than kidnapping innocent people and placing bombs in mailboxes. It might take me longer to get what I want, but at least I'm not hurting anybody in the process."

Serge straightened up and brushed his hair back. "Easy girls." He slapped his hand on the newspaper. "This is serious business. Pierre Laporte died yesterday. He was found dead in the trunk of a car. The paper claims they've got arrest warrants for all the cell members."

Sylvie stepped back, staring at Lisette as if she had just barged into a private meeting. Pit pulled his hand out of his shorts and leaned against the table.

"Dead?" Lisette's mouth fell open. "Shoved in the trunk of a car with the spare tire like he was garbage? That's gangster crap. They've gone too far. If anybody supported the FLQ before, they sure won't now. Laporte was a good family man. Where did they find him?"

Pit blew out his cigarette smoke in her direction. "On the south shore, near the St-Hubert airport." He lifted his chin up high. "And they're liberators, not frigging gangsters. For someone doing a major in political science, you don't know much. Don't they teach you nerds about the means justifying the end?"

Lisette tugged her housecoat closer. "The way things are happening these days, it's more like the ends justifying the means." She could usually manage to rise above Pit's simple-minded comments by changing the subject or pretending she wasn't listening. He never caught on, mistaking her silence for adherence to his views. With that angry look cemented on his face and a ready snarl for anyone who disagreed with him, challenging him was pointless.

Pit lowered himself on a chair. "Same damn thing. Switching the words around doesn't make you any smarter."

"Right. This isn't getting us anywhere. We don't have all the details. Maybe Laporte tried to escape and there was an accident. They weren't about to call the cops, so they put the body in the car." Sylvie shot Lisette a look of disapproval and then smiled at Pit before heading for the stove. "I'll make you a coffee, babe. It's too early for silly word games."

Lisette focused on the black eyeliner smudges under Pit's eyes and the oily strands of hair hanging down his back. A sure sign he hadn't showered after last night's gig at the club. "That's possible, Sylvie. But that doesn't make everything right." She looked straight at Pit. "And we're not talking about the same thing. There's a big difference. You're saying that FLQ activities are backed by moral reasoning that has ethical consequences."

Pit shoved his chair back, his fists by his side. "Frigging right they're playing by the rules. The workers' rules. Not what the damn oppressors decide."

Serge glowered at Lisette from across the room. She avoided his eyes, staring at Pit instead with no intention of backing down. The sight of Pit standing around in his girlfriend's underwear gloating about the death of an innocent man made her want to scream.

"In my books." She stiffened and folded her arms across her chest. "Real books, Pit, not like those Superman comic books you leave hanging around." A wave of heat crept up her neck and face. "Liberators—as you like to call them—don't kidnap someone who's playing football with his family on his front lawn. If you tell me what's happening out there is a good example of the end justifying the means, that's another story. I agree that the FLQ will stop at nothing to get what they want."

Sylvie placed the kettle on the stove and glanced at Pit, an anxious look on her face. Lisette dug her fingers into her crossed arms and braced herself for his counterattack. She had been walking on eggshells around Pit and Sylvie since she moved in with them. It was time she spoke her mind. Pit Nadeau, streetwise, from a hard-drinking family in the tough district of St-Henri, didn't take well to an affront.

Pit took a step towards Lisette, and Serge slid in between them. "Everyone take a time-out. No need to fight about this."

"I don't like her attitude—pregnant or not." Pit gave Lisette a black look and leaned back to stamp out his cigarette in the already full ashtray on the table.

"Cool it, Pit." Sylvie reached in the cupboard for a mug. "A sad thing happened yesterday. But if anyone is to blame, it's Trudeau for sending his army here. Instead of solving anything, it's made things worse."

Lisette leaned sideways against the door frame, willing herself far away from this scene. After almost a year of listening to all the ranting against Ottawa, it all seemed like grandstanding to her. That the English had always had a tight hold on political and financial matters in Quebec was a known fact. And yes, it was about time Quebecers asserted their autonomy. But Sylvie and Pit talked about it *ad nauseam*.

Sylvie was like a political parrot, repeating everything she read in newspapers or picked up at political rallies. Her father, a successful federal criminal lawyer, had severed all ties with her when she moved in with Pit. Her attacks on his position within the federal system were her way of getting back at him. Pit's brand of song was all about the Quebec working class and the need to revolt against the English elite. The spectators always roared for more when Pit did his angry anti-English-establishment numbers. But nobody paid much attention when he switched to the non-political songs. Serge seemed to be the only one of the three who wasn't self-serving.

Happy to be close to Serge, Lisette hadn't let Sylvie and Pit's antics bother her at first. She had believed in an independent Quebec since her early teens. But when the movement became more violent, she distanced herself. Her lack of proper sleep lately had eroded her tolerance level to way below the zero mark. She turned to Sylvie. "You're forgetting something. The army was brought in after the FLQ threatened to kill Laporte. I agree it didn't help matters, but his death wasn't a direct consequence of army tanks rolling down Beaver Hall."

Serge raised his palms up in the air. "Why are we having this conversation? Laporte is dead, so now the cops don't have to tiptoe around us anymore. They can storm in and arrest whoever the hell they want. That's crap about them having a warrant out for the cell members. We're under martial law, so they don't need damn warrants to arrest anybody." He gestured towards Lisette. "They'll even pick her up if they figured she knew something. They've got ways to make anybody talk. They've been on my trail for a while now, so we all have to stop bickering and watch our backs."

Sylvie pulled the bottle of instant coffee out of the cupboard. "Daddy will just freak if I get arrested. I suppose he'd send his secretary to bail me out." She looked back over her shoulder at Lisette. "Being pregnant must make it easier for you to break down under pressure."

Lisette glared at Sylvie. "The only thing that can make me break under pressure is listening to more of your bullshit. Let's go, Serge. I'm getting dressed and we're out of here." She spun on her heel and marched to the bedroom, slamming the door behind her.

Pit scowled before sitting back down. "She's nothing but trouble, man." He shifted his gaze to Sylvie. "Don't forget, babe. Three sugars and only a drop of milk."

"Don't worry about Lise. She'll come round." Serge zipped up his jacket. "There's bigger things to think about, Pit. I can't be the only one they're after. They must be onto you too. Try taming your gigs down a bit. Get off their radar for a while."

"It's not like we're responsible for the damn kidnappings." Sylvie poured hot water into two mugs and reached for the sugar bowl. "So what if we support our Patriotes by sending cash? Those guys are risking their lives for our freedom. The least we can do is back them."

Serge cocked his head at her. "Aiding and abetting, Sylvie. We share responsibility for whatever they do with that money. And that's all OK—we accept that. We're all doing our part. All I'm saying is that we have to lay low for now."

Pit leaned back in his chair and yawned. "Chill, man. My songs are part of my brand. I sing for the working class, not the frigging oppressors. If I were you"—he pointed his chin in Lisette's direction—"I'd worry more about why they're following you."

Serge's shoulders dropped and he stared at Pit, incredulous. A long moment passed before he spoke. "I told you, man. You two can't stand each other, but that doesn't mean she'd blow the whistle. You're not making any sense. You've got to stay alert. You know what I mean, man. Cut back on the booze and the drugs. You've got to keep your mind clear." Hands clenched, he headed for the bedroom.

Lisette followed Serge down the winding metal stairs to the sidewalk. Her stomach churned. Their discussion in the kitchen had left him stone-faced and silent. Pit and Sylvie hadn't painted a glowing picture of her: a blabbermouth who'd break under pressure. And Pit's last comment to Serge, which she'd overheard as she was dressing—what was that all about? Serge had stood up for her, but did he also suspect her? Rumours that informers had infiltrated the FLQ had been going around for a while now. One of their demands on a manifesto broadcast by a local radio station was that police release the name of any informers to the public.

The diner was a short couple of blocks away. Serge remained tight-lipped and stone-faced. She'd been a little brutal with Pit and

Sylvie but it wasn't the first time she'd had words with them. They dished it out as much as she did. Serge never got involved with their arguments. Her stand against violence shouldn't be a big surprise to him.

They had agreed not to let their differences come between them. He drew a line between his love life and his cause. He saw himself as a defender of the Quebec working class, enabler of an independent Quebec. That Lisette didn't approve of his way of operating didn't deter him. He had promised her to come up with other ways besides robbing banks to help finance FLQ activities. Yet she wasn't convinced where his loyalties lay. He was loving and attentive when they were together but could turn on a dime to his militant mode.

She admired his independent nature and his dogged ability not to let anyone sway him. Her previous love relationships had never gone past the physical. He had surprised her by blossoming into the grand symphony conductor of the reason why she got up in the morning. She was ready to do anything not to lose him. With his hand pressed to her belly, he had sworn, tears in his eyes, to always be there for her and the baby. Our child, he'd promised her, will never experience the pain your mother made you go through.

Serge chose a corner booth at the end of the small diner and signalled to the waitress to bring coffee. Lisette slid her belly across the table from him and watched him crack his knuckles. "What's this all about? Pit's getting paranoid. All that toking up is warping whatever brain he's got?"

He lifted his gaze. "Pit's OK, but he doesn't take prisoners. Attack him and he won't give up till you're down. Pushing him against the wall like you did wasn't a good move on your part."

"So he figures I'd squeal on you guys? That's sick! In any case, I never know what you guys are up to. What's to squeal about?"

He looked away. "There's been a lot of talk about infiltrators. The cops know too much, too often."

"And what—" A tightening in her chest made her pause. "What do *you* think about all that?"

He waited until the waitress had placed the coffee in front of them and walked away. "It doesn't make a lot of sense. Sylvie and Pit can't figure out why I'm the target and not them."

She let out a soft sigh. If Serge had shared Pit's suspicions, it would've meant the end of them as a couple. Trust was a vital part of what they had together. But the way he kept on pulling at and bending his fingers, there had to be something else he wasn't telling her. "Nobody knows for sure. They might be on the radar without even knowing. Sylvie's too busy fussing with her hair and adjusting her sunglasses every two minutes to notice what's happening around her. And Pit... well... being the center of attention is what he expects. Someone watching his every move is an everyday thing for him."

He grimaced. "They're kind of special alright... but I know a softer side of them than what you see. Pit has always been different, always caught in some scrap when we were in school. I'd be there for him each time. He was the kid brother I never had. I think Sylvie is attracted to the neediness in him. He depends on her for everything. I know you resent the fact that she's had it easy all her life. But it isn't her fault her parents are well off. She got everything she asked for growing up, but her parents were never around. And both of them are real loyal to the cause. Pit can sure get a crowd all riled up and Sylvie's great with large group activities. She can organize a sit-in or a march in the bat of an eye."

"Loyal... it's not how you'd describe me... not after this morning. But something else is bugging you, right? Whatever it is, spit it out."

He pressed his palms flat on the table. "You might not be as passionate as they are about what we're doing, but you're loyal to what you believe in. That makes you strong and I love that in you. Sylvie and Pit, though, aren't convinced you're on our side. They don't think you bring much to the table."

She sipped her coffee and stared at him from over the top of her glasses. "Looks like you guys have been discussing me. You know I go to all the demonstrations and wave all their banners and posters around. Sometimes I might not agree with what's going on. That doesn't mean I don't believe in the cause."

He pressed his hands together and gazed down at the table.

"You haven't even touched your coffee. If something's up, Serge, you better come out with it."

He raked his fingers through his hair. "What you said to them before sure didn't help. There's no easy way to say this, but... they figure it'd be better if you lived somewhere else." He leaned back on the bench, biting down on his lip. "By the end of the week... if possible. They're real paranoid about being busted."

She straightened, her look incredulous. "You mean... move out? Because of the baby? At least they're right about that. It'll be a lot more crowded in there when the baby comes." Why had he hesitated to tell her this? He wasn't giving her the whole picture.

"It's not about the baby." He fidgeted in his seat. "Sylvie sort of likes the idea of having a kid crawling around."

"Can't see Pit going for that or anything else that has to do with me." She and Pit had never hit it off. "Hey! Don't look so down. It's not a problem. They're actually on my side for once. I've been wanting us to get our own place for a while now. So what's the big—" She fixed her eyes on his. Something in the way he was staring at her made her pause. "You're not in any trouble, are you? You didn't order a big breakfast like you always do. And your coffee must be stone cold by now. What's going on?"

"I can't take any chances, Lise. I can't sleep nights thinking about it." He twisted his mug back and forth. "I spotted that car trailing me again last night. I'm sure the cops have been watching us for a while now. They haven't moved in on us because they think we can lead them to Laporte. Nothing's stopping them now that's he's dead. They're on the warpath. There's a massive manhunt for FLQ members. They'll haul in anybody who they think might know something."

"What's that got to do with me moving out?"

"Don't you see?" He tugged at his hair. "If they bust down our door, they'll haul all of us in. I won't let them throw you behind bars. What if the baby comes early? They'd probably grill you while you're giving birth. We have to find you a safe place where they won't find you. And we've got to stay away from each other... at least till the dust settles."

Her breathing stopped for a split second and she tightened the grip on her coffee mug. He too wanted her to move out. On her own. Was this his way of breaking up with her? Where did he expect her to go? Eight months pregnant. No steady job. No money. He was the father of their child—they were a family. "So... it isn't only Sylvie and Pit who want me out." She felt a stirring in her belly. He had let her down—like everybody else before him.

"I'll work more hours. I'll help you out." He reached out to grab her hand. "It's too dangerous for you and the baby. I'll help you find a place."

"So come with me. We'll lay low together. If you disappear for a while, whoever's following you will forget about you."

He shook his head. "I can't just drop out of the action like that. We have to keep on resisting. Our support is needed even more now that the cops have stepped up their search. You're asking me to give up my soul. Louis Riel said it all just before his English oppressors executed—"

"Stop." She raised her hand in protest, her voice cracking. "No need to quote him. Your poster is the first thing I see when I open my eyes in the morning. His words are etched in my brain like blood on a wool blanket: 'I have nothing but my heart and I have given it long ago to my country.' Spare me the drama. If you're breaking up with me, leave me a bit of dignity."

"Keep it down. People are staring at us." He lowered his gaze and shoved the sugar container back in place beside the salt and pepper. "That's what I'm all about, Lise." His voice low, insistent. "You knew it when you moved in with me."

"Look what it got Riel, eh? The guy devoted his life to Métis rights and what did it get him? The English hung him by the neck and in the end, nothing changed for his people. I get it—politics comes before me and your child. Have you thought about who's going to rent to me in my condition—and with no job to back me up? I've got no place to run to. I know you gave your heart away, but what about your sense of responsibility?" The smell of her coffee made her nauseous and she swallowed hard to block the tears from falling. Why was he doing this to her? They were a family. She had never trusted anyone like she did him.

"This isn't a breakup. We'll be back together in no time. You know I've got to see this thing through. And I'm scared as hell the cops will pick you up. We can't be seen together, not until it's safer. I promise we'll look for a place together. I wish we had located your mother, I'm sure she'd want to help, especially when she finds out about that unclaimed amount I told you about."

"Is that why you've been so helpful about searching for her? You figured it was a convenient solution—dumping me with a complete stranger."

"I don't believe I'm hearing this crap. I've been helping because it's important to you. And yes, I think it'd be a damn good idea if you met her and she turned out OK. We'd need furniture if you rented and you know we can't afford it. It will only be for a few months while all this shit is going on. All you need is a room. Somewhere safe for you and the baby right now."

Her shoulders relaxed. He wasn't breaking up with her after all. "Maybe you're right, Serge. Check in that database for anything on my mother's uncles. Maybe you can come up with something. I'm not very hopeful, but you never know."

"It's our only safe option right now. If your mother doesn't help, you'll know she's not worth seeing again. We'll have to figure something else out." He paused to wipe a hand over his eyes and looked away. "You know I can't afford to pay for two rents, but I'll work double shifts. We'll be a family soon. I promise."

The intensity in his voice and the tears she had seen him wipe away quelled the turmoil in her chest. She had reacted too quickly. He was right about her being at risk. He was only looking out for her and the baby—being a family man after all. A temporary breakup, for the good of all.

In any case, he was right about her mother. She owed her at least this. It was time she found out what the woman was all about. If she refused to help, she'd know where she stood with her.

CHAPTER 10

Lisette rang the buzzer a second time and checked her watch. The residence was supposed to be open for visitors at this hour. She had woken up early and tiptoed around the apartment so as not to wake anybody up. Both Serge and Pit had come home late from work the night before. Nothing had been said about yesterday's argument. Crossing each other in the hallway that evening before he went off to the bar, she and Pit had nodded at each other as if they were strangers. There were no words left to be said. They wanted her out. She wasn't a good fit. She'd shove her belongings into garbage bags and find another place to stay. That's how it had always been with her.

Sylvie had come to sit beside her on the sofa after Pit left. Lisette had closed her textbook, thinking she probably wanted to watch TV.

"I don't want to disturb what you're doing, Lisette. I'm working on my school project too, but I wanted to talk to you before you went to bed."

"You didn't go watch Pit's gig?"

"Not this time. He's playing at some dive in the east end. The toilets there are disgusting." She flinched. "I always feel like I've just been attacked by millions of tiny crabs when I sit on the bowl."

Lisette laughed. "I never sit down. I'd rather squat."

"It can't be easy for you to do that nowadays."

"You're right about that. Even using toilet paper is a challenge with this big belly."

Sylvie reached down behind the couch, pulled out a shopping bag, and placed it beside Lisette. "Here. A little something for the baby."

"Really? You didn't have to do that, but it's sure nice of you." She glanced at the bag. "And from Ogilvy's too. This must have cost you a few bucks."

Sylvie shrugged. "What the heck. My mother gives me a good allowance."

Lisette opened the bag and pulled out four pairs of baby pyjamas, two white and the other two bright blue. "Thanks, Sylvie. It's very generous of you. Especially after what happened yesterday."

"Pit chose the colours. He thought they looked patriotic."

Lisette looked up. "He did? I'm... surprised he'd even bother."

Sylvie stretched her arms out and yawned. "I have to get back to my project." She hesitated, her eyes pensive. "Pit might talk big, but he's really just a softie. He never says anything bad about you behind your back, but when you two get together, sparks fly. He's just as worried about you getting busted as Serge is."

Lisette pressed her lips together. She had misjudged them both. "I never... thought of him like that. Maybe I can... tell him I'm sorry. I was a little patronizing with him."

Sylvie grimaced. "You can try, but don't expect him to apologize back. His parents were drunk half the time, so he grew up dodging punches at home and on the street. You never apologize where he comes from—once a fight is over, you just get ready for the next one." She made a beeline for her bedroom. "I need to get back to my work or I'll never finish."

Lisette rang the buzzer again. It had taken her a long bus and metro ride to get here. Two unfinished term papers were waiting for her at home. She was about to head back to the bus stop when the receptionist hurried out of the office and rushed to open the glass door.

"Sorry to keep you waiting." She forced a smile. "Quite a coincidence. I was just on the phone with Mr. Pritchart. I had no way of contacting you, so it's a good thing you came by. I called him about your request for his phone number. He's left a message for you. Come with me and I'll give it to you."

Lisette followed the woman into the office. Good news at last. She'd have someone else besides Stella to help her with the search.

The receptionist tore off a yellow slip from her message pad and handed it to her. "He left you his lawyer's number."

"His lawyer?" She scanned the message "What for?"

The woman sat down at her desk. "He also gave strict orders not to allow you to visit his mother without his presence."

"What's he talking about?" Her body tensed. "He can't do that. She's my great-grandmother. I can visit her whenever I want to."

"Peter Pritchart is her legal guardian. He has the authority to make any decisions about her financial and her personal welfare. He feels your visits might worsen her heart condition."

A wave of heat surged up her neck. "She seemed happy enough to see me last Friday. It didn't look like she needed to have someone make decisions for her."

"It might seem that way at times. The residents have good days and bad ones. The odd visit won't give you the whole picture." She leaned back in her chair and crossed her arms. "The poor dears put on a brave show of smiling and pretending they know who you are. You'll never hear them mention your name until you say it first. All that effort it takes to pretend they're on top of things drains them of all their energy." She skimmed the open file in front of her. "Mrs. White noted that Mrs. Pritchart had to rest right after your visit and she refused to eat her supper."

"She seemed a little excited about seeing me, but that was about it."

"That's because you don't know her situation." The woman closed her file and lifted her gaze. "Her son doesn't want his mother too stimulated. If you want to discuss this further, please call his lawyer."

Lisette bit her lip and shifted from foot to foot. This uncle sounded a little too controlling for her liking, but then, Grandpa Pritchart hadn't seemed any better. There had been no problem during Friday's visit. Grandma Stella had appeared a little tired at the end but that was to be expected. That didn't mean she wasn't allowed to come back and visit her. She pulled her shoulders back.

If they were going to refuse to buzz her in next time she came, she may as well see her now.

"I promised her I'd come back today. Since I'm here, I'll just pop in to say hi. You don't want to disappoint her, do you?" She turned on her heel before the woman had time to react and headed towards the lounge. "I won't be long."

Lisette heard the receptionist call out to her. She continued down the hallway without looking back.

Grandma Stella sat in the same armchair, a thick wool sweater wrapped around her shoulders and a blanket covering her lap.

"You feeling OK, Grandma?" Lisette hung her jacket on the back of the armchair opposite from her and sat down.

Stella beamed at her. "You came back, dear. I thought you'd stay away after I bored you silly last time." She tugged her sweater closer. "I have the chills this morning. I get like that when I don't get much sleep—it happens a lot even with those pills they give me. I'll just have to rest after lunch."

"You didn't bore me." She glanced back over her shoulder to see if the receptionist had followed and reached into her bag for her notebook. "That's why I'm here. Now that I've discovered I have a family, I want to learn a bit more about them. I can't stay long, though. I don't want to tire you."

She reached over to pat Lisette's knee. "Quite the opposite, dear. The residents here might seem tired and a bit depressed to you. It looks like it's always autumn here. Not because of the service. We're all well-fed and kept safe like baby chicks in their nest. Not having any contact with anybody outside of here is what gets us. Sometimes the family visits, but they can hardly wait to leave as soon as they set foot in here. You can't blame them. Being here reminds them of how they'll end up one day." She smoothed out the wrinkles in her blanket and raised her head. "Bless you for coming, dear. Talking about old things with you might've tired me out, but it's the same as being sick. You feel like you're going to die, but once you've heaved it all out, you feel great again. It had to come out. My family means well. They never talk about things that might upset me. But burying something doesn't stop it from hurting. You don't see it, but the spirit of what you buried still lives on." She fell silent and stared down at her lap.

"We don't have to talk about sad things, Grandma. Some things must've made you laugh over the years."

That made her look up and smile. "Yes, when the boys were small. And your grandmother Claire was funny, a real joy to have around." She paused a moment and looked away. "I know I was supposed to side with our John, but I always felt sorry for her. She lit up any room she walked into. The poor girl didn't have a happy end." She shook her head, her eyes far away. "Had she lived, she would've found a way to forgive John. That's just how she was.... There's a story she used to tell—although John always marched out of the room when she started on that. It made us women laugh the way she mimed each part of the story. It must've happened in the autumn, just before she met our John.... "

CHAPTER 11

'

Rivière-au-Renard, Quebec
November 1932

Claire clutched the old canvas carryall on her lap. The batch of tea biscuits and cold ham slices Ma had wrapped for her sat snug on top of the few pieces of clothing she had packed. Her twin brother's trousers felt tight over the bloomers and extra underwear she had on. But a northeaster had started and she had no idea when and where she'd end up.

She braced herself on the seat to avoid leaning sideways into the driver each time he took a sharp curve. The old guy drove with a lead foot but the quicker they got there the better. The black Roadster pickup smelling of stale codfish and screech rum had pulled over minutes after she jerked her thumb up. Said he was driving nonstop to Quebec City but she'd have to sit closer to him on account of the passenger door that sometimes swung open when he hit a bump.

The old guy wasn't much of a talker. Dried and yellowed farmers' fields of early autumn, humbled by the whims of the sun and rain, rolled by on one side of the gravel road. She tried to focus on the cedar posts leaning windward at the edge of the ditches. On the other side, the dark grey-blue waters of the St. Lawrence River flowed northeast back towards her village. Whenever the cedar posts stopped, she knew they were approaching another village along the coast, closer to her living out her dream.

A present for her sweet sixteenth birthday. Leaving her suffocating maritime village for the bright lights of Montreal. No more limits on when to boogie, chew gum, blow smoke in a guy's face, or smear herself with tons of makeup. No more going to confession, ever again.

The cedar posts leaning over from the wind and rain reminded her of Ma, shoulders hunched in her long, faded grey housedress. She stood on the sagging steps of their tiny clapboard house, her head tilted, watching her daughter set out for the side of the highway. Claire's twin brother waved goodbye through the broken window beside the front door—another reminder of Pa's drunken visits from the lumber camp. There'd be hell to pay when he found out his golden girl had left without his blessing.

Ma had reached into the cracked cookie jar just as Claire picked up her bag before heading for the front door. Get yourself away before it's too late, she'd said, handing her the grocery money for the month. Claire swallowed hard and shoved the small bills in the side pocket of her long twill coat. Her brothers would be eating only turnips and lard for the next few weeks.

No man's going to shove me around, Ma. Not like Pa does, she'd yelled over her shoulder, marching towards the road.

More cedar posts. It'd be a while before they drove by another village. She reached into her bag to pull out her red lipstick. No need for a mirror. A quick stroke and she smacked her lips together to spread it out.

"That sounds right good. Shakes a man up that does."

His gruff voice made her shift on the seat. She took a quick glance at him. He hadn't said a single word since she hopped into his truck over an hour ago. "What's that?"

"That smacking sound you just did." He kept his eyes on the road. "Putting something in your mouth sure makes you feel right good, eh?"

Her whole body tensed up and she inched over towards the passenger door. "Nothing went in my mouth, mister. I just put some damn lipstick on." She liked the old guy better when he stuck to his driving. He had just popped up and started babbling like a slimy old jack-in-the-box.

He glanced at her and smirked. His two front teeth were missing and the rest were tobacco-stained. "Sexy red mouth... well, little girl, that makes a man want to party all night long. A pretty blond chick like you—guys must want to touch the merchandise a lot, eh?"

"That's where my feet come in. A girl's got to learn to hit where it counts the most." Her heart raced. She made an effort to swallow down breaths so he didn't detect her panic. The old guy's tongue kept on darting in and out of his mouth and he swallowed hard a few times. She wanted to yell at him to stop the damn truck but she didn't want him thinking he had any power over her. Rabid dogs can smell your fear. That's when they attack.

"A scrapper, eh? Makes the prize even sweeter." He clutched the steering wheel with one hand and placed the other palm-down beside her on the seat. His fingernails, ringed with dirt, were as tobacco-stained as his teeth.

She edged a little closer to the door. His arm movement had unleashed the acrid odour of his unwashed body and soiled clothes. Spasms of nausea surged up her throat. She grabbed the door handle and scanned the side of the highway. The deep ditches brimmed with tall reeds and cattails, but it was better than landing head first on the hard gravel at the speed he was going. Diving straight into the ditch was her best bet. But he was crazy enough to reverse and come back for her. Nowhere to run. Fields and bushes on one side of the road and steep cliffs going down to the river on the other. Hardly any traffic on the road and no house in sight—better hold on till—

"Hang in there, chickadee." He swerved the truck onto a narrow dirt road, reached out to grip her upper thigh and dragged her back beside him. "Thinking of jumping, eh? Right sexy chick you are, but you're sure three bricks shy of a load."

She struggled to pull away but her left arm was pinned under his. The smell of his rotten teeth and cigarette breath made her want to gag. He clutched her crotch so hard she thought his fingers would tear right through her trousers.

"Going to be some good... yes sir... right fresh catch this is." He gasped, drool trickling down the crevices at the corners of his mouth.

"Let go, you greasy bastard." She raised her right fist and swung for his private parts. He jerked his arm up to stop her, lost control of the steering wheel and crashed into a thick stand of hawthorn shrubs alongside the road. Her body slammed against the passenger door, swinging it wide open.

She came to with her head and shoulders dangling out of the cab. How long had she been hanging there? Her head throbbed. Her first reflex was to make a run for it. She pushed against the rocker panel to pull her legs out. Nothing budged. The old guy must've collapsed on top of her. She froze. Gasping sounds from inside the truck. She reached for the side of the cab and managed to yank herself high enough to see inside. Her heart pounded through her chest.

The old guy straddled her, his pants lowered to his knees, staring down in disbelief at a milky stain on the front of her bloomers. Her trousers, buttons ripped off, were pulled halfway off her hips. She strained to pull her legs out from under him. "Get off me. Old greasy perv. I could be dead and there you are trying to stick your dirty dink inside me."

He jerked his head up, spittle in the corner of his mouth, and backed up, fumbling to pull his pants up. "No good little cock teaser. Causing a man to waste his shot with them tight trousers of yours. Out of my truck before I kick your sorry ass into the river."

She dove out before he was able to button his pants, kicking her bag out from the floor of the cab at the same time. The Roadster did a quick U-Turn and spun off in a cloud of dust. She wiped down her bloomers with a handful of dried grass and pulled up the trousers. She had just reached in her bag for a safety pin to replace the missing button when she noticed the black leather wallet on the ground. Must've dropped out of his pocket when he tugged his drawers down and then flown out of the cab when she kicked her bag out.

She counted the wad of paper dollars and grinned, thanking her brother for the discarded trousers that had protected her from the old pervert. Looked like a whole year's pay there from the fish-processing plant down east. Enough to keep her going for a while and to treat herself to a trendy pair of women's trousers. She brushed the dried grass and twigs from her coat and marched back to the main road.

Stella paused after she finished her story and tucked her blanket around her lap. She gazed out the window and seemed to have forgotten she had a visitor.

Lisette waited a moment before speaking. "So… Claire made her way to the bright lights, I guess?"

Stella turned to her, a puzzled look on her face, and nodded. "Yes… if I remember right, she said she got a lift from a couple driving to Saint Joseph's Oratory in Montreal. Our John met her at a Christmas dance that same year and"—she paused a moment—"they married two months later."

"Sounds like it wasn't a happy event."

"Such a beautiful couple. They only had eyes for each other." She fidgeted with the folds of her blanket. "Timothy was dead set against it from the start." She pulled her sweater closer.

Lisette hesitated before closing her notebook. The conversation seemed to be draining the woman. Besides learning the names of her grandparents, she hadn't progressed too far in her research. But at least the mystery of her origins was starting to fall apart. She knew for sure that she belonged to some kind of family chain. She was about to get up when Stella glanced at her. "You're not leaving already, dear? You just got here."

Lisette leaned back in her chair. "I thought you were too tired to continue."

Stella smiled. "Not seeing my loved ones is what makes me tired. Besides Janette coming once a week, I don't get many visitors. Both my sons are always too busy. Having you here makes me forget how long the day will be." Her face softened, a faraway look in her eyes. "I think of Claire often. I was always happy to see her. But my family won't mention her name anymore. They've always blamed her for what happened. Our little Nadine suffered because of it. Timothy and the boys had nothing good to say about the poor child."

"So what happened with John and Claire?" Lisette kept an eye out for anybody walking down the hallway, expecting the receptionist to barge in any minute now and tell her to leave. Maybe what Stella had to say wasn't going to take too long. If they wanted to bar her from coming back, she intended to find out as much as possible while she had a chance.

Stella clasped her hands together. "Claire was like an open book. She'd share intimate details about her and John... things I preferred she keep to herself. If only I had listened more...."

CHAPTER 12

Montreal
September 1939

Claire and John sat at opposite ends of the hospital waiting room. He in a vinyl armchair, smoking and staring out the tall picture windows at the traffic below. She on a hard metal chair facing the corridor leading to the observation room, her stomach a tangle of knots. Claire had hoped they'd keep the child overnight, giving her a good excuse to stay by her bedside. John needed time alone to gather his thoughts. No use trying to reason with him when he was in such a tizzy.

She stared at him across the room. "You told the landlord about that metal railing, right? Five years we've been living there and the damn thing's still broken."

He stubbed out in the floor-standing ashtray beside him and blew the smoke in her direction. "Yeah, it's my fault, right? The kid rolled down two sets of stairs and sliced her leg to the bone." He pounded his fist on the arm of his chair. "Good thing the neighbour looked out her window and saw the kid in a pool of blood. Her own mother was too busy dancing to notice her own kid was bleeding to death."

Claire lowered her head, twisting her wedding band back and forth. "You know I like my music loud, John. I didn't hear a blasted thing. I was listening to *Strange Fruit*, that new Billie Holiday record I got last week. Last time I checked, Nadine was on the front landing colouring in her book."

He shook his head at her. "You and your damn negro music." He lit another cigarette and continued staring at the traffic. "Nothing matters to you when that's playing."

She dug her nails into her palms. He had it all wrong. Music made everything matter to her. It opened her heart, her eyes, her soul. But it was no use telling him that. He just didn't understand. To him, music went hand in hand with booze and office parties. And of course, it made people forget how foolish they look when they dance.

That's what he wants people to think.

That he's the doting father, and I'm the negligent one.

They hadn't been to a nightclub on a Saturday night since he found out she was pregnant. No more dances and fancy restaurants with friends after that. All these guys looking her way pissed him off. In his mind, being a mother made her sacred. His alone to touch and admire. The rounder her belly grew, the more obsessed he was with her body, measuring her belly and the swell of her breasts every evening. He oiled and massaged every inch of her body after each bath. Speaking to the baby through her navel. Asking the baby permission to make love to her. When Nadine was born, the first thing he noticed was the colour of her eyes, and… that she wasn't a boy.

Nadine came into the world five weeks short of nine months after the wedding. That's when John's pouting and dark moods began. The baby was too much for her, he claimed. She had no time left to even put lipstick on. His snide remarks were the worst, said with that irritating boyish smile of his: *Funny how the kid has brown eyes and both of us are blue-eyed*—or—*she don't look at all like anybody in the family.* But he'd never even set eyes on anybody in her own family. Always too far to travel, or never the right time.

She had tried to include him in some of the parental duties, but he refused to change diapers, burp the baby, or pick her up when she cried. He insisted she breastfeed in bed to give him a chance to suckle on one breast while the baby fed from the other. She happened to catch a reflection of her breasts, mottled with bruises and teeth marks, in the mirror one morning. Right at that moment, she decided to wean the baby. John started working more overtime after that and sent the child to Stella most weekends. He claimed to need more alone time with his wife. The only perk of having a baby around, he'd told her, was that sweet breast milk spraying my lips and throat.

Claire had, in a real sense, become a single parent, while John bragged to his fellow workers how easy fatherhood was for him. The only time his father self-image became a problem was when he was obliged to take part. Nadine's accident had pulled him away from his desk and forced him to rush to the hospital. The girl had lost too much blood and needed a transfusion. Claire wasn't compatible, so the doctor assumed the father would be.

She shifted position in her seat, crossing her arms with her clenched fists tucked under her armpits. Her insides boiled.

How dare he blame me for this.

Music and dancing had always been her passion. That's what had brought them together when she first moved to Montreal. She had felt sorry for the short guy sitting by himself at a table in the back of the dance hall. A few of the girls refused his request to dance. Not because he wasn't good-looking—he was handsome in a boyish kind of way—but because girls like to look up at the guy when they're dancing. So she sauntered up to him and tilted her head towards the other dancers. They hit it off, big-time. You bowled me over, he'd told her. He'd never met such a spirited blond bombshell. She'd never come across a guy who loved to help her put on her makeup and sometimes slept with her frilly undies tucked under his pillow.

She shot him a dirty look and bit down on her lip. He sat forward, legs spread wide with his arms resting on his thighs. His mouth closed tight with that fixed hardness in his features. The next few hours promised to be tough being around him. She hated it when he was in a tizzy like this. Instead of mellowing with age, his temper tantrums were getting worse. She had left her small village back east to get away from Pa's violent fits, swearing no man was going to push her around like he did Ma. She remembered that hard black glint in Pa's eyes just before he swung at her—the same cold look John had when he got pissed. But John always backed down when she left the room. He never hunted her out.

A hot mass, like embers of black coal, stuck in her throat, blocking her from speaking. If she voiced her anger, the air flowing in would cause the embers to burst into flames.

He has no right to—

Her fist trembled with the urge to up and smack him.

He has no right to—

"Mr. and Mrs. John Pritchard?" The doctor stood in front of them, a clipboard in hand.

Both John and Claire jumped up from their seats. She let out her breath. "Is Nadine OK?"

The doctor smiled. "Your little girl will be fine, Mrs. Pritchard. She's lost a lot of blood, but she'll be OK to go home an hour after the transfusion." He turned to John. "Our tests show that your blood, as well as Mrs. Pritchart's, is incompatible. We'll need your consent to use our own blood supply."

"There must be some mistake, doctor." John had his eyes riveted on him. "We can't both be incompatible."

The doctor adjusted his glasses. "It turns out both you and your wife have the same blood type. Your child, unfortunately"—he lowered his gaze—"does not." He showed John the clipboard. "Please sign this form and we'll have Nadine home in no time."

John didn't say a word after he signed the consent form. He looked daggers at her and marched back to his seat by the window. A layer of unease settled around her shoulders. Nadine's blood had spoken. A whirlwind affair with a sailor on a week's furlough in Montreal.

Claire only found out about her pregnancy a few weeks after she met John. They were already crazy for each other by then. She was sure, once she told him everything, that his love for her would help him go forward with it all. But the right moment never came. He was forever embroiled in some conflict at work or with his family. Always fighting to get the approval he thought he deserved. She had imagined the remote possibility the child was John's—weird and wonderful things happened everyday—he had, after all, come to her bed the night they met and returned each night after that.

His silence continued on the ride home. Mouth pursed and hands clutching the steering wheel. Claire braced herself for a showdown. The air around him smelled sulphuric, like the heavy moments before lightning strikes.

The full moon, a distant beacon in the early evening sky, shone through Nadine's bedroom window as Claire closed the door behind her. She prayed for sleep to protect her daughter from the storm brewing in the other room.

She stepped into the kitchen from the hallway. He was leaning against the counter, an open bottle of whiskey in hand. She headed towards the fridge, her stomach tight. He was nasty when drunk. He had never put a hand on her, but it had come close a few times after an outing at the cinema, a concert, or a walk in the park. He always imagined some guy or other had looked at her the wrong way.

He'd smash the wall with his fist a hair's width away from her head. Or pin her throat to the mattress with his open hand, pressing down till she gasped and took a swing at him. The I'm-so-sorry song followed soon after, swearing he'd never hurt her. Claire knew better, having heard the same song each time Pa threw Ma against the wall in their little clapboard house back east. She'd told Ma she'd never stay with a man that shoved her around, and although John hadn't yet, she knew it was time for her to move on before it happened. She'd wait till he passed out to pack a few things.

"You haven't eaten yet. I'll warm up the beef stew and boil water for tea." Ma made sure she kept Pa's meal warm in case he came stumbling in drunk. He'd shovel the food down, distracted from his intent to slap her around. On numerous occasions, Claire had walked into the kitchen to see Pa lying face-first in his plate of mashed potatoes and gravy. Let sleeping dogs lie, Ma would tell her.

"How long were you going to keep your dirty little secret from me?" He swigged the whiskey straight from the bottle.

"There's never been any dirty secret. It was always a matter of you being ready to hear it." Her hand trembled as she placed the pot of stew on the stovetop and switched the burner on.

Keep moving. Don't let on you're scared.
He'll hit harder if he sees you're weak.
The sooner he eats, the faster he'll pass out.

It was clear to her now. The right moment would never have come. Nobody need ever know—or care, one way or another—but he'd always hold it against her and the child. He wasn't man enough to accept that Nadine deserved love just like any other child.

"It had to come from a complete stranger." He raised the bottle and gulped down more whiskey, gasping and sputtering as he lowered it. "Do you know how stupid I felt when the doctor informed me I wasn't the kid's father? I'm sure they had a good laugh when they got the results at the lab." He banged the bottle on the counter. "Just like you did, stupid slut." His voice was now louder, angrier. "You must've laughed all the way to the altar." He lifted the bottle again.

She reached into the cupboard for a plate. He never was good with alcohol. Two shots and he'd have a glow on him. That's when the poor-me talk started. Nobody showed him any respect. Everybody was out to stab him in the back.

She'd feed him quick like Ma did Pa. Shovelling food down makes drunks sleepy—either that or they fall flat down on the floor in their vomit. She wasn't going to wait for morning to see him snoozing in his plate of beef stew and dumplings. As soon as she heard him snoring she'd get Nadine dressed and they'd be out the door. She scooped some stew out of the pan and slapped it on the plate.

Lukewarm will do. He's too drunk to tell.

"Knew it... soon as I—" He downed another shot and the bottle slipped out of his hand, smashing and scattering shards of glass all over the kitchen floor. "Knew that little bitch wasn't mine from the start." He stared down at the broken glass. "My life is in pieces because of you—" He kicked the shards in her direction. "Just like this broken glass. Father always said not to marry a French slut. He saw right through you."

Her body tensed, her vision clouded. She swerved and heaved the plate of stew at him. Gravy and chunks of meat and potatoes slid down his chest. "The hell with you and your uppity family.

Your father didn't think I was good enough? Well, the hell with you, buddy. Marrying you was the worst mistake of my life. Lots of guys will be more than happy to have me. Nadine might not be your seed, but you haven't come up with any of yours either. A short guy with empty balls—that about sums you up. Even the army rejected you."

There. My words spilled out.

No turning back now.

His eyes widened and his mouth fell open. She might've gone too far. He'd never pass out now. "As soon as I get Nadine dressed we'll be out of your hair forever."

"Maman!" Nadine wailed from behind her mother.

Claire's head shot around. "Go put your coat and shoes on, Nadine." All that shouting and breaking of glass had woken her. The child stood clinging to her teddy bear at the edge of the hallway. "Go on, sweetie. Get dressed and wait for me at the back door." The sight of her would only fuel his anger.

Why had she lashed out at him like that? Ma always shut herself down when Pa got mean drunk. She'd tiptoe around him like he was some bomb ready to go off. Even the sound of her pouring his tea set him off. But being invisible wasn't her intent when she escaped her clapboard home back east.

She had just hit John where it mattered most—his height and his failure to produce a son like both his brothers had. And being rejected by the army wasn't going to sit well with his father. The truth was out, flapping in the breeze like a shredded sail. Little Nadine would be sure to foot the bill. She needed to calm him down enough to make a run for it before anyone got hurt. She looked over her shoulder at him. Her heart skipped a beat.

He lurched towards her. A long kitchen knife in his fist. "Figure you can find someone better, don't you? Some tall guy with a big dick that'll keep you barefoot and pregnant. Is that what you want?" He staggered forward, his eyes cold and hard. "Think again, bitch. If I can't do it, nobody else will."

She had never seen him like this. She stood frozen in front of the stove.

"Maman! I'm scared."

Nadine's cry shook her out of her stupor. No reasoning with a guy holding a knife. She grabbed the kettle of boiling water, hurled it at him and turned on her heel. He cried out. She snatched up Nadine and tore out the back. Halfway down the second flight of stairs, she heard him kick the door open.

"I'll get you, slut." He pounded down the metal stairs after them.

Claire held on tight to Nadine, her heart pounding through her chest. She only had to reach the gate to the back alley and run down the half block to the bright lights on Ste-Catherine Street. He wouldn't try anything with all those people walking around—not with a child in her arms.

She'd almost reached the gate when she tripped over an old tire and fell face down on wet grass. Nadine screamed. A sharp burning pain exploded in Claire's lower back.

Run, Nadine.

Push up. Run to the lights.

Get yourself away…run—

The second searing wave surged from her right shoulder and tore like lightning throughout her body. Nadine's screams echoed beneath her.

CHAPTER 13

Lisette rooted through the Biographies section in the used bookstore and pulled out a title about Louis Riel. A lot of the pages were dog-eared but the cover was still in good condition. Required readings for her many courses had taught her to look out for such well-used books. The author's main points were usually found on the bookmarked pages, saving her from having to read the whole volume. She sauntered over to the old sofa facing the front window of the store.

Louis Riel's biography wasn't at the top of her preferred reading list but she'd give it a try. Posters of the Métis leader covered all the available space of Serge's bedroom walls. Curious how Serge was so devoted to a man who had been hanged for treason close to a hundred years ago. What was it about him that held the power to tug so hard at Serge's heartstrings? She didn't expect him to feel the same devotion towards her, but if she understood what attracted him, she might accept coming a close second. She dropped the books she planned to buy on the sofa and looked outside.

From where she was sitting she could distinguish the front of the café across the street. The call from Social Services yesterday afternoon had made her heart race, but had also left her with the urge to flee and leave the past undisturbed. What was she getting into? She hadn't expected to hear from them so soon. A disclosure form in her birth mother's file gave them permission to contact her in the event that the adoptee requested her personal information. Her mother had to go by the office to sign another form allowing them to give Lisette the phone number. The proper paperwork was now in place. Her birth mother hadn't wasted any time. Nor had Lisette. Serge had urged her to call right away.

The last visit with Grandma Stella had left Lisette with a sinking feeling in her stomach and she had stopped by the library to verify her story in the archives. It had checked out, and the husband had later hung himself in his prison cell on the day of her funeral. The image of her mother, a young child, being witness to this violence had troubled her sleep two nights straight.

This wasn't the family she had wished for. Her mother appeared to belong to a family just as dysfunctional as the foster homes she had known. Was it worth continuing her quest? It felt like another letdown—the same disenchantment she experienced as a child when she realized her new family was just as screwed up as the previous one.

She had been excited to meet Grandma Stella. At long last, a link confirming she belonged to an actual family. As it turned out, after listening to Grandma Stella's story, she was only her adoptive great-grandmother. Still, it was better than no grandparent at all. And to make matters worse, the receptionist at the senior's home had caught up to her as she was leaving to warn her she'd have to be accompanied by Peter Pritchart next time she visited. Just when she had discovered a loving grandmother, she had to let her go.

Serge had found the addresses of both uncles in the database, but since nobody had heard from Nadine in twenty years, contacting them seemed futile. She was wary of calling her Uncle Peter after he had blocked her from visiting his mother. In any case, she'd have to go through his lawyer if she wanted to speak to him. Uncle Denis was probably just as unapproachable.

When Social Services had called her, Lisette had hesitated. She had survived well enough so far without knowing her mother; her life could go on without her. But a nagging urge persisted to confront the woman who had caused all the pain she had suffered as a child. When she told Serge about the call, his face lit up.

He insisted that she go meet her to discuss her family's medical history and find out more about that unclaimed account he had discovered. "Your mother will be glad to know about this. You never know, she might even feel generous enough to share some of it with you."

Now that she had time to think it over, she wasn't sure she wanted to go ahead with the meeting. The woman had cast her aside at birth and given her away to complete strangers who had abandoned her into foster care. She was responsible for all the pain and humiliation she had endured. The social workers had never had time to listen. As soon as a problem came up, they'd switch her to a new home and another set of problems. Lisette placed a hand on her belly. She'd never do to her child what her own mother had done to her.

She owed the woman nothing. If it wasn't for her eye doctor, she would never have started searching for her. Yet the longing to see what her birth mother looked like coaxed her to forge ahead. Grandma Stella had seen a resemblance right away, except for the difference in bone structure. Lisette's large hands and feet had set her apart from the other schoolgirls her age. 'Sasquatch' had been her nickname all through high school. But having a resemblance to someone implied that you belonged to a certain group—a family. Lisette had never felt any sense of belonging. In grade school she had been the tall kid who never fit in, never staying around long enough to form any real friendships. High school had brought out the rebel in her and she learned to use her hands and feet to get her point across.

"Did you find the books you were looking for?"

Lisette glanced up to see Nicky, the owner of the bookshop, smiling down at her. Her first job after high school had been shelving tons of used books from the storeroom and helping customers find what they were looking for. Nicky had been more of a friend to her than an employer. They had stayed in touch after Lisette quit to take a job at the local depanneur near Serge's apartment.

"Well… I know Serge will like *The Diaries of Louis Riel* and"— she picked up the dog-eared copy of *Dr Spock's Baby and Child Care*— "I hope this one comes in handy."

"That was my bible with my first kid." Nicky sat down on the sofa beside Lisette. "I saved my old copy in case she decides to have her own one day. Though it doesn't look like she'll slow down long enough to even consider it." She cocked her head and studied Lisette. "You must be due soon. How are you coping?"

"Mid-November." Lisette sighed. "Can't wait to get it over with. The only time I get any sleep these days is when I'm sitting on the bus."

"The last month is tough. Do you have all the baby things?"

Lisette removed her glasses and rubbed her eyes. "We picked up a crib and a stroller at the Salvation Army last week. They're in pretty good shape for the price."

"Are you OK for baby clothes?"

"Got a bagful at a church bazaar and Sylvie—my roomie, remember?—gave me a few baby pyjamas."

"That'll do for a start. Babies don't need a big wardrobe. What about Serge?"

She rolled her shoulders back and put her glasses back on. "Same. Driving cabs—for now. He plans to continue his major in social science one of these days. He took some time off to… take care of things. We're looking for another place to live, although we can't really afford it right now. Serge is putting in more hours at work to put money aside for us, but that means I hardly see him." A movement from across the street caught her eye and her head jerked in the direction of the café. Someone had just walked in. She waited to see if the person chose to sit at one of tables close to the street. Not that she'd be able to tell if the person was male or female, but any new customer going in could be her. A window seat had been mentioned during their telephone conversation.

"Is something wrong?" Nicky checked to see what she was looking at.

"I'm supposed to meet someone over there." Lisette frowned. "I came early to see what she looked like first."

"A stranger? What if you don't like what you see?"

She grimaced. "It's more about my gut feeling when I see her."

"Now you've got me curious." Nicky cocked her head and stared at her friend. "Out with it. You know you'll end up telling me sooner or later."

Lisette placed her books in a neat pile on top of her bag. Nicky was like an older sister to her. They talked together about everything. But if she told her who she was meeting, she'd get all excited and encourage her to go ahead and do it. She wanted this decision to be hers alone, not influenced by anybody else.

Nicky glanced across the street. "Somebody just went in."

Lisette straightened in her seat and peered out. "That's what I figured. Can you see where they sat? Is it a woman?"

Nicky stared at her. "You can't see that far?"

"Well... if they sit close to the front, I can see the general shape of the person."

"But you can't tell if it's a human or a gorilla, right?"

"Get off it, Nicky. Did they take a window seat or not?"

"There's someone sitting at the far end table, right beside the window."

"So? Is it a woman or not? You're making my blood pressure rise."

"Good. I'm not giving any more clues until you tell me what this is all about. Since you only have about ten feet of vision with your glasses on, you're going to have to come clean. Your only other choice is getting your ass off the sofa and crossing the street."

Lisette leaned back against the sofa. "You have a real mean streak."

Nicky smiled. "And you have a stubborn one. Now give it up. I've got customers filing in." She waved to a long-haired man heading to the back of the store.

"For your information, it's because of my eyesight that I looked her up. I'm not sure it's even worth the bother."

"Your eyesight?" Nicky thought for a moment. "Didn't your eye doctor suggest you look up your medical history? Are you trying to say that—"

"You have to promise me you won't play the big sister act and try to guilt me into going over there. The decision belongs to me— only me. I don't want to hear any Hallmark card emotion about the healing balm of motherhood. I've had a lot of mothers, both birth and adoptive, as well as eight foster ones. Not one of them shone with that famous unconditional love crap. Life doesn't always fit into those Hallmark sentimental slots. And parents don't always love their kids, nor the other way round."

"Relax, kid. No one's pushing you against a wall."

Lisette took her glasses off and rubbed her eyes again. "Sorry, Nicky. There's a lot going on these days. Sylvie and Pit are pushing me out the door and I've got some heavy term papers to finish before my due date. And it doesn't look like Serge is moving in with me for a few months, not until he gets his act together."

Nicky reached over to take her hand. "Don't be sorry. It's me that's in the wrong. Bugging you like—" She looked outside. "Bingo, kiddo. There's a woman in a red sweater sitting right next to the window."

Lisette straightened. "What does she look like? Young? Old?"

"In her late thirties, maybe forties. Shortish hair—" She looked back at Lisette. "Hair colour like yours. The waitress just brought her a coffee."

An older woman approached them at the sofa. "Excuse me. Do you work here? I need some help finding a book."

"No problem, madam." Nicky stood up and before following the woman to the bookshelves, turned back and gave Lisette a thumbs-up.

Lisette leaned back and took a deep breath.

CHAPTER 14

Nadine nodded to the waitress at the café to pour her a refill. More caffeine wasn't going to help settle the acidity in her gut but the woman had already approached her table twice with her carafe. Nursing an empty cup made her look like she had nowhere to go. She'd have to make this coffee last longer than the last two.

No sign of... Lisette—not a name she'd choose, but what did it matter? She wrapped her hands around the hot mug and contemplated the late afternoon crowd streaming down Ste-Catherine Street. If only she had an idea what she looked like, she'd spot her right away as she entered, gaining a few moments to ease the pounding in her chest.

She had thought of nothing else since receiving the registered letter after Papi's visit last Friday.

This letter is for Nadine Pritchart. The Archives Department of Social Services received a request this morning concerning the disclosure of some of your identifying information. Since the permission for disclosure in your file has been updated on a regular basis, we would appreciate that you call us as soon as possible. Our offices are open from nine to four, Monday to Friday.

Nadine Pritchart—nobody called her that anymore. The letter had left her breathless. She read it over six times before calling and reaching the woman minutes before she was about to leave for the day. Before they could give out any of her personal information, Nadine needed to drop by their office to sign the necessary form. She had made arrangements to take care of that before work on Monday.

Her daughter—the child they had stolen from her—was searching for her. A wave of warmth radiated through her chest. Her dream had come true at last—her daughter had come back to her. She imagined them jumping into each other's arms. They'd be best friends to the end of time. Her daughter would love her as much as she had always loved her.

Nadine had made a point over the years of checking with Social Services on her daughter's birthday to make sure they still had her disclosure form on file. It gave them permission to contact her if ever her daughter requested a meeting. Somehow she had always known the reunion was to happen. Social Services wasn't aware that she no longer used the Pritchart name. She worried that telling them might screw up their search system and delay any possible meeting. She and her daughter had shared the same last name—at least until after the adoption. Informing them of her name change might rock the boat and make it harder for them to make the link.

The weekend before she was to stop by the Social Services office had dragged on and on. No sleep to speak of and no energy to cook or clean. She drank tea after tea while leafing through her scrapbook, dreaming about what her daughter might look like.

The next two days at the office had been a blur. She had taken copious notes at the meetings. After rereading them, she noticed certain comments appeared more than once. Other notes had nothing to do with the subject at hand. She'd have to check with her colleague before submitting her final report.

Papi was the only person to understand her excitement. She had to tell someone. She called him to share her news and he promised to drop in when he drove back to Montreal on the weekend. He came to mind when the telephone rang yesterday evening and her heart skipped a beat. No one ever called her after the late news. Had he had an accident? He had mentioned going to visit a couple of bush camps in northern Quebec. The gravel roads in that part of the province were often narrow and unlit. She took a long breath before picking up the receiver. When it dawned on her who was on the other end, her heart almost burst right through her chest. Her stomach churned so hard she had come close to being sick right after she hung up.

She wrapped both hands around her refilled mug and breathed in the warm coffee aroma. Her mind was in a whirlwind. The tight walls of her world had broken down and the tingling in her heart made her feel like she was flying amok in a huge beehive. First there had been that chance meeting with Papi. Then the letter from Social Services, and now—her heart gave a slight lurch—she had heard the voice of her own daughter. The actual telephone conversation was a total blackout. She had blurted out yes to everything the girl said.

She twisted around in her chair and took a look around the café. No new customer had entered since she had sat down almost an hour ago. A young couple holding hands across a corner table. An older woman sipping her coffee with the open pages of *The Montreal Star* covering the whole table in front of her. The two young men sitting at the table behind her had the *Journal de Montréal* open between them, poring over the details of the latest bombing.

She tugged at the collar of her wool turtleneck and fidgeted, crossing and uncrossing her legs. Lisette might have spotted her through the window and decided not to come in. Or… she hadn't bothered to come at all. Something also might have happened to her. She bit the inside of her lip and glanced up at the darkening sky. If she got up and left now, she'd be going back on the promise she'd made so many years ago. Her dream had been with her too long to give it up. The girl had sounded keen on the phone and had even insisted that they meet as soon as possible.

Nadine tightened her grasp on her mug. She didn't want to risk leaving—not now—and have the girl appear a few minutes later. Maybe she'd taken down the wrong directions to get here. She remembered her hand shaking so much she had a hard time holding the pen, dropping it once and asking Lisette to repeat the address. She groped in her jacket pocket for the slip of paper where she had scribbled a few sketchy details. This was the right café, but it was also part of a chain with several locations downtown. Maybe she was waiting at the wrong one.

No, she wasn't ready to leave. The girl was just late. There had to be a good explanation. She had never thought of asking for her phone number. She'd order three or more refills if she had to. The promise she had made twenty years ago was about to come true.

CHAPTER 15

Montreal
October 1950

Nadine clutched her small brown valise and hurried down the cement steps of Maternité Catholique. The early autumn breeze brought a welcome coolness to her face and neck. She paused when she reached the sidewalk facing Dorchester Boulevard and turned around. She tilted her head back to look up at the four-storey greystone that had housed her for the last nine months. No tears. Enough had been shed in the large communal dormitory she had shared with the other girls on the fourth floor.

Her quick exit from the cheerless building had been her sprint to freedom. Yet each step taken down the long dark hallway to the vestibule tore away at her heart. A part of her soul would linger there forever. Her pain impregnated the fabric of the walls, joining the chorus of grief left behind by previous women who had exited through the same oak door.

Six months of domestic work for the nuns had paid off her debt for board and medical bills. Now she was free to leave. At sixteen with no work experience, her only chance at full-time work was the garment factories in the east end of the city. She had enough money hidden in the lining of her valise to pay for a few weeks rent at a cheap rooming house. Bread and butter, and maybe a bit of cheese, her only food till she saw a paycheque.

All she had left to do was walk away and forget what had happened. She was leaving her past self behind. It was time to detach herself from that scared sixteen-year-old who had first entered this building. Time to start a new life.

Isa, her friend and soulmate, had promised to wave from one of the windows, providing the nuns weren't watching. Blinds on the street side of the building remained lowered at all times. Residents of the maternity ward for unwed mothers had to stay hidden from passersby. The nuns agreed to allow sunlight to filter in through the windows facing the cathedral in the back, except during the hours of public worship. Contact with family or friends, either by letter or by phone, wasn't tolerated. Any reminder of their past selves, especially talk about the lives they had left behind, was off-limits. Their normal street clothes, pictures, trinkets from home, or any money they owned, had to remain hidden in their suitcases. The safeguarding of the family honour was paramount, so residents had to keep their real names secret and go by ones given to them by the home.

The nuns had declared that the name Isa sounded too much like Louisa, her birth name, and chastised her each time she used it. She resisted, refusing her assigned name, even for the few months of her stay. She didn't care what the nuns said and stuck her tongue out each time they had their backs turned.

Lifting the blinds to wave goodbye no matter what extra chore the nuns punished her with was something Nadine expected Isa to do. She always managed to either be late for the 6:30 wake-up prayers, forget to do part of her daily chores, or worst of all, talk back to one of the nuns. The punishment was scrubbing the toilets on the first and second floors where the married women were. The residents there weren't like the penitents on the fourth floor. They were the good mothers—the ones who made sure they had a wedding band on their finger before getting pregnant. Free to share their family stories and to get visitors. Proud and strong with the new life growing inside them. No need to hide these model Catholic mothers from society. They even had their own private entrance on the St-Hubert Street side of the building. The nuns encouraged them to treat Isa like a lowly servant and to order her to empty their bedpans and change their soiled sheets.

The nuns' rigid rules proved difficult for Isa. She ignored the one forbidding penitents to talk about their lives outside the maternity ward. The women had to reinvent themselves during their stay and blot out all references to their past lives. They lived in limbo with two versions of themselves. Their sinful past selves had propelled them into this period of repentance. The new penitent selves waited to emerge cleansed and ready to reintegrate into society. Isa missed her five younger brothers and sisters too much to pretend they didn't exist. Nadine often woke in the middle of the night to find her curled up beside her on her narrow cot.

"Not again." She'd edge over to give Isa more room on the bed and tuck the coarse grey blanket around her. "It must be hard for you to know your baby is at the crèche here. But stay away from there. It's for your own good. He'll be gone soon and your heart will explode in a thousand pieces."

Isa slid her head under the blanket and clutched Nadine's arm. "I'll go crazy if I have to stay here another six months. No one talks to me apart from you. Being around babies and pregnant women makes me want to be with my own baby more and more. I stay awake nights thinking of ways to kill all these stupid nuns. I told Sister Blain I changed my mind about those adoption papers. 'Nobody can love him the way I do,' I told her." She poked her head out from under the blanket. "And do you know what that old biddy answered me? 'Love?' she said, like it was a dirty word. 'You don't even know what that means. You're too immature and selfish to be a mother,' she almost spit at me. I wanted to squeeze my hands around her neck till her eyes popped out of her ugly face."

"Let go of me." Nadine pried off Isa's grip. "You're hurting me. If you'd wring her neck as hard as you're squeezing my arm, we'd all be attending her funeral." She pulled her closer. "Sister Blain only knows about spiritual love. She doesn't know anything about a mother's love. Separating a mother and child is like splitting a soul in half. The soul won't rest till it's back together again."

"That's right." Isa sat up straight. "Those nuns have their noses stuck so tight up God's robes, they have no idea how real people feel."

"Some nuns are OK, Isa. A few here—I'm not sure which ones—took their vows after giving away their own babies. It must be harder for them with all those babies reminding them of their own. At least we have the hope of one day reuniting with our child—they never will. You can't give up. Your child will want to meet you one day."

"Wish I was as sure of that as you are. But what if they give my baby boy to some mean rich people who mistreat him? No one can be sure they'll love my baby boy. In my nightmares, I'm looking through the window of a fancy Westmount house. My baby's there crying his eyes out in the biggest crib you've ever seen and his little arms are all black and blue with bruises. A woman in a nanny's uniform is sitting in a shiny new rocking chair beside the crib. She's examining her nails and yawning at the same time. I start banging on the window for her to let me in, so she gets up and jerks the black drapes closed tight. I can't see my baby anymore, but I can hear him wailing."

"It's the mother in you. You'll worry about him for the rest of your life. That's how you'll keep him in your heart." Nadine eased Isa back down beside her under the blanket. "You know how the nuns keep on reminding us... that if it wasn't for what they're doing here, a lot of babies would die. In the old days, before the nuns took care of finding homes for the babies, unwed mothers didn't know what to do once they left this place with their newborn. Some darted across Dorchester Boulevard right in front of the building here. They'd run down Woodyard Street past the old railway tracks and throw the poor baby in the St. Lawrence River."

Isa was quiet for a long while. Muffled sounds of traffic and the rise and fall of women's snoring swirled around them in their scratchy grey cocoon. Her voice, when she spoke again, came out soft, almost childlike. "Throwing him in the cold water all alone like that... that's just mean. I'd hold on to him real tight and jump into the St. Lawrence with him."

"Try not to think too much about all this. Give your body time to get stronger. Your heart will heal in time." Nadine held her hand. "It's only been two weeks since you gave birth."

Isa sat up again. "Nobody can tell you're three years younger than me. It's my job to give advice and not the other way around." She placed her head in her hands and let out a soft moan. "I won't make it here without you. I have to get out before I dunk someone's head in the toilet bowl. Everybody looks at me like I've escaped from the asylum. Sometimes it feels like the walls are closing in all around me and I can't breathe."

"Hush. Not so loud." Nadine smoothed Isa's long tangled hair away from her face. "We don't want Sister Gagnon finding you here again. And you know you can't leave this place before you pay off your debt to them. Promise me you'll work hard and stay out of trouble. Time will go faster for you that way."

"I swear I didn't try to pick him up this time. All I did was look at him through the glass." She slammed her fist down on the mattress. "I hate them. It's my baby. If I don't bother going to see him, they'll say I'm not interested in him so they can give him away faster. If I do go, I get scolded like a child. I wish they'd all drink poisoned tea and die in their sleep tonight. We'd all get up next morning and walk out with our baby—" She paused and stared at Nadine. "Oh no... I'm so sorry. I wasn't thinking."

Nadine looked away. For two weeks after the birth of her daughter, she had thought only of breaking into Sister Blain's office files to find out where her baby had gone. She plotted nonstop to escape from the maternity home to get her child back. Lying awake nights imagining ways of sneaking her baby girl out of her adopted home... and... that's where her plans fell through. She had no idea where to bring her. To feed herself was a challenge, to feed a baby on top of that would be overwhelming. Getting a job in a factory was possible, but what about the baby while she was at work? She had nightmares of the baby howling in a crib with large grey rats scurrying all over her.

"You've seen your child's face, Isa. You've touched his soft hair and smelled the perfume of his small body. I know you're suffering, but at least you have that precious image of him. They bundled mine into another woman's arms long before I even woke up from the labour.

My child is faceless—like a dream baby. But in my heart, she has brown eyes and hair like me... and she smiles each time she sees me. She's six months old now and must be sitting up by herself. There's a big sunny room full of colours of the rainbow for her in my heart, with a bunch of pretty dresses and lots of dolls and stuffed animals in her crib. She'll always be with me no matter where they've sent her."

After taking a long breath, she managed a weak smile. "You see, no matter how many nuns you knock off, nothing will bring my baby back right now. I have to wait and grow strong for when she comes back to me." She twirled a loose strand of her friend's hair around her finger. "I wanted to call her Isa, like you. I never told anyone. It seemed pointless after they took her from me. Who knows what her name is now. She'll always be Isa to me."

Isa leaned down to hug her. "Like me? You mean I'd be her godmother?"

"Of course. I wanted her to be a rebel like you. I wanted her to change the world."

Isa pushed the blanket away and stood up beside the bed. "I don't want my kid to be anything like me. I hope he grows up patient and understanding just like you. The nuns are right about me. I only think about myself—only my problems matter to me. You never complain, but I know you're hurting too."

"It's no use whining, Isa. Nobody listens." She reached under her pillow and took out a small piece of paper. "Here, I copied this for you. Don't lose this address. One of the girls told me they've always got plenty of rooms to rent there. Come see me when you get out. Now lie back down and tell me more about your family. I'd like to meet them all one day."

Nadine closed her eyes and listened to Isa give a rundown of her family back in her village north of Montreal. Their likes and dislikes, their happy times together, as well as their frequent quarrels, were familiar to Nadine. She never tired of hearing Isa talk about them. No one argued where Nadine was from. No one spoke out of turn and disagreements were rare. Talking about her family helped Isa reunite in spirit with her loved ones. Nadine imagined the family she had always dreamed of—loud, stormy and loving. She held Isa's hand till darkness had faded enough to distinguish the shapes of the other beds in the dormitory and then nudged her away.

It was greyish dawn when Nadine threw her blanket off and swung her legs off the bed. A few of the women were already up tucking their blankets under their thin mattresses. A bell sounded announcing the 6:30 morning prayers. Whoever still lingered in bed bolted up and made a grab for their clothes.

No rushing to the chapel with the other penitents today—her first and only act of disobedience. With her debt paid off and her release papers signed, the nuns didn't have the power to inflict any punishment. She'd be off after the morning bread and tea—the only meal she'd have today. The thought of not getting hired at one of the garment factories on St-Hubert Street made her stomach clench. Restaurant work, her second option, didn't always offer full-time. She needed a steady paycheque and a job that kept her too busy to think about the emptiness in her heart.

She snapped her valise closed and glanced up at the *Prayer of the Unworthy* posted on the wall above her metal bed frame. This had become an automatic gesture since the first day of her stay here. She clenched her fist and looked down, wishing she had the courage to tear it down. Isa hadn't hesitated.

Dear Lord, I am not worthy of being a mother. I have blasphemed against the sanctity of marriage. I have transgressed your command-ments. I have gone against all your divine inspiration and guidance, and because of my folly, you have imposed the heavy yolk of maternity on me.

She'd never have to read it again, although the words had grown deep roots in her mind. The nuns welcomed every occasion to remind them how they had disgraced themselves and their families. Their lives now ruined, they had to make amends. Hard work and religious dedication were the only ways to make them fit for marriage and prepare them to reintegrate into society. The rate of infanticide had dropped, the nuns often pointed out, because of their devotion to finding respectable parents for the poor children born of unwed mothers. Because of them, infants were no longer found floating down the St. Lawrence River, frozen in back alleys, or abandoned in garbage bins.

Dear Lord, I am unworthy, without means and support, abandoned by the father of my child. My dishonour finally opens my eyes.

What would I do without your pity? Please have pity on this unworthy mother, but more so for the small child within me. In the name of Mary, your Holy Mother, please disregard the sins of this child's parents. Let him be beautiful, healthy, intelligent, docile and brave. Let him love you and make him a faithful follower so that he may never offend you as his parents have sinned and offended you.

I pray for my unborn child. I pray that charitable parents welcome my child into their home.

I beg you to give this child the gift of the new life of baptism and welcome him into the Holy Church. I beg you to find him charitable adoptive parents. Most of all, I beg you to show him mercy. Take his young life from this earth if he must carry within him the sad inheritance of the passions that have made his parents sinners.

Reading the prayer three times a day was part of their daily chores. Isa refused to even look at the poster and had ripped it off the wall by her bed on her first day. Sister Bélanger forced her to copy it out again. It took a good part of the morning to erase her errors and start over. When she posted it back up, the sister ordered her to read it out loud in the dormitory for everyone to hear. Isa paused and stumbled on every single word. The girls complained they'd miss the morning prayers if they had to wait for her to finish. The sister shook her head and marched out. Further attempts to have her read it aloud each day for the next week made Isa stammer even more. The nuns declared her not only an unrepentant sinner but a stupid one as well.

Nadine felt a tightening in her chest and she stepped back to scan the third-floor windows again. Isa might be waiting for the right moment to sneak up to one between chores. That defiant wave—that show of solidarity—was needed to boost her courage to face what she had to do. She planned to get an early start to find lodging and drop off her valise before looking for a job. She'd also need more time to find her way around these streets and alleyways. Besides taking the streetcar to visit Grandma Stella, at no time had she ventured outside of her neighbourhood on her own. Montreal's east-end array of nightclubs, restaurants, shops and factories was both foreign and scary to her.

Come on, Isa. I need to get going.

If she lingered too long in front of the building, Sister Blain was sure to notice her from the office and come out to scold her. The thought of finding a place to stay gave her stomach cramps. What if everyone refused to rent to her? She remembered the cozy bedroom she had left back home. She and Aunt Jan had fashioned her light blue curtains and a matching quilt by canvassing everyone they knew for their discarded dresses, blouses and shirts with blue designs. Chances were her aunt was flipping through her favourite book, *The Joy of Cooking*, at this very moment. Uncle Denis loved it when she cooked something special just for him. *He'll eat fried rat on a stick if he thinks I made it special for him,* Aunt Jan often joked with the local butcher.

Aunt Jan had insisted she go back and finish high school after the birth was over. But to face the other girls at Saint Mary's Academy was out of the question. They had never given her a moment's thought. The gossip must've started as soon as they heard she wasn't finishing the school year. Facing the girls at Saint Mary's was one thing, but having to live with the Pritcharts' eternal disapproval would be purgatory. Uncle Denis had never wanted her around in the first place. He only tolerated her because of Aunt Jan. Now that Nadine had brought shame to the family, he was sure to hold it against her and make her life miserable. The Pritcharts' claim that she took after her mother's French side was now confirmed in their eyes. Going back to live with them was out of the question.

She checked the windows of the third floor one last time. No sign of Isa. She sighed and turned around. Time to get on with her new life. She reached into her pocket, pulled out the note with the address, bit her lip and looked towards St. Timothy Street. It was a long uphill trek to the rooming house.

Just then a woman clutching a baby wrapped in a green hospital blanket appeared from the St-Hubert Street side of the building. Two nuns, their black robes ballooning around them, ran behind, screaming at her to stop. Nadine froze when she recognized Isa, her wool coat unbuttoned over her blue hospital dress.

Isa glanced back over her shoulder, a frantic look on her face. The nuns were gaining on her. She pressed the child to her chest and bolted.

Nadine cried out her name. Isa shot her head around to grin at Nadine and continued running. What had possessed her to take the child? Where was she going? She must've sneaked into the crèche while most of the staff were at breakfast. Nadine's heart skipped a beat when she saw her stumble off the sidewalk and dodge an oncoming car.

She had almost reached the middle of the boulevard when a milk truck made a sudden turn off Woodyard Street onto Dorchester. The sound of brakes came too late to avoid Isa. Traffic came to a full stop in each direction. The truck driver jumped out of the cab, yelling for help.

The two nuns, hunched over Isa's body, were doing the sign of the cross when Nadine reached them. Isa lay flat on her belly against the pavement. The baby's white wool sweater and matching mittens, bloodied and tangled in his mother's hair. His tiny arm poked out from beneath Isa's broken body, reminding Nadine of the universal white flag hoisted in battle. Her heart lurched. Isa's fight was over. The nuns continued their litany, the hems of their long dark skirts darkened with the blood from the unwed mother and her child. Nadine leaned down to smooth Isa's hair away from her face and tucked the baby's arm into the folds of the stained hospital blanket. Their souls were to forever travel together as one. No one had the power to separate them now.

Sister Blain touched Nadine's shoulder. "Don't linger here, my child. They're in God's hands now. There's nothing you can do but pray for them."

Nadine refused to budge until the gurney had wheeled the bodies away and the nuns had trudged back across the street. Praying for

Isa didn't make any sense to her. She had departed on her journey to a place where no one would judge her ever again. They had been soul sisters for a short period on this earth but were now linked till the end of time. Nadine blinked back her tears and made a silent promise to her friend.

Watch, dear Isa.

Watch my baby girl come back to me.

CHAPTER 16

The door to the café lurched open. A young woman wearing a green canvas hooded poncho and loose jeans entered clutching a knapsack in one hand. She scanned the room, hesitating when her eyes landed on Nadine. She remained staring a long moment, then crossed the café, her face expressionless.

Nadine stood up and clutched the back of her chair, her heart pounding. It had to be her. The same full lips and high cheekbones she saw in the mirror every day. She had the urge to run and throw her arms around her, but the intensity in the girl's eyes made her hold back.

What do I do? Wait. Smile.

She's… so beautiful.

What if she turns back?

Social Services had advised her to choose a neutral meeting place and not to expect too much. She had only been waiting thirty minutes this time. Better than last time, with a no-show after two hours of endless waiting. The girl had called back last night mumbling some kind of excuse, which Nadine didn't remember or care about. She was here. Walking straight in her direction. Right back into her life.

The young woman came to a stop beside her table. "Nadine Pritchart?"

She shook her head, biting down on her lip. "Brochet. My name is Nadine Brochet. I go by my mother's maiden name now."

Lisette stood tall and strong, raindrops dripping off her green poncho onto the ceramic floor. "That's why you were so hard to find. I went through all the Pritcharts listed in the telephone book. Stella

Pritchart was the only one I found who knew you. That led me to a seniors home in NDG, but that's where the trail ended."

Nadine sat down again and gestured for the girl to do the same, her words blocked by a burning ball in her throat. If she opened her mouth to say anything else, tears were sure to fall. She remained frozen, mesmerized in front of this beautiful girl—this long-lost daughter. "There's... two Pritchart uncles still living," she managed to slip out. "But I don't think they'd have been any help to you. Was Grandma Stella shocked to hear from you?"

Lisette leaned forward to shrug off her wet poncho, spraying the tabletop between them. "More happy than shocked. She thought I was your mother Claire when I first visited last Friday. Later, she seemed to think I was you."

Heat rose to Nadine's cheeks. She had avoided seeing Grandma Stella for twenty long years, and here was her daughter going to visit her as soon as she found out about her. Why did she let this happen? How heartless she must appear to Grandma... and to Aunt Jan, who must've heard by now.

"Grandma's not far off. My Aunt Jan always said my mother had a lot of pizzazz, something I never had, but you seem to. I remember her being delicate, with hands no bigger than a child's."

Lisette spread a hand out in front of her. "Can't say that about me. I must take after my father."

Nadine averted her eyes. If the girl only knew how close she was to the truth. But now wasn't the time. "Did... she ask about me?" She swallowed the tepid mouthful of coffee left in her mug and braced herself for the answer. Why did she expect Grandma to care about her after she had neglected her for so long?

The girl straightened, holding the poncho in front of her. "Ask about you? Not really, I had to interrupt her a few times to remind her who I was. But I heard all about Grandpa Pritchart, and how your mother was killed by her husband. Nice lady, but she sure loves to talk."

Nadine's shoulders stiffened at such a casual mention of her mother's death. The subject had been taboo while she was growing up and she had never once talked about it to anyone.

Lisette hung her poncho on the back of her seat, dropped her knapsack on the floor, and lowered herself into the chair. Her black and white sweatshirt outlined her swollen abdomen.

Nadine's eyes widened at the sight of her round belly. She swallowed hard and clutched the seat of her chair. "How... far are you?"

"Eight months done." She leaned back in her seat and placed both hands on her stomach. "It feels more like eight years. I don't know how elephants manage, but I'll sure be glad when the kid pops out."

Nadine was at a loss for words. That Lisette would be pregnant had never crossed her mind. She had planned to warn her about Grandpa's genetic disorder—the girl had to be told about the risks involved. But not now. Not when the girl was about to give birth. Better to have Lisette resent her later for not having said anything rather than worry her in her last month. She stared at the girl's wide hands and wrists—big-boned like the Pritcharts. "How's it going with you?"

"OK I guess, if you're talking about the pregnancy." She pressed her hands on her hips and arched her back. "Not so sure about everything else."

"There's someone?" The girl was gorgeous. Dark glowing eyes, smooth skin, and the outline of her mountainous belly bursting like a proud monument through her shirt. Her daughter's show of pride in carrying her child triggered a pain in the back of Nadine's throat. She had felt such shame while pregnant with her.

Lisette wiped the raindrops off the table with the sleeve of her shirt and looked up at the waitress. "Coffee, please. Two creams, no sugar." She turned back to Nadine. "Serge—he's the one who nagged me to call you back after I didn't show up yesterday—he's the baby's father. So, yes there's someone. I know who the father is, if that's what you're asking. Didn't you?"

"Black for me, please." Nadine ordered her coffee and waited for the waitress to be out of earshot. That Lisette was so willing to discuss personal matters in front of strangers meant she expected the same honesty from her. She swallowed hard to stop the bile rising up her throat. "Yes, Lisette... I did... know. I only asked because I wondered if someone was helping you out. Sorry if that offended you."

The girl's gaze locked into hers. "I assumed if I have... a Mommy"—she tilted her head sideways, a look of defiance in her eyes—"I'd have a Daddy to match. Looks to me like you're the one who took offence."

The waitress returned with the coffee and creamers and headed towards her other customers.

"It's not something I thought we'd talk about... not here, in any case." Nadine forced a smile. "All I can say right now is that... he's dead. Your father died a long time ago."

Lisette stirred two creams into her coffee. "You make it sound like it's a good thing. Was he some kind of creep or something? Is that why you pawned me off?"

Nadine took in a long breath to try to ease the knots in her gut and pushed her shoulders back. This wasn't how she'd imagined the meeting to be. No flash of recognition. No weeping and throwing their arms around each other. She had felt the urge to run to her the moment she entered the café, but the dark look on Lisette's face had stopped her. It was too soon. They were strangers, after all. They had to give themselves time to get to know each other. "It wasn't... like that—" She faltered and looked down at her hands. "They, uh... took you away before I set eyes on you... I've waited so long for this moment. I—" Her words stopped dead in her throat.

Lisette pulled her glasses off and cleaned them with her napkin. "Here we go. The Harlequin moment when mother and child meet for the first time in twenty years. Spare me the drama, please. I had enough of that in the foster homes they dumped me in."

Nadine stared at her, perplexed. "Foster homes? I was under the impression that a young couple adopted you."

"Right." She crunched the napkin and tossed it on the table. "The model couple got divorced one week after my fifth birthday. First they told me I was adopted, and then they announced they couldn't keep me anymore. Seven screwed-up families later, here I am, survivor of abuse and neglect in the commendable foster care system.

But hey—" She leaned back and folded her arms across her chest. "None of that is your fault, is it? All you did was give birth to me and go on with your life."

"I—" Nadine started to protest, but a hardness in the girl's eyes stopped her. She was blaming her for whatever rejection she had suffered as a child. The girl was right. She had kept her safe inside the walls of her womb for nine months and then let her go into the unknown. They had promised a better life for her, better parents. The girl didn't know how much she had wanted to keep her, or imagine the shame it was at the time to be an unwed mother. She'd come round. She had waited and dreamed too long for this moment to lose her again. "I guess you must hate me right now. I—"

Lisette put her mug down hard and glared at her. "Right now, you say? I've hated you all my life. Each time Social Services switched me from one home to another I'd draw a picture of what I thought you looked like. And after I'd tear it into tiny pieces. It was never the foster family's fault; always my bad attitude, always a bad fit."

Nadine pressed her lips together and turned away. She didn't know what to say or do. The girl had a right to be angry, to want to hurt her. How to make her understand she had always loved her— always wanted her—that she had never lost hope they'd reunite one day? Social Services must've kept a record of all the calls she'd made through the years to make sure they still had her permission to give out her contact information to the girl. It was probably something they weren't at liberty to tell Lisette. Would this have made a difference to her? Her anger might be too entrenched. She had hated too long to understand right now.

The silence was heavy between them. Nadine fiddled with her napkin, pressing her fingers along the fold. Lisette had been leaning forward clutching her coffee mug when she straightened and placed her hand on the side of her belly.

Nadine's head shot up. "Is it moving?"

"More like dancing a jig." She grinned. "It always seems to happen when I'm hungry. Kid's already looking out for me."

"You better eat something then." She signalled to the waitress, who headed towards them. "The baby takes up all your energy at this stage."

"I am feeling pretty tired these—" She glanced up at the waitress, "Do you have something small I can order?"

"Why don't you try their chicken special? It's close enough to supper time." She needed to buy more time with her daughter. Having a meal together might ease the tension a bit.

Lisette raised her palm in protest. "That'll bust my budget. I'm trying to save up for a new place to stay. Plus I've got to find some kind of furniture—used will do, but free would be better."

"Don't worry. I'll take care of the bill." She turned to the waitress. "Make that two chicken specials with a coffee refill, please."

The waitress scribbled in her order pad and trotted away.

Lisette studied Nadine for a brief moment. "You look kind of young to be my mother. I guess it's because you were only sixteen when you had me." She paused to sip her coffee. "Being pregnant, I can see how things must've been tough on you. But I'm a big girl now. I don't hate you as much as when I was a kid, and it doesn't mean we can't be on talking terms."

Nadine let out a soft sigh. If the girl claimed she hated her a little less, that was encouraging. "You're looking for a new place to stay? Because of the baby, I suppose."

Lisette frowned. "My roommates—it's kind of complicated—want me out. It's their place, so I have no say in the matter. I don't pay actual rent, but I work it out by cleaning up after them. Not paying rent plus working three days a week at the depanneur helps me out with school. It gets a little crowded sharing the place with Serge and the other couple. And... there's the baby coming soon. I've got till next week to find a place. I don't imagine they'd physically throw me out, but it can get a little awkward."

"And Serge?"

"What about him?"

The sharp look in Lisette's eyes made Nadine hesitate. "Will he... be helping you with the move?" Maybe she was probing too much. Yet the girl wasn't giving out too many details.

"I've only got my books and my clothes to move… and then there's the baby's crib." She paused. "Serge will be joining me"—she fiddled with her hair, tugging a fistful, releasing it, and grabbing another—"as soon as he can… but he'll help me with the rent and all that. He hasn't said anything about letting me have his bed, so I'll have to rent something furnished." She cocked her head, a faraway look in her eyes. "I suppose I can always apply for a student loan after the baby comes. It'll tide me over till I can get a better paying job." She stared down at her hands. "And… well I'll have to think about daycare." She reached in her bag for a Kleenex and wiped the sheen of sweat on her forehead. "All these things to think about. But it'll all work out… once Serge joins me. We can be a real family then."

The waitress came back with the chicken platters, refilled their coffee mugs, and scooted off to the next customer. Lisette attacked her food as soon as it landed in front of her.

Nadine poked at her chicken with her fork. Nothing appeared appetizing. The girl was eight months pregnant, broke, and moving out by herself. No furniture. No steady job. Who would rent to her? The father of her child didn't appear too concerned about her situation. Who was this guy, and where were his brains? Something didn't seem right. Nadine hesitated to ask too many questions. She watched how fast the girl wolfed down her food. Had she even eaten today? This was her own flesh and blood. Her daughter. Would the girl be too proud to accept help?

"Please don't take this wrong." Nadine put her fork down and Lisette looked up from her plate. "It looks to me like… you can use some help. I have a spare bedroom at home. You're welcome to stay till you get back on your feet… or longer… if you want."

Lisette shot her a sardonic smile and reached for her glass of water. "Isn't this a little late to play mother?"

Nadine's heart raced. She had gone too far. The girl hadn't asked for help. She was pushing herself on her. Judging her situation. What did it matter that the father of the child wasn't going to be around? It was none of her business. If the girl walked out, she'd never see her again. "I only… wanted to—"

Lisette lifted her palm to stop her. "Right, well. You do owe me." She stabbed her chicken, cutting it into bite-sized pieces. "Supposing I take you up on your offer, I'd have to check out the place first. The room has to be big enough to fit a crib. It'd only be for a short while—that's if I decide to go ahead with it. Serge and I are getting back together soon. So don't go making any long-term plans for me. It's not as if we can pick up and pretend we're family after twenty years."

Nadine clutched her fork. The thought of eating anything made her stomach churn. The girl was right. Twenty lost years. No memories connecting them. Strangers with nothing in common. Her life had ceased to exist when they took her daughter away. She had plodded along all this time, reacting to, but never participating in what was happening around her. Sharing a meal with her own daughter right now was a gift from the gods. If there was a price to pay she'd have to deal with it, but at this moment, her heart was bursting too much to even think about that. She'd have to keep their conversation going and try to find some kind of common ground. She noticed a rolled up newspaper sticking out of Lisette's bag. "Who do you think will win the municipal elections on Sunday?"

Lisette glanced up at her. "Jean Drapeau is scaring the shit out of the people to get himself elected. He's got everybody thinking the opposition is full of terrorists and revolutionaries."

Nadine's stomach relaxed. Politics seemed to interest her—a good start to connect. "From what I hear, Drapeau's Civic Party will get most of the seats."

"And that'll be the end of democracy in Montreal." Lisette frowned. "He'll keep his dictator billy club hidden in his desk as long as you vote for him every four years and keep your mouth shut the rest of the time."

"He's still a popular choice. He brought in the metro system, Expo '67, Place des Arts, and now he's planning for the 1976 Summer Olympics."

"What has he done for the poor and the people he made homeless to make room for his grand ideas?"

"You talk about Drapeau using fear to get elected, but what about the FLQ? Haven't they been using fear and violence to get what they want? How is that different from the way Drapeau operates?"

Lisette thought for a moment. "I'm OK with their mission, but I've never approved of their methods. Sylvie and Pit will shoot me if they hear me say this, but the FLQ is only a small militant group aiming to blow up democracy for the sake of democracy. Just as Drapeau is sabotaging democracy with his lies and fear campaign. Democracy is like a good marriage. You need to have trust and respect from both sides."

"I'm glad to see we already agree on something." Nadine smiled at her.

Lisette looked at Nadine's untouched plate. "Hey, if you're not eating that, ask for a doggy bag and I'll bring it home for Serge."

**

Nadine shook the rain from her jacket into the bathtub and hung it on a hanger to dry on the shower curtain bar. Peaches meowed nonstop from the kitchen. The cat's feeding time was two hours ago but her rendezvous with Lisette had lasted longer than expected.

She had daydreamed of this meeting too often to convince herself it had really happened. She had longed to reach across the table to touch her hand, to feel the warmth surging through her veins. They had shared the same blood for nine months twenty years ago. But her daughter had erected an invisible barrier with all those angry remarks each time Nadine attempted to get to know her better.

She had tried to focus on what seemed to interest her daughter most: Serge and politics. Her face softened when Serge's name came up. Without asking too many questions, Nadine gathered he drove a taxi part-time and was active in some political group. Lisette babbled on about breastfeeding and making her own baby food. Nadine swallowed hard recalling the drugs the nuns had forced down her throat to dry up her own breast milk. Each time Lisette mentioned what a good mother she'd try to be, her chest tightened.

They agreed she'd come and visit Nadine's apartment the next day to see if the extra bedroom was what she wanted. They went their separate ways; Lisette headed for the university while Nadine traced her way back home.

The rush hour trip home had seemed to take forever. By the time she stepped off the bus she had almost convinced herself that Lisette would one day forgive her for not having been a good mother to her. Yet a nagging thought plagued her all the way home. She'd probably never hear from her again. Payback for having left Aunt Jan, Papi and Grandma Stella without a word so many years ago.

Peaches meowed louder.

She went to the kitchen pantry and took out the food bag. The cat circled round her feet, purring and rubbing against her ankles. "Move, you silly, beautiful old cat. I can't fill your bowl with you blocking my way."

Peaches sprang to her bowl and started nibbling her food before Nadine had finished serving. If only life were that simple. She loved and took great care of this furry orange beauty and he reciprocated with loyalty and companionship. Peaches always stood guard beside her on her pillow when she woke confused and sweating from a bad dream. He stayed perched on the bedroom dresser when a lover stayed for the night—although that hadn't happened in over a year. The cat was privy to all her fears and longings without ever betraying her. If only the world had more people as loyal as Peaches.

So much to do before Lisette came over the next day, yet she didn't know where to start. The apartment needed a thorough cleaning but she'd tackle all the clutter in the extra bedroom first. Things had to be welcoming enough for Lisette to want to move in. The bedroom was more like a storage area for anything she didn't use. Piles of books, old magazines, winter clothes and boots occupied a good section of the room.

The receptionist from work, Diane, came to sleep in that room each time she had a heated argument with her boyfriend. Nadine had offered her a place to stay the first time she noticed the bruises on her arms. The blue marks had faded away, but when they reappeared, Diane came back for a couple more days. Nadine enjoyed Diane's company but wished she'd let go of her loser boyfriend. Not that she was in any position to talk, having held on too long to certain undeserving men over the years.

Her first serious relationship had been short-lived, ending the same day her doctor told her the itchiness in her groin was due to a bad case of crabs. Her partner at the time, Dany, had turned the story around and accused her of infecting him. Then there was Mike. It took her three years to figure out why she'd find cat after cat mutilated in her backyard—two of them she had adopted as kittens. She caught him red-handed one day smashing a stray cat in the head with a bloodied brick. Fucking cats are evil and full of diseases, he'd yelled at her. I can't sleep with a damn cat lurking around the bedroom.

There were three others after that. Two lasted beyond the lusting stage but dropped her, alleging her lack of commitment. Gilles, her last one, insisted on looking at his lesbian porn magazines before making out. He claimed it made him a better lover and when she broke up with him, he mailed her a dildo with the words *think of me* scribbled with a black marker.

What was it about her that attracted such men? Was she tainted, or damaged like the nuns had drummed into all the unwed mothers at the maternity home? Had she not paid enough when they took her infant child away from her? Grandpa Pritchart's repeated remarks that she came from bad blood echoed within her. Troubled men had populated her childhood, starting with a jealous husband murdering her mother in cold blood. Uncle Denis, agreeing to adopt her without acknowledging her as his own. Grandpa Pritchart, whose weakness had ruined any chance of her having a normal childhood. And then there was Uncle Peter... she had almost forgotten about him.

CHAPTER 17

Montreal

1951

Nadine lowered herself into her chair at the long wooden table and unwrapped her bread and cheese-spread lunch. She tried to avoid glancing at Manon's thick ham and lettuce sandwich across from her. She had scraped the bottom of her jar of cheese this morning. She'd have to settle for lard sandwiches for her lunches until her next payday.

The factory foreman had agreed to try her out at the sewing machines. The raise in wages would only appear after her six months of apprenticeship. If only she'd stop making those stupid mistakes all the time. She worked overtime most nights, always at regular pay—no overtime paid before she was eighteen.

Working late was better than staring at the damp walls in her shabby room at the boarding house. After wolfing down her usual boiled egg and slice of bread for supper, the only thing left to do was go to bed for the night. The landlady, her only visitor, did her weekly rounds to collect the rent, sometimes bringing her a bowl of her leftover vegetable soup. The long hours at work left her drained and sleep took over as soon as her head hit the pillow. No time to think. Nor time to focus on the intimate noises coming from the other lodgers and the shared washroom down the hallway.

Manon finished half of her sandwich and rewrapped the rest. "Can't eat all this. I sliced the ham too thick. Here—" She slid it over to Nadine's side of the table. "I'd bring it home for my supper but I'm going out right after work. Go on, take it. It'll go to waste if you don't."

"Thanks, Manon. You're a good friend." Nadine placed the half sandwich in her lunch bag. A welcome change to the boiled egg she had planned for supper. "It's been a while since I've tasted ham."

Even with the extra hours at work, her pay only managed to cover rent and basic food items. Meat wasn't one of them. Often one of the women at the table happened to have brought an extra tea biscuit or had an apple she wasn't hungry for. It usually found its way to Nadine's place at the lunch table. At first, accepting this food had triggered an uneasiness in her chest. But the handouts were always accompanied by a warm smile, a gentle tug on her hair, or an affectionate touch of her arm. She came to understand that these hard-working women looked out for her as if she were a family member. Their small gifts of food came straight from the heart. They helped ease the hunger pangs that woke her up in the middle of the night, and gave her more stamina at work. One day she'd like to help make working conditions a little easier for these kind women.

She looked at the women sitting around the table and her throat tightened. Some came from immigrant backgrounds, but most were from poor French Canadian families. All chatted together like old friends, hurrying to finish their meagre meal before the end of their half-hour lunch break. "Everybody has been so good to me here."

Manon cocked her head. "Everybody?"

Nadine made a face and shrugged. "The section foreman has been yelling in my ear a lot lately. We're not allowed to talk with the other operators while we're working, so I can't ask them for help. How am I supposed to learn the trade if no one shows me how?"

"He's supervising your apprenticeship, so he's supposed to instruct you on how to do things. Isn't that what he's doing? He's often at your workstation."

"I try hard to do things right. He throws the work on my table and lets me figure it out. If I'm lucky the operator next to me gets the same type of work and I can copy what she's doing. When he catches me sewing a piece wrong, he yells at me that I'll never make it to the end of my training. Last week, he docked my pay because I pricked myself on the needle and left a teeny blood stain on the seam of an inside pocket. Had I noticed it, I could've snipped it off."

"He's the biggest jerk on the floor." Manon's eyes narrowed. "I'll let the other girls know what's happening." She leaned forward, her voice lowered. "Leave your lunch bag on the back of your chair here. The undergarments we're working on are pretty skimpy. They won't take up much room in your bag. We'll figure out who's working on which piece. Each operator will stitch up a different sample for you and sneak it into your bag on their way to the toilets. Study the stitching at home and you'll be OK." She paused to smile at her. "Hey, don't look so discouraged. The girls did it for me too when I first started. Believe me, it sure made my life much easier. The better you get at your job, the fewer excuses he'll have to put his slimy hands on you."

Nadine glanced up, wide-eyed. "How do you know? The boss told me to shut up about it."

"The guy's a creep. Everyone knows that." Manon brushed her sandwich crumbs off the table. "He likes sweet young ones like you. Report the asshole if he tries anything."

Nadine cleared her throat and looked around to make sure no one was listening. "At first, he'd only put his hand on the back of my neck when he leaned over to say something to me. Then he started rubbing my back each time. It made my skin crawl, but I need this job so I didn't say anything. Two weeks ago, he squatted beside me to tell me I hadn't sewn a piece right. He put his hand on my lap under the table—out of everyone's sight—and pulled my skirt up past my knees. I pushed his hand away but he did it again and started rubbing my thigh with a big grin on his face. I wanted to run out of there and never come back. Before I knew it, I had pushed my chair back and marched straight to the boss's office."

"Brave move, kid. What did the boss say?"

"What do you think, eh?" Nadine slapped her lunch bag down on the table. "He told me to stop making trouble. 'Get back to your sewing machine and stop spreading rumours,' he yelled at me." She clutched the edge of the table. "Like I was a silly kid telling lies. If I didn't need this stupid job, I'd tell them all off and never come—" She studied the other women sitting at the table. "Was I talking too loud? The boss will fire me if he hears I said anything."

Manon grinned. "Don't you worry. What you say at this table, stays at this table. They might pretend they're not listening, but they're not hard of hearing either. Good thing, too. If one of the operators hesitated to sew up a sample for you before this, she sure won't now. The foreman must know you snitched on him, that's why he's giving you a hard time. The better you get at your job, the less he can harass you." She pushed her chair back and motioned for Nadine to follow. "Come on. I'm going out back for a smoke."

Nadine took a quick look at the round wall clock. Twelve minutes left on their lunch break. Enough time to grab her coat and get a breath of fresh air before starting back. The full, dark blue coat Aunt Jan had bought her two winters ago still served her well and—stylish or not—she intended to keep it a few years longer. It also doubled as an extra bed cover during the cold winter nights when the wind whistled through her drafty window.

Manon wasn't in the habit of inviting anybody to go outside with her. She sometimes joined the group of smokers who hung out along the back wall of the factory during the break. Most times she stood away from them near the back gates, her cigarette smoke blending with the fumes of noon-hour traffic.

Nadine hooked her lunch bag on to the back of her chair and followed close on Manon's heels. When her friend passed by the coat rack without stopping, she reminded her how cold it was outside.

Manon gave her a playful shove. "Don't be such a baby, Nadine. It's not even winter yet and you're bundled for the North Pole. The cold will help kill off some of the germs from this moldy dump."

They continued down the hallway and pushed the door open to the back yard. Nadine admired Manon's elegant, wide floral skirt and dark blue cashmere cardigan. Her pastel blue blouse, nipped-in at the waist, outlined her slim figure. Manon wasn't that much older and had been at the factory only a year longer, but she always showed up wearing clothes Nadine only dreamed of having. The navy-blue Baby Dolls on her feet cost a good week's pay. How did she do it? The few items of clothing Nadine owned all came from the Sally Ann and church basement thrift shops.

Wages for a sewing machine operator were higher than what Nadine got as a simple needle worker. The raise in pay she'd get if she passed her training in six months would allow her to buy more food, but not cover other expenses. None of the others in the sewing machine section came to work dressed like a model. Manon was pretty evasive about her personal life. The other girls suspected a rich boyfriend—married, of course. They liked to rib her about the sugar daddy she was keeping from them. That's right, she'd joke back, I'm head of the Secret Sugar Daddy Club. You're all welcome to join.

Manon waved to the other smokers by the brick wall and headed for the gate at the back of the yard. She slid her Export A pack and small silver lighter from the pocket of her skirt, pulled out a cigarette, and offered one to Nadine, who declined. "Wise girl." She cupped her hand over the lighter and drew hard on her cigarette. "I'm sorry I started this dirty habit."

Nadine laughed. "I can't afford it anyway."

"Right." She blew out her smoke over Nadine's head. "That's why I wanted to talk to you. It's plain you're having a hard time getting by. Same as me when I first started here. But it doesn't have to be that way. Some of the women here have husbands who help out—or else they're supposed to be helping, though I know it's not always the case. Most of the younger ones still live at home and they're not stuck paying rent like us." She studied Nadine. "I've got a gig for you. But you've got to promise me this conversation stays between us."

"You can trust me, Manon. You know I don't talk much to anybody here."

"I know you won't shoot your mouth off." She took a drag, inhaled the smoke deep into her lungs, and let it out in long jets. "This shitty job is more of a front for me right now. I've got myself an easy gig for big bucks."

"Any chance for me to get in on it?"

"Sure thing. All I have to do is sit for an hour and watch some guy put on women's clothes." She waved her smoke away from Nadine's face. "Don't look so shocked. There's nothing to it. Sometimes he talks to me and I answer, but no touching, ever. The madam has other girls who do those things on the upstairs floor. The guy takes about thirty minutes to dress up and get made up before coming out from behind a screen. Sometimes he asks that you wear something special. The madam has a walk-in closet full of weird outfits."

Nadine pulled her coat closer. "Can you get arrested for that?"

"No law against watching a guy parade his new clothes. Most never wear the same outfit twice. It's damn good money. What I get for two one-hour gigs is the same pay as a full day's work at the factory. So if you do three each time, you can cover a week's pay in three nights. The extra cash can help you move out of that crappy rooming house and get yourself some furniture. Say goodbye to lard sandwiches and get some decent clothes. What do you think, kid?"

Nadine cleared her throat and dug her hands deeper into the pockets of her coat. She didn't know what to say. The mystery of Manon's sugar daddy had just disappeared down the drain along with the aura of glamour that had accompanied her friend. What she was asking her to do didn't feel right. If she told her that, she'd look like she was judging her, and refusing to go along might create a barrier between them.

Manon leaned back against the gate with her arms crossed. "What's the matter, Little Goody Two-Shoes? Not prudish enough for you?"

Nadine backed up a couple steps, her stomach in a knot. Manon was the only one at the factory who knew about her past. She hadn't planned on telling her. It had slipped out last summer at the company's family picnic at Beaver Lake.

The joyous laughter of young children darting in and out of the crowd of employees had tugged at her heart. If only for a few short hours, their grimy playgrounds of garbage-strewn alleyways, broken cement sidewalks, and tilted front stoops were forgotten. They tore around the adults, chasing each other over picnic tables and vast expanses of greenery and sand.

She sat at a picnic table with the women from work, sipping cheap wine offered by the bosses. It burned her throat at first, but after the second glass it tasted less like medicine. When a grubby little girl stopped running to grab onto Nadine's leg and beam up at her, something shifted inside her.

Manon found her sitting on a flat boulder beside the lake and nudged herself into the narrow space beside her. She asked her what she was doing there all by herself and Nadine's tears burst out.

Her confession had cemented a bond between them and they made a habit of sitting together at lunchtime after that. Nadine didn't want to lose her friendship, but what she had proposed left a sour taste in her mouth. Manon had never judged her when she told her about the baby, nor had she probed her for details, but had remained silent with her arms around her shoulder. There had been no mention of it afterwards. "It's not that, Manon. I —"

"Hey, kid. I'm only showing you a way out. You want to spend the rest of your life eating lard sandwiches every day except for the occasional hard-boiled egg, and rooting through somebody's hand-me-downs in smelly thrift shops, that's your business." She ground her cigarette butt with her heel and squinted at Nadine through the smoke. "Take control of your own life or someone else will do it for you."

"I have no right to judge you, Manon. The money is sure tempting but I don't know if I can do something like that. Let's not be at odds about this."

Manon's face softened. "Hey, kid. Don't look so upset. Of course, we'll stay friends. You're always so sensitive about things." She brushed the cigarette ashes off her sleeve and took Nadine's arm. "Time to get back. This autumn wind is getting nippy. We'll have to start wearing our woollen bloomers soon."

She came to a halt after a few steps and grinned at Nadine. "Hey, I've got an idea. Why don't you come along with me after work tomorrow? You don't have to do a thing but watch my gig through a secret opening in the hallway. You'll see, there's nothing to it. I watch the guy, I listen to his dumb comments, sometimes I say a few words, and the madam gives me cash when I'm done. I'm only booked for two gigs so I'll have time to treat you after to a smoked meat sandwich on Ste-Catherine Street." She shivered and continued towards the factory door. "It'll be nice to have someone walk with me to the bus stop afterwards. I hate being out alone in that part of town. It's pretty dark and gloomy along Saint-Dominique Street. I'm always scared some creep will jump out of a dark alleyway and ambush me. You can be my bodyguard for tomorrow night. What do you say, kid?"

Nadine smiled, her eyes glowing. They were still friends after all. She'd tag along with her and put this disagreement behind them for good. Where was the harm in that? And no overtime was scheduled for tomorrow. All she'd do in her drab room was lie on her narrow cot and rehash her problems all evening. This thing might bring them closer, just as her confession about her past had done. That's what good friends do, support each other no matter what. "Can't afford to refuse a free meal, especially smoked meat with lots of mustard. It reminds me of my Aunt Jan. Each time we went shopping downtown we'd stop and share a sandwich at Ben's Deli."

Manon yanked open the back door to the shop and gestured for Nadine to enter. "No need to head all the way to the other side of town for that. I know a great little restaurant that serves a smoked meat that towers over Ben's, and tastier too."

Wooden stairs stood next to the two glass facades of Simon's Provision Store on the ground floor. They led up to a faded red door on the balcony of the second level of the old three-storey brick building. The lights from Bob's Bar Salon on one side and Ti-Guy's Tattoo Art on the other lit up the grocer's darkened store windows. A thick layer of dust covered the cans of food and drinks.

A second set of more narrow stairs, almost hidden from view between the walls of the tattoo shop and the grocer, also led to the second floor, but to a black door further down from the red one.

All the shades of the upper floors were down, although a faint light filtered through most of them.

Manon pulled her hands out of the deep pockets of her box coat and turned to Nadine before climbing the stairs. "Remember, you're my cousin from out of town. And call me Fern, that's my working name here. Let me do the talking and things will be OK. And don't leave your gloves on your chair or you'll forget them like you always do. Stuff them in the arm of that big coat of yours. Madame Anna's not the giving-back type."

Nadine glanced at her wool gloves. "No one will want these. Three of the fingers are coming apart." She looked up at the stairs and bit her lip. The sight of the deserted grocery store and shabby building made her hesitate. What was she doing here? Her decision to support her friend might not have been such a great idea. "I can just go on home if my being here is a problem."

Manon climbed on to the first step and paused before going up. "Don't worry. I can handle Madame Anna."

"Is this the only way in and out of this place?"

"Customers use the other stairs beside the tattoo place. It leads to a tiny locked foyer with a telephone on the wall. Once they pick up the receiver, the phone rings twice on Madame Anna's desk and she decides whether to buzz them in or not. They can't get to the rooms without first seeing her about business. The two rooms where I work have a door on opposite sides where the guy can slip in behind the dressing screen to change clothes in private. Makes it easier for the girls to escape in case of trouble. This door here is only for workers. Madame Anna likes to keep things separate. She doesn't want anyone figuring out that the men going to the black door are heading to her side of the building. She always sits at her desk up here to keep an eye on things—her boarding house business, she calls it. Let's go. I'm booked for two gigs and she doesn't like to keep her people waiting."

Manon sprinted up the stairs two steps at a time. Nadine followed, clutching the loose wooden banister. She swallowed hard but the knot in her throat remained. Manon rapped four times below a small peephole on the door. A brief pause and the door swung open halfway. A woman's wide-boned hand appeared, gesturing them to come in. They entered a foyer crowded with a long overstuffed sofa along one wall and several armchairs lined against the opposite one. Large glass ashtrays and ornate boudoir lamps sat on the wooden end tables between the armchairs. An array of framed pictures depicting women in various stages of undress decorated the walls. A heavy odour of cigarette smoke lingered in the air.

A tall stern-looking woman with blond hair twisted back into a tight bun slammed the door behind them and clicked the deadbolt into position. "Who the hell's that?" She stood rigid, staring with arms crossed over her ample chest. The pink and white polka dot scarf wrapped around her neck accentuated the severity of her calf-length black wool suit. Nadine's shoulder's stiffened when she saw the disdain on the woman's face. A brutal reminder of the nuns at the maternity home. She took a step back and Manon grabbed her wrist.

"Good evening, Madame Anna." Manon flashed a wide smile. "Love that scarf. Polka dots are the latest rage." She leaned her head towards Nadine. "This here is my cousin, Rosa, all the way from back east. I had to meet her at the train station after work. But if I brought her back to my place, I'd get here late. I didn't think you'd mind her sitting on a chair outside the room till I'm finished. She won't be in the way, I promise."

Madame Anna studied Nadine. "No minors. Get her out of here." She walked to the wooden desk in the corner behind her and pulled out a black notebook from the top drawer.

"But she's going on nineteen."

"She can wait outside and away from my building. Don't want cops sniffing around."

Manon's eyes widened. "You're asking my cousin to stand outside in the cold for two hours with all those creeps lurking around?"

Madame Anna tilted her head towards the door. "Show the kid out and get to work. The first client wants you in cop clothes, and you'll be a nurse for the second one."

Manon took a step forward. "Sorry Madame Anna, but my family depends on me to keep Rosa safe. The girl has no idea how to get around Montreal. Leaving her on her own outside in this area is like throwing her to the wolves. If she can't stay here this one time while I work, I'm going to have to escort her home right now."

Madame Anna's eyes narrowed. "My other girls are all busy upstairs. The clients won't like being stood up. If you leave now, forget about coming back."

Manon grabbed Nadine's arm and headed towards the door.

The telephone on Madame Anna's desk rang twice. She reached for it, stopping mid-way. "Another damn client calling and I've got two others waiting already." She grabbed the receiver, covered it with her hand and glared back over her shoulder at Manon. "OK. She can stay. But that's only because I'm stuck. She better keep her mouth shut about this and stay out of my way."

Manon smiled at Nadine. "Come on, kid. I've got to find that cop outfit." She rushed to the end of the hallway and pushed open the door to the changing room. "Check in that chest over in the corner." She started sifting through the colourful assortment of outfits hanging on racks on both sides of the large walk-in closet. "You'll find a pair of handcuffs and a police baton."

Nadine rooted through the pile of kinky gadgets in the chest and pulled out the two items Manon asked for. She took a long breath and slumped back against the closed door. Her knees were still wobbly from the confrontation with Madame Anna. She cursed Manon under her breath for insisting she stay. Why did she ever agree to come? "That woman is a real terror. I can't believe you can speak to her like that without pissing your pants. She had me tongue tied."

Manon laughed. "I told you I'd handle her. I knew she'd never turn a client away. She makes big bucks on each gig I do." She pulled her shoulders back and lifted her chin. "How do I look? Threatening enough for you?"

Despite the knot in her gut, Nadine managed to smile at how gawky her friend looked in the loose-fitting police uniform. She stepped forward and straightened the cap. "This can fit a head three times fatter than yours. The holster looks like it's weighing you down.

You're not as scary as Madame Anna, but you can still put the fear of God in a grown man wearing frilly pink undies."

"Let's go, kid, before the guy starts bitching I'm late." She hurried to the room across the hall. "See this?" She pointed to a small knob at eye level on the wall beside the door. "Slide it sideways when you want to see what's happening. It opens up a vent in the wall heater and gives you a pretty good view. You won't hear Madame Anna admit to this, but I know she uses it to check up on us." She reached for the doorknob. "Whatever you do, don't let her see you peeking through the vent. She figures no one knows, but one of the girls saw her do it. She's liable to kick you out now that I'm on the job. We'll have a minute together when I change outfits. Get the folding chair from the next room to sit in the hallway here. We'll crack up about this later at the restaurant." She disappeared behind the closed door.

The legs of the old folding chair wobbled back and forth. Nadine hadn't figured out how to secure it, so she tried not to move around too much in case it collapsed beneath her. Her position at the end of the dim-lit hallway sheltered her from whatever was taking place in the foyer. From the corner of her eye, she caught a glimpse of the customers as they crossed the end of the hallway to Madame Anna's desk. She pretended to be busy with something in her lap in case one of the men happened to glance down the hallway. She didn't dare turn her head in their direction. If one of them asked Madame Anna what she was doing in the hallway, she'd be in for it. She had to look like she had a reason for being there. What if she met up with one of these men on the street one day? He'd probably think she was one of the workers here.

The men didn't wait very long for services. After a short exchange with Madame Anna, they'd sit in the foyer for a short while before she sent them up the creaky staircase to the rooms on the upper floors. The telephone rang every few minutes, bringing a new customer shuffling to her desk. Nadine's wait for her friend appeared endless. All she heard were the scraping of shoes across the foyer floor and the rumble of male voices interacting with Madame Anna.

The upstairs noises were more pronounced, giving free rein to the imaginings of those waiting to take part. Steady, rhythmic banging of bed posts against walls. Squeaking of mattress springs. Muffled moans, and at times, the eruption of shrill laughter.

Not much noise came from the room behind her. Muffled comments from Manon's client about garter belts, false eyelashes and padded bras at times broke the silence. Manon hadn't moved from her chair against the wall behind Nadine. Her remarks, though vague and never exceeding two or three words, filtered through the wall, loud enough for Nadine to know she was doing OK.

She controlled her urge to slide the vent knob open to peek at the guy in girlie clothes—cotton bloomers didn't seem very likely. She hadn't dared to try this when Manon was busy with her first gig. The thought of Madame Anna catching her in the act had kept her sitting almost motionless. Plus it hadn't seemed right to spy on the guy like that. He paid good money to live out his fantasy in private and not have someone sneak a look at him through a hole in the wall. But if she took a quick look, she and Manon might have something to laugh about later.

There had been no time to talk when Manon finished her first gig. She had rolled her eyes at Nadine and rushed to the changing room, giving her the thumbs up as she trotted back dressed as a nurse.

Nadine yawned and stretched her back. A man had just darted past the hallway, and from the sound of the terse voices, seemed to be insisting on something. The image of the thick, succulent smoked meat awaiting her made her belly growl.

Manon's voice cut through the wall separating them. "You've got the girdle on backwards."

Nadine straightened in her chair, imagining the hilarious scene behind her. Manon must want her to see this or why else would she raise her voice like that. She'd only take a tiny peek and sit back down again. The guy won't know... and it might be possible that he didn't mind a bigger audience. If he was already parading in front of Manon, it must mean her gig was almost over. Madame Anna seemed less menacing to her knowing the woman stayed glued to her phone not to miss out on any clients.

She sprang to her feet without first steadying the chair. It snapped back, crashing down on the hardwood floor. A head popped into view at the end of the hallway. Before Nadine had time to haul the chair back up, the person had disappeared. She hesitated before reaching for the vent knob or even sitting back down again. If it was Madame Anna's head she had seen, standing up to confront her seemed less humiliating than having to stare up at her angry face.

A short while went by with no reaction from the foyer. Maybe the noise hadn't bothered anybody. She reached up to slide the vent open, reminding herself to snap it back as soon as she caught a glimpse of the man with the girdle on backwards. The narrow rectangular opening only showed the tip of Manon's head and a large-sized bed with a frilly bed cover. The client must have been standing out of view away from the bed. She decided to adjust the vent opening when someone jerked her hand away.

"Getting our undies wet, are we?" Madame Anna stood beside her, eyes blazing and her voice a low rasp. "Nothing's free here. You owe me two hours of service, you little bitch."

Nadine didn't have time to protest. Madame Anna gestured to a tall bald man hovering behind her. He grabbed Nadine's arm and steered her to the next room. Madame Anna carried the chair back, clicked it back into place and shoved her down.

Nadine's heart pounded through her chest. She struggled to push herself up but Madame Anna shoved a hand over her mouth and snapped her head back.

"Listen good, little lady. Nobody gets their rocks off here without paying." Saliva spurted out of the madam's mouth. "A regular of mine is waiting with no one to service him. So you're going to sit here and watch him do his thing just like Fern's doing next door. You're lucky I'm letting you off with only that. My bouncer here hates peepers as much as I do. Once he gives them a good going over, they can't ever peep again. So if you want to keep that little goody-goody face of yours in one piece, you better sit here quiet on this chair. The client's coming through that door right behind that screen to get himself dressed up. And when he comes out, you'll be watching and getting your pussy as wet as you did before in the hallway."

Nadine squeezed her eyes shut, her stomach knotted up tight.

"Perk up. You better look like you're enjoying yourself. Any complaints and you'll be starting over with my next customer." Madame Anna cuffed the back of Nadine's head. "My loyal bouncer's going to keep watch outside this door. No funny business. Forget about opening this door till the client has zipped his pants back on. Don't show your face here again unless you plan on paying for my services."

The door closed behind her. Nadine jerked her eyes open, her breath coming in short gasps. She gripped the side of the chair with shaking hands. She needed to get out before the guy showed up. The door on the opposite side of the room might lead to the black door and she'd bypass the foyer. But what if it didn't and she came face to face with Madame Anna? Sitting here made her just like all the girls working here—exploiting men's sexual fantasies for cash. Not her. She didn't have the stomach for this. She tried to focus on how to get off the chair without it snapping closed again and alerting the bouncer.

Then the other door opened and closed. A bulging duffle bag dropped down between the stubby legs of the screen. Too late. She hadn't moved fast enough. She swallowed the hard lump in her throat and gasped for air. The Harlequin ladies on the wallpaper inched in closer and closer. She dug her fingers into her wool coat to block a scream from escaping. She had to get a hold of herself. The bouncer was ready to spring through the door any moment. One hour, Manon had told her. About thirty minutes for the guy to get dolled up before he springs out from behind the screen.

She held her breath. She had no choice.

I can do this... I can.

If the guy attacked her, the bouncer was in the hallway—one good thing going for her.

Deep breath, Nadine. You'll get through this.

All she had to do was pretend she was Manon.

We'll laugh about this later.

We will.

The folding screen, painted the same shade of pink as the Harlequin ladies on the wallpaper, stood on four short legs. The man had removed his shoes and socks and was standing beside his duffle bag. He hung his shirt and pants over the top of the screen, let his underwear drop to the floor and kicked them out of the way. Her stomach tensed. Did he have a wife at home keeping his dinner warm? What about that duffle bag full of sexy undergarments—did he store it in the trunk of his car, or hide it in a secret locker at the train station?

The sound of a zipper ripping open. The soft thud of clothes hitting the floor. He must be leaning down, naked, rooting through his bag. Red stiletto-heeled shoes appeared on the floor below the screen. "Finally found a pair my size." His words tremulous, almost boyish.

She squeezed her knees together. No way was she going to encourage him. He could talk all he wanted, but she didn't have to answer him.

Loud grunts and sighs, and the occasional thump against the screen. He must be struggling to force delicate undies onto a hairy, angular body.

Sweet Jesus.

Please don't make the screen come crashing down.

The guy dressed in girlie things is bad enough.

But not with his private parts flapping all over the place.

"Love these silky undies. My mother always wore rough cotton ones and my wife buys the cheaper ones that look like cut-off bloomers. These are a little tight around my weenie, but... what a feeling." He dropped a pink garter belt on the floor and leaned down to pick it up.

She pressed her lips together and averted her eyes at the sight of the tufts of dark hair on his wrist.

"These stockings will take a while. I've got to be careful to pull that back seam nice and straight. Don't want to snag these black fishnets after paying so much for them." He fell silent a moment and continued, louder, sterner. "Helen never buys these. She thinks only sluts wear them. God forbid. Just thinking about wearing fishnets would make her run to confession."

Nadine cocked her head towards the screen. His abrupt change of tone caught her attention. The authoritative way he pronounced the name 'Helen' triggered a vague memory of someone she knew—with an identical name and addressed in the same harsh manner. The only one who came to mind was Aunt Helen, married to Uncle Peter, but she had only ever seen them together at Christmas or Easter. He'd always been gruff with the timid woman. She might also be thinking of an old classmate. The nuns at school didn't always speak kindly to their students, especially the poor ones who were too hungry to pay attention.

"Now for my makeup." His tone soft and excited again. "I didn't forget my hand mirror this time, so I won't take too long."

She clasped her hands together on her lap and then shoved them deep into the pockets of her coat. It was one thing to listen to him while he stayed behind the screen, but having to face a grown man wearing feminine underwear was another ball game. What was she supposed to do when he made his grand appearance? Look away? Stare down at the floor? But pretending he looked sensuous in his girlie clothes was part of the bargain. He'd complain to Madame Anna before she had a chance to escape.

And what if she got the giggles? That bouncer was bound to hear. He was probably peeping through the vent.

Run. Now.

Before the guy shows himself.

That damn bouncer. He'd attack as soon as she stood up. She'd have to force a smile and keep it fixed until the end of the ordeal. Manon's gig would be over soon. Thinking of that juicy smoked meat sandwich would keep her smile going. She'd imagine the spicy smell of mustard and the crunch of the dill pickle.

A sigh from behind the screen.

The red stiletto-heeled shoes were now on his feet.

A soft moan.

He stepped out and——to her surprise——inched out with his back to her. She gripped the seat of her chair, holding her breath.

Stay like that.

I won't have to face you.

Legs wide apart, shoulders pushed back, his hips wobbled in his stiletto heels. He massaged his rump, flattened in the tight pink silk panties with matching garter belt. His long blond wig reached down to the pink nylon bra that dug into the folds of the loose flesh of his back. Patches of dark hair covered his shoulders and lower back, contrasting with the delicate silk undergarments. One of the back straps of the garter belt had unsnapped, showing a large expanse of bluish white skin above the top of the black fishnet stocking.

The musty smell of the room along with the clumsy shape in red stiletto heels wobbling in front of her triggered a wave of nausea that surged up her throat. He turned to face her. She shot a quick glance around the room for a wastebasket. Her heart skipped a beat. His gyrating movements had shifted his blond wig sideways, revealing oily black hair pushed back from his forehead. The sloppy eye makeup accentuated his thick black eyebrows and five o'clock shadow.

She recognized him right away——the same telltale cleft chin and full lips as the other men in the family.

"Uncle Peter."

She spotted the wastebasket under the bedside table and bolted for it.

CHAPTER 18

Lisette examined the front of the apartment building before opening the car door. "Don't come up just yet, Serge. Give me a few minutes to check things out before you haul everything up to the second floor. I've already told her that I'd have to see it before I decided." Maybe she should've waited to tell him about Nadine's offer until after first going to visit the apartment on her own. He had acted like it was a done deal. She'd expected him to get cold feet about them living apart. But his face had lit up when she mentioned it and he started rooting through the cupboard right away for black garbage bags to help her pack.

"I'm sure the room will be just fine." He reached into the back seat and tugged on one of her bags. "It's rent-free. Can't get any better than this. And it can't be too shabby judging by the looks of the front of building."

"What if there's no room for a crib?" She had asked him to leave the crib behind in case the place wasn't to her liking.

But Sylvie had insisted. "If they bust us, they'll see the crib and connect the dots." Connections—the focal point of Sylvie and Pit's daily menu of platitudes. Cops only operate with connections, Pit liked to repeat. Without dots to connect, they attack the pawns.

"Wait till we bring the bags up. I'll just leave the crib in the car if I don't see enough space in the room. There must be some kind of dresser in the room. Slide one of the drawers out and use it as a cradle for a few months." He pushed his door open, dropped the bag on the sidewalk and reached for the other two. "Stop stalling, Lise. Jump on the chance. You can't beat free rent and board. Once the panic about Laporte has died down and you're back on your feet, we'll get our own place. Let's go. We're in a no-parking zone." He grabbed hold of two bags with one hand and the third one with the other.

She let out a long breath and reached down for her knapsack. "Why do I feel like… I'll never see you again? You won't even let me call you."

He hesitated a moment, set the bags down, and walked around to the passenger side to open the door for her. "Come on, Lise. We've gone over this. I can't take any chances in case they've tapped the phone. If they trace your mother's number, they'll haul you both in for questioning. I'll be staying somewhere else from now on, so you can't reach me at that number anymore. Pit and I decided it was best we stay at separate locations." He took a quick look around at the neighbouring apartment buildings. "Try to be reasonable. You'll be safe here. I even took the company car today to make sure no one followed."

She climbed out of the car and swung her bulky knapsack over her shoulder. "You're making a mountain out of a molehill about all this. Or maybe it's only an excuse for getting rid of me."

It wouldn't be the first time a guy had come up with a sorry excuse to drop her. I don't see her showing much loyalty to the cause, had been Pit's lame objection to her living with them. We all have to be of one mind to move forward, his favourite mantra.

All nonsense.

Pit had resented her from the moment she moved in. Not that Serge went along with all of Pit's foolishness. But Laporte's death had put a damper on things. Pit and Sylvie had jumped on the chance to stress the danger of a pregnant woman being exposed to police raids, long interrogations and jail time.

"Don't start, Lise. Even Pit says someone's on his trail now, so I can't be imagining things."

"But what if there's an emergency and I need to reach you? I'm sure my mother won't mind you staying here with me. That sacred mission of yours can survive without you for a few months—at least till after the baby is born." Wrong choice of words, but his refusal to put family before his political activities got under her skin. "The fight for an independent Quebec has been going on for over a hundred years. What are a few short months in the grand scheme of things? I hate to shatter your illusions, but the fight will continue with or without you."

He turned on his heel and snatched the bags from the sidewalk. "Where do you want me to dump these?"

"Hold on, Serge." She hurried after him. "That didn't come out right. I didn't mean what I said." They had discussed his political vision many times over. He had never budged from his position before this—why did she expect him to do so now? Arguing would only keep him away. One of these days she'd learn to think before opening her mouth.

He stopped in his tracks, his eyes blazing. "Didn't you mean it? You say you believe in what I'm doing. But you've never once encouraged me."

"Don't say that. I don't always agree with the way you choose to go about things, but still, I've never doubted your passion for justice." She tried to swallow the hard lump in her throat. "It's just that… this is like a damn breakup."

He continued to the entrance of the building and placed the bags down before pulling the door open. He waited for her to catch up, shamefaced. "Sorry for being such a prick. But how many times do I have to repeat it?" He wrapped his arms around her. "I know this is bad timing with you being pregnant, but I've got to see this through. Staying with you won't stop them from following me. I'm relieved your mother is taking you in. It's only temporary. You can always leave a note at the taxi stand and my boss will make sure I get it. He knows about the baby. So don't you worry. I promise I'll be at the hospital as soon as I get the word. You have to trust me on this. Take advantage of the little time you have left to finish up your term papers and put your feet up. Get to know your mother."

"Is the room OK, Isa? Sorry, I mean Lisette." Nadine stood in the kitchen doorway. "There's plenty of room for the crib against the wall by the closet. If you want a place to work on your term papers, there's that small storage room I use as an office. I sometimes use it when I bring work home, which doesn't happen often these days. The receptionist has been taking over a lot of my paperwork. The room has become a dumping ground for bills, old books and magazines."

Lisette gazed up from her seat on the sofa, a pained look in her eyes. "Yeah, I guess. The bedroom will do. It sure beats the cramped space I shared with Serge at the other flat. At least there's a window in this one. He's assembling the crib right now… before he takes off." She folded her arms over her belly. "The least he can do before vanishing from my life."

"He doesn't have to rush out." Nadine detected the shakiness in her daughter's voice and controlled her urge to take her in her arms. "He's welcome back anytime."

"He's got things to take care of." Lisette stared down at her lap. "He won't be back. If he does, it won't be for a few months."

"A few months. You're liable to give birth any day now. Is it because of his work?"

"I suppose so—" Her voice wavered. "Yeah. I guess you can say that."

Nadine took a step forward. "Is something wrong? Can I get you something? Water or a coffee? Do you need to rest?"

Lisette sagged against the back of the sofa and turned to stare out the window.

Nadine struggled between her urge to comfort her and her intention to let her be. She headed to the kitchen, stopping when Serge stepped into the room.

"All done. The crib is set up. I've got to bring the car back or my boss will have a fit."

"I was just about to make coffee. You must have time for that."

"Thanks, but I've got tons of things waiting for me." He raised his palms up. "And the car's in a no-parking zone." He stepped up to the window and looked out. "The cops haven't left a ticket yet. Better take off before they spot it."

Lisette followed him to the door while Nadine walked into the kitchen.

"Don't go." She put her arms around him.

"Hey, don't make this harder. We'll be together… soon as the dust settles. You'll be safe here." He leaned down to kiss her.

Nadine came back with two mugs and placed them on the coffee table just as Serge closed the door behind him. She sat down on the sofa and Lisette did the same, reaching out to wrap both hands around a mug. "Exactly what I needed. Having someone else make my coffee. I've been so tired lately."

"Looks like a heavy baby to cart around." Nadine glanced down at Lisette's belly and pressed her lips together. "What did Serge mean about you being safe here? Are you in some kind of danger?"

Lisette lifted a shoulder. "He likes to exaggerate at times."

"About what?"

"All the crap going around about the FLQ." She hesitated a moment. "He's deep in the politics of it all. He doesn't want me involved and figures it'd be better if I stay away from him till things settle down."

Nadine decided not to probe any further. She had spotted the large, blue fleur-de-lys tattooed on the inside of his right wrist when they shook hands earlier, and had blurted out how difficult it was to get rid of a tattoo once you get tired of looking at it. Etched on for life, he'd replied and winked at her. Yes, she'd answered. Such a beautiful flower.

"Interested in politics, is he? It's good to keep up to date with what's happening."

"Well, he sure does. But he doesn't just sit around thinking about things. He believes thoughts are a call to action. And when he says he's going to do something, you can be sure it's going to happen. He's as solid as they come."

"He strikes me as being honest enough." Nadine noticed the twitch in Lisette's left eye. Was she that anxious about Serge leaving—or was it an eye problem? "Is he a member of some kind of political group?"

"Not a card-carrying member—" She paused to stare at Nadine. "What's with the weird look? He's part of a group that believes in supporting Quebec's independence. Nothing wrong with that."

"If I get what you mean, then he's smart to keep you away from all that. Let's not talk about that right now. The media will let us know what's happening. We'll leave the politics to him and we'll concentrate on you and the baby." She got up to lock the front door. "Why don't you have a rest and I'll call you for supper?"

Lisette nodded and grabbed on to the arm of the sofa to pull herself up. "Guess what Serge said made sense. I need quiet time to finish off my term papers before the baby comes." She headed for her new bedroom. "I sure won't miss pitching Pit's dirty undies into the wash, or listening to Sylvie complain about the way I fold her towels—though she can be nice at times." She stopped to place her hands on her belly. "Hey. This baby sure likes to kick. Time for a nap, kiddo."

Nadine lay still, disoriented. Had she been dreaming or was her daughter actually sleeping in the spare room? She threw the blanket off, swung her legs off the bed and tiptoed down the hallway to make sure. She always kept the door to the spare bedroom open for Peaches—his favourite lookout being the windowsill with a view of the back alley.

Closed.

Nadine let out a soft sigh. She hadn't dreamt it. Only a plywood door separated her from her daughter. She felt her way in the dark to the front door and groped on the mat for Lisette's runners.

Yes, she's here.

Thank you God for giving me back my daughter.

She felt her way back to her bed, hoping to catch another couple hours of sleep, only to spring back up again at the sound of sobbing. She rushed to her daughter's bedroom door. But the cries had stopped by the time she got there, so she slid down to the floor and waited until her daughter's soft snores filtered through the door.

She spent Saturday morning helping Lisette sort out her clothes from the plastic bags and setting up a workspace in the office for her.

There hadn't been time for laundry before the move, so a good part of Lisette's clothes, as well as a bag full of used baby clothes, went into the washing machine. At times their hands brushed against each other as they worked—Nadine's heart soared when Lisette didn't flinch at the touch. They reserved the two top drawers of the dresser for baby items, leaving the bottom two for Lisette's own use.

The afternoon shopping outing for baby clothes and toiletry items took longer than planned. The army, checking for bombs, had sealed off several blocks of the downtown area. Nadine and Lisette stood among the small crowd of bystanders outside the cordoned-off area. Stern-faced soldiers with semi-automatic rifles stood at attention.

Nadine shuddered. "It's a creepy sight. I've got to walk by this twice a day when I go to work. You'd figure they'd take the weekend off."

"It's just grandstanding." Lisette's eyes narrowed. "I'm sure it's not even necessary. Serge is right when he says Trudeau's manipulating us."

"Well, I don't want to stick around in case there's a real bomb." She took Lisette's arm and guided her back in the opposite direction. "Lots of shops on Ste-Catherine East have what we're looking for. Not worth hanging around here."

"Serge and I went to the Sally Ann store up ahead. You can pick up a whole garbage bag of baby clothes for next to nothing. I got more baby things from a church bazar." Lisette paused, pressing her palm on her belly. Her eyes lit up. "This kid is going to be a dancer."

Nadine smiled. "You can't dress a dancer in old clothes. Forget about the Sally Ann for now and let me be a grandmother. Although I was only able to afford to buy at thrift shops before you were born, I used to dream about shopping for lace baby dresses at Eaton's department store. Sometimes I'd luck out and happen to visit the church basement on days when they gave out free stuff." She steered her ahead. "Come on. The shops are only a couple of blocks away. It's OK for grandmothers to spoil their grandchildren and mothers have no say in the matter."

"You don't have to do this. Serge said he'd send me some money."

"So use it for something else. This is my treat. You can't leave this to the last minute. What if the baby comes early?"

Nadine avoided mentioning Serge's name and kept her busy shopping around in the various small boutiques. She often caught her staring into space when she spoke to her. Last night's sobbing most likely had something to do with him. The sight of the soldiers must've brought back the reason why they had to live apart.

As pleasant as Serge had appeared to her, she had a feeling her daughter wasn't going to see much of him. If he was being followed as Lisette had explained, he had to be doing something illegal. And if he thought it too risky for Lisette to stay with him, it stood to reason that he had to be in danger too. It was best Lisette started getting used to living her life without him. The baby would set her priorities straight.

They shared a bowl of Hostess potato chips while they watched the Habs take on the Flyers on Hockey Night in Canada. Lisette stayed focused on the game, only getting off the sofa during commercials to use the bathroom. Nadine, not a sports fan, had hoped to use that time to clear up any questions Lisette might have about her birth. Social Services had disclosed only general details to her, while Grandma Stella—the poor woman must still be traumatized—had focused on the death of Nadine's parents. But Lisette appeared uninterested in it all and hadn't bothered to ask questions.

The girl had, nevertheless, initiated the search for her biological parents, so why didn't she wonder who her father was? The thought of revisiting that part of her past made Nadine's stomach clench. She had told no one. She was ready, though, to break her long silence for her daughter. She owed her that. But it also involved warning her she might be a carrier of her father's kidney disorder. Telling her now was only going to cause her stress. Better to wait a few weeks until after the child was born. Nowadays, blood tests detected these problems at birth. Treatment options were possible, though the cure remained a mystery.

The high-pitched siren signalling the Montreal Canadiens 3-1 win over the Philadelphia Flyers blared from the screen. Lisette bolted up, holding a fist high above her head. "Way to go, guys!" She turned to Nadine with a grin. "Serge must be cracking another beer open as we speak."

Nadine smiled back and switched off the TV. "I've got a few bottles of Labatt 50 on the bottom shelf of the fridge if you feel like celebrating. It'll give us a chance to talk about things." She got up and headed for the kitchen.

"Only a small glass for me. One bottle and I have to pee three times within a half hour." She sat back down and leaned over the side of the sofa to root through the wicker magazine rack.

Nadine came back with two glasses of beer and placed them on the coffee table in front of them. "I see you found my old scrapbook."

Lisette looked up, puzzled. "It was at the bottom of the magazine pile. What's it about? Looks like someone—you, I guess—cut out a bunch of images of kids from magazines and pasted them in here. Was this some kind of high school project of yours? Judging from all the yellowed pages, it's been around for a while."

Nadine took a sip of beer and nodded. "Did you notice the name on the cover and all the different dates written inside?"

Lisette closed the scrapbook and looked at the big block letters on the cover page. "Isa?" She paused a moment. "That's what you keep on calling me."

"Sorry about that." Nadine grinned. "I'm trying to get used to calling you Lisette. I had already chosen a name for you before you were born. Isa, if you were a girl, and Paul, for a boy. But none of that mattered after you got adopted."

"Paul? Grandma Stella said your father's name was John?"

"Paul is Aunt Jan's father's name—my adoptive grandfather. He's driving back from Saint-Roch tomorrow, so you'll have a chance to meet him."

"Can't. Maybe next time. I'll be at the library most of the day working on my paper. I have to get it done soon." Lisette flipped the scrapbook open again. "So what's this scrapbook all about? Hey! That's my date of birth!" She pointed to the top of the first page.

Nadine pressed her lips together. It had been a while since she had leafed through her scrapbook. Each image she had glued on the pages had come with a deep ache in her chest. "Count yourself lucky, Lisette. No one will take your child away from you. When I left the maternity home—apart from knowing you were a girl—I had no idea what you looked like. No smell. No touch. It was like a bad dream. When I got settled I did my best to keep your memory alive—to make you real. I picked up old magazines people left on the bus and some came from garbage cans I passed by on my walks. You were always in my thoughts. When I found an image of what I figured you might look like at a certain age, I'd cut it out. You'll find lots of pictures of newborns—I was pretty messed up at the time. Each year on your birthday, I'd take out the old scrapbook, write the date, and add new pictures of you a little older, a little taller. That was my only way of keeping track... of keeping you real."

"I don't have any pictures of me as a kid. My adoptive parents might've snapped a few. I know for sure my foster ones didn't." Lisette studied each page, pausing at times to look up at Nadine. "You even have one of a kid doing her First Communion."

"I thought the nuns must've placed you with a Catholic family." Strange to have her own daughter alive in front of her, inspecting images of what her mother had imagined she'd be like. What was she thinking? Was she measuring, comparing the distances between the imagined and the real?

"I didn't have one of those." Lisette turned to the next page.

"What's that?"

"A First Communion." She scanned the page. "My foster mother said it wasn't fair to her daughter to celebrate the two of us at the same time." She browsed through a few more pages. "No Second Communion either"—she lingered a few moments near the end of the scrapbook—"Couldn't afford a dress for my grad, so I didn't bother." She slapped the scrapbook closed. "I packed my bag after the last high school exam, left that sick foster home to go crash with a friend, and never went back."

"Sick? What do you mean?" Nadine tightened her grip on her glass, dreading her daughter's answer. Why hadn't Social Services contacted her after the adoptive parents placed her into foster care? She had been working five years by then and had been in a better position to take care of her child.

Lisette remembered her beer and reached for it. "Same shit, different foster home. It was my word against theirs. He said I lied— claimed he never touched me. His wife said I wasn't a good fit. When they mentioned a group home, I made a dash for it before the social worker got there."

Nadine bit down hard on her lip and stared at her empty glass. Was she ever going to be able to make amends to her child and ease some of the pain from her past? The only thing to do now was show her unconditional love. "I had this recurrent dream for a long time after your birth where the nurse in the maternity room placed you against my chest. You hadn't cried out like newborns do. I could see the outline of your face, but not your features. Your skin was still warm and moist from being inside me and I reached out to put my arms around you. But something blocked me—I don't know what, a strong force, maybe. My arms weren't able to reach you no matter how hard I strained. I yelled over and over again that I wanted to touch my baby. The nurses went about their business without even looking at me."

"Sounds more like a nightmare to me." Lisette placed her glass down, tilted her head sideways and studied Nadine. "That scrapbook sort of gives me another vision of things. You've got to be pretty lonesome and sad to build an album about another person like this— to imagine the life of someone you've never even seen. I guess you must've wanted me around after all."

"You'll never know how much." Nadine swallowed the hot lump in her throat. By recognizing her pain of having lost her at birth, Lisette had also accepted the primal bond between mother and child. A tingling warmth radiated in her chest.

"So what's the verdict?" Lisette smirked. "The last images in the scrapbook are all beautiful, smiling young women who look pretty successful at something. The real me is rude and antisocial. A plain Jane with thick glasses. Hates dressing up. Refuses to wear makeup. Wears wide, size ten shoes and has large peasant hands. She's two weeks behind in her term papers and eight months pregnant with no plans of getting married. How's that for a letdown?"

Nadine laughed. "You're right about all those things except the plain Jane part. I couldn't have asked for a more beautiful daughter. I'm so very proud of you."

Lisette cleared her throat and looked down at the floor. "That's a first. Nobody's ever told me that before. They always said I wasn't a good fit—too moody, too disruptive, too rude… one even said I was too high and mighty—she never did tell me why. I don't remember anything about my adopted mother, but one thing I do know for sure, I never once hugged any of my foster mothers."

"How about starting with your own mother?" Nadine reached for her daughter, her eyes brimming with tears. It was more of a one-sided hug, with Lisette's arms stuck to her side, but still, she was able to wrap her arms around her and hold her close for the very first time.

Nadine poured a second cup of coffee and sat down at the kitchen table with the Sunday *Gazette*. They had stayed up talking late into the night, about Serge for the most part, but Nadine had managed to bring up Papi and Aunt Jan quite a few times. Her attempts to broach the subject of Lisette's father hadn't worked out as planned.

"By the look on your face, I can tell you're about to tell me something weird. So don't bother." Lisette raised her palm each time she tried to bring the subject up. "My mind can't take another family gloom story tonight. When I started searching for you, I expected to find a normal family. The first person I found was Grandma Stella. The story about your father stabbing your mother to death really got to me. I went through enough crap growing up. I don't need to learn any more gruesome details about my so-called real family.

If Social Services hadn't called me, I wasn't going to continue the search. So let's talk about positive things right now. I need to know I come from a boring, loving family."

"It's too bad Grandma Stella brought that up right away. That's a pretty rough start for you." Nadine remained silent a while before speaking again. "She's probably never gotten over what happened. I know I haven't. But you're right. Let's enjoy our evening together."

Lisette emerged from her room in pyjamas, eyes swollen, and clutching a Kleenex in her hand. Nadine's heart went out to her. If only she could offer her a magic potion that would make her pain disappear.

"There's a plate of pancakes keeping warm in the oven for you. The butter and maple syrup are both on the counter." She continued with the *Gazette* crossword puzzle.

Lisette pulled the plate out of the oven, placed it on the table across from Nadine and dragged her feet back to the percolator to pour herself a mug. She leaned against the counter to sip her coffee, a distant look in her eyes.

Nadine waited a moment before looking up. "Don't forget to turn the oven off."

Lisette blinked, reached out to push the off button and shuffled back to sit at the table.

Nadine went back to her crossword, not knowing how to address her. The girl might not be a morning person—there was so much to learn about each other. She didn't want to jinx anything after the pleasant time they'd had yesterday. Lisette's initial hostility towards her had toned down and she seemed more trusting. She watched from the corner of her eye as Lisette ate a mouthful of her pancake and pushed her plate away.

"Serge and I always go for breakfast at our local diner Sunday mornings." Her eyes dull, her voice flat. "He loves their roasted potatoes. I always have to watch he doesn't steal some from my plate."

"You must miss him a lot." Nadine jotted down another answer, pressing the nib of her pen hard into the thin newspaper. The girl seemed completely obsessed with a guy who placed his politics before his personal obligations.

Lisette leaned her elbows on the table and placed her head in her hands. "I called him late last night. He told me not to, but I just needed to hear his voice." She closed her eyes and took a deep breath.

"What did he have to say?" Nadine restrained the words rising in her throat. The guy had completely isolated himself from Lisette without allowing her any way of reaching him. Public telephones were still a safe way to contact her. If he loved her as much as Lisette believed, he'd be there for her. But Nadine didn't have the courage to tell her how unfeeling she thought he was. Lisette wasn't ready to hear anything negative about him. It was only going to sabotage whatever relationship had started to blossom between her and her daughter.

"That's the problem." Lisette lay her head on the table. "There's no more service at that number. I don't know if Sylvie got her number changed, if they've all moved out, or if they're all at the police station. I don't know what the heck's happening." She sat up straight. "He's made it all up. Nobody's following him and the phones aren't tapped. He said all that to get rid of me. Pit and Sylvie never liked me from the beginning. I'm just a bad fit for them." She paused. "But that's nothing new."

That Serge might have fabricated his situation didn't surprise Nadine. She'd heard enough lame excuses from men wanting to break up with her to recognize the signs. "Well, you're a perfect fit to me. I know it's easy for me to say, but try not to worry too much. You've only got a short time left to rest before the baby comes. Why don't you come visit Aunt Jan with me and Papi. It'll be an emotional visit for me, but I'd really like you to meet her. It'll take your mind off things."

Lisette pulled her glasses off and rubbed her eyes. "Sorry about the outburst—just a pregnant woman with hormones gone wild. I'll pass on that visit for now. You'll probably cry and talk about sad things. Listening to Grandma Stella go on about your father was enough for me. But he wasn't really your father, right? According to her story, that's why your parents had that big fight." She wiped her glasses on her cotton nightshirt and pushed them back on. "I think I'll skip the library too and go back to bed. My eyes have been acting up the last few days so I'll avoid straining them today. My papers can wait till tomorrow."

Nadine's head shot up. "What's with your eyes?"

"I'm not sure. I didn't have that problem before I got pregnant."

"So what is it exactly?"

Lisette pushed her hair away from her face. "Nothing much. It only happens sometimes, but more often lately. I'll be reading for a short while and big white blotches appear on the page like I've got openings in my eyes. I can only see disjointed patches of what I'm supposed to read. It sure doesn't help with all the reading I've got for my courses. I've tried compresses of cold tea bags, cucumber slices, eye drops, but nothing works. The problem will go away after the baby comes."

Nadine skipped a breath. "Have you seen an eye specialist?" She remembered, as they spoke, sitting on the old sofa in her pyjamas beside Grandpa Pritchart. He'd point to the bold headlines while she'd read the article in the newspaper out loud to him. The small newsprint strained his eyes, making the words fade and disappear on him. Your grandmother never went to school long enough to learn how to read proper, he'd say to her. His thigh pressed into the side of hers. His hard fingers massaged her lower back, sometimes sliding down below the elastic waistline of her pyjama bottom.

"He wants to try a new operation." Lisette grimaced. "But it can be risky, so he won't do it if my problem turns out to be genetic. That's why—" She stopped to think. "It was one of the reasons I looked you up in the first place. With everything going on, I keep on forgetting to ask you. It's no use asking about your father, but did anyone from your mother's family have these problems?"

Nadine let her pen drop on the table and pushed her crossword puzzle aside. She clasped her hands together under the table to hide her trembling. Lisette's question had triggered a thickness in her throat.

It was time to tell her about Grandpa Pritchart's disorder. Lisette needed to know. Yet besides giving her something else to worry about, telling her the truth wasn't going to change much. That baby was well on the way no matter what. Waiting till after the birth might be a better time. She'd get a proper diagnosis from her doctor, and a more informed decision about possible eye surgery from the obstetrician. But still... keeping this from her might jeopardize whatever trust had formed between them.

She bit down hard on her lip, determined to tell her. The words froze in her throat. A wave of cold sweat surged over her body. If bolting from the room and hiding under her blankets without appearing too neurotic had been an option, she would've taken it. She had kept the secret of Lisette's father festering inside her so long, she wasn't able to dislodge it. She took a deep breath. "The only thing I know about my mother's family is that they came from back east."

CHAPTER 19

Quebec City, Quebec
October 1970

It was early morning when Paul exited off the Quebec Bridge to take Highway 132 towards Montreal. He was looking forward to seeing Janette but he knew emotions were sure to run high today. He had called her as soon as he arrived home from Montreal to tell her about Nadine—bad move, telling her in person would've been easier on her. Janette had sobbed a good while after he broke the news to her. When Nadine phoned afterwards to tell him about reuniting with her daughter, he decided not to tell Janette. It was up to Nadine to announce the good news.

Denis had always acted as if he was Janette's saviour. Not that she needed saving. Paul's daughter was solid, from a long line of strong independent women who never backed down in the face of adversity. She might appear meek and docile at times, but she was the one who held the reins in her marriage. Paul had always left his daughter's parenting to his mother, trusting her to handle all the tears and temperamental outbursts of a growing girl. His role had been the cameo father, bringer of gifts on work breaks and holidays.

The three-hour drive to Montreal didn't bother him. He had a lot to think about. His family wasn't the only thing on his mind. The two logging camps he had visited on the north shore of the river yesterday had left a feeling of heaviness in his chest. The forestry industry wasn't the same anymore. The good old days when he first started working for the Forestry Workers' Union after World

War II were no more. No more shaking hands with the lumberjacks, or listening to their wild stories about life in the camps. Gone was the camaraderie—the satisfaction of doing a good day's work.

Bush workers at one time used to welcome him to the camp, trusting he could help make their working conditions a little easier. His sole contacts these days were the operators of powerful chainsaws and machinery. These sub-contractors dealt only with large players in the pulp and paper industry. Their main concerns were contract renewals, not food, lodging, or working conditions. Axes, bucksaws and sleighs were tools of the past.

The traditional crude logging camps he had frequented as a young axeman had disappeared. Chopping at the trunks of gigantic pines from sunrise to sunset was no longer required. The isolated woods had once been a man's world, where his masculinity was on the line. Strength and endurance with axes and crosscut saws defined his identity. A man's performance nowadays was no longer judged on brute strength, but on the ability to operate the different chainsaws and machinery. Improved roadwork and easy access to vehicles now made it possible for workers to have their weekends off. No longer was it necessary for loggers to live away from their families six long months at a time.

He found himself thinking of Rose and how much easier it might have been on their marriage had they seen each other every weekend. His young wife had found their months apart at his parents' home especially difficult with a newborn always crying for attention. If only he'd been by her side those last precious days before she died. Not only had he failed as a husband, but by giving his mother free rein to bring up his daughter, he had failed as a father too.

Janette had grown up in the shadow of a dead mother and a part-time father who, apart from the few days at Christmas and Easter, was only present a few weeks during the summer season. His long absences had weakened the God-given bond offered to him on the day of her birth. Absent on that important day, he had decided to stay at the bush camp rather than risk the long journey home during the spring thaw. The fissure that had opened between them deepened as she grew older.

When it came time for her to marry Denis, she had gone ahead without asking his blessing. He had forfeited his right to such respect. His visits with her as a married woman had always been tense. Denis had never been welcoming, and Janette had done her best to balance her sense of duty to both her husband and her father. Paul had formed an instant bond with his adopted grandchild, Nadine, a child who like him had lost the love of her life. Her disappearance at age sixteen had shattered him as much as it had Janette.

His regular visits to Rose's and his parents' tombstones made him hesitate to move from Saint-Roch. All his childhood friends were long gone. His neighbourhood no longer resembled the one he grew up in. His apartment was close to the union office yet it was getting harder for him to motivate himself to even show up for work. It was time to move closer to Janette and try to mend a few of the broken fences he had neglected for so long.

Meeting up with Nadine last week had awakened painful memories—the sharpest one being the day he had learned of Rose's death. Every thought, every image that had crossed his mind when he hopped off the train on that fatal Christmas Eve were as vivid to him now as they had been fifty years ago.

CHAPTER 20

Saint-Roch, Quebec
December 1918

Paul Brault lowered his gauze mask before hopping off at the Saint-
Roch station, in the working-class town just below Quebec City.
The air was safer... healthier, outside the train. Though most of the
passengers wore the required mask, there was still a lot of wheezing
and coughing.

The late afternoon winter sky had already started to darken. He
glanced around a few times, puzzled not to see Rose waiting for him.
Not once in the four years since he had started taking the train to
the logging camps had she missed his arrival. Saying goodbye was
another story—It's bad luck, she'd say. Paul always made sure to
throw his knapsack over his shoulder and head for the train station
while she was busy in another room. It was a little weird at first and
it sure ruffled his parents, but it's what Rose wanted and that was
plenty good enough for him.

Except for a few stragglers standing around or sitting on benches,
the station was empty. All had cloth masks covering their mouths and
noses, including the ticket agents behind the counters. He dragged
his feet towards the exit, an empty feeling in the pit of his stomach.
In the few short months he'd been away in the bush, the Spanish
flu scare had reached his hometown. The Great War had at long last
come to an end in November. All those recruiting war posters that
had instilled fear and anguish in the hearts of Canadians for the last

four years had disappeared. Plastered over them were newer ones warning against the deadly epidemic:

COUGHING AND SNEEZING SPREAD DISEASE!
EAT MORE ONIONS!
STOCK UP ON GARLIC AND CAMPHOR!
WEAR A MASK AND SAVE YOUR LIFE!

He remembered the newspaper story he had read on the train about a San Francisco health officer shooting a man in the downtown area for refusing to wear an influenza mask. He let out a long breath and quickened his step. Fear of death from the Spanish Flu, like the fear of dying during the war, brought out the worst in people.

Before stepping out of the station, he paused to look back over his shoulder, a little uncomfortable about leaving without the comfort of Rose's hand tucked into his. He squared his shoulders and set out on the long trek down to his parents' home in the lower part of Saint-Roch. The walk had never seemed long with Rose trotting by his side. She chatted nonstop about the things she'd forgotten to write to him in her letters. Private conversations between them were rare with his parents always at home. She took advantage of their short time alone to reveal all the things that had bothered her since they had last spoken. As soon as they reached his parents' home, she resumed her usual taciturn self.

She always wore her best outfit to greet him at the train. For the most part, it was something borrowed from her Aunt Lea, a seamstress who worked from her Saint-Roch flat. Most of her creations were meant for her wealthy English customers from uptown, although she'd sometimes get an order from a local woman. When one of her rich customers decided the finished dress wasn't exactly to her liking, Lea turned around and sold it to someone else. The English clientele always paid up front, not like the locals who could only pay her a few coins each week. Lea never came up short and was happy to let her favourite niece borrow a dress any time she fancied one.

His face softened recalling how elegant Rose looked the last time she came to the station. The loose one-piece frock of beige charmeuse took his breath away. A short vest front of light brown crepe stopped a little above her ankles. The matching veiled hat enhanced Rose's dark hair and eyes, and when she beamed up at him and took his arm, he felt he was walking with royalty.

Rose's last letter mentioned their eight-month-old daughter was coughing a lot. That his wife was staying home today because Bébé Janette didn't feel well made sense to him, although his mother Anne was always willing to lend a hand with the child. As far as he knew, it was normal for babies to catch colds, and Rose had finished her nursing training last month. The baby was in good hands. Anybody who coughed and had a fever these days was convinced they were dying of Spanish flu. Paul picked up speed. If the child was still sick, he'd get a doctor to come to the house. He didn't want his daughter going to the hospital with all those flu victims corded like logs into all available spaces.

His eyes widened at the sight of his neighbourhood almost deserted on a Christmas Eve. Most people heeded the ban on public gatherings and stayed home until the flu was under control. All churches, schools, theatres, and taverns remained closed. Big department stores and banks were allowed to stay open if the employees wore gauze masks. He peered up the street expecting to see Rose running up to meet him. She might've been too busy with the Christmas preparations to remember he was coming home.

Bébé Janette was born during the hectic spring drive, when loggers work nonstop on the river drive, floating the logs downriver to the mills. He hadn't been able to take time off to be with Rose and didn't set eyes on their daughter until she was five weeks old. He tried to explain how the melting snow had submerged the camp's only road, making it impossible to travel.

"Well, you're here now"—she glared at him—"and I suppose that's all a woman can expect." She grasped the baby from his arms, placed her back in the crib, and marched down the hall to the kitchen to help Anne with the meal.

Her cold response made his mind race. Had he done something to offend her? Wasn't he trying his best to provide for his family? His mother had warned him about the shifting moods of pregnant women and the warrior blood of new mothers.

"Once you plant your seed in a woman, she leaves her old self behind. Forget the silly girl who smiled at your every word and embrace the strong woman who will nurture your child." Anne rarely gave her opinion about things, but when she did, Paul listened.

Thinking back, he might have pulled it off without too much trouble along the arduous trek through the woods. A good six-hour walk along a muddy logging road to the nearest village. Hard terrain with hungry black bears roaming around that time of year. He was sure she hadn't wanted him to risk making a widow out of her, but why expect him to get home at all costs? His mother and Aunt Lea never left her side during the long agonizing hours of childbirth, and the doctor arrived just as she gave the final push. Her cries of pain would've paralyzed him, making him no help to her at all.

Her sharp comment had wedged a slight fracture in their young marriage, embedding the seed of guilt of a long-distance husband and father. When he left again in the fall, he swore on his grandmother's grave that he'd be with her and Bébé Janette for their first Christmas as a family. He'd only go back to the bush camp after the New Year, in time to haul the logs to the banks of the river for the spring thaw.

Rose had received her diploma four weeks ago and had already started nursing at Hôtel-Dieu Hospital. The stress of starting a new job and taking care of the baby might be the reason she had missed his train arrival. The kerosene lamps at the camp hung from the pine rafters in the kitchen area. The men sat around the long rough table drinking tea and playing cards at night. They liked to bug him about his letter writing, insisting he forget about his wife for five minutes and play cards with them. He didn't appreciate them hovering over his shoulder and commenting on everything he wrote to Rose, so he'd go and perch on the edge of his cot. The lighting wasn't too good but at least there was a bit of privacy. With all the shouting coming from the card players, he might have jotted down the wrong arrival time.

Only two trains arrived from Montreal each day, an early one at nine in the morning and the next one at four o'clock in the afternoon. Rose knew that if he missed the morning train, he'd be sure to be on the later one. No matter the weather, she was there to greet him with that broad smile of hers. It was a chance for her to take a break from the constant grumbling of her father-in-law Roger. Bébé Janette, a happy, curious child, had started crawling earlier than most babies her age. Roger would often look down from his rocking chair to see her little fingers plucking at his shoelaces and shoving them in her mouth. He'd roar for Anne. "Get this brat away from me. All that Indian blood in her, sneaking up and robbing you while you're not looking."

That his first grandchild's mother was a Huron-Métis from Loretteville was beyond his comprehension. His son, handsome and hard-working, had first pick of any good *Canadienne* from Saint-Roch. Why settle for an Indian girl from the northern outskirts of Quebec City? Her ancestors had long ago embraced the same Catholic faith as his, but he remained convinced they still lived in cedar longhouses.

They dig up the bones of their dead, he intoned to anybody who listened, and carry them to whichever hunting ground they move to.

Anne was forced to drop the pile of laundry she worked on and rush to rescue the child. Roger never mentioned his objections to the child's ancestry in front of Rose. He was happy for the extra pair of hands to help with the laundry that Anne took in from the English families. Rose's help allowed more meat to appear on their dinner plates. She never once talked back to him but flinched each time he'd say the baby crawled around naked "like a savage," or that her wailing in the dead of night was just like "Indian war cries."

Roger hadn't been any easier on his twin boys when they were toddlers. He had an aversion to grubby little fingers clutching onto his pant legs. Their disgusting habit of rubbing their snotty noses on the sleeve of his Sunday shirt turned Roger off. Sunday mornings got a bit easier when the boys got old enough to sit at Mass without tugging on Anne's rosary and scattering the beads on the church's ceramic floor.

The tips of Paul's fingers tingled with the cold. He stopped on the sidewalk to root through his knapsack for the wool gloves his mother had given him when he last left for the woods. He had left the ones he used for work on his cot, bringing only the other unused pair he saved for outings. She had never given up her role as a mother of twins, always knitting or sewing two of everything, even for Bébé Janette.

He crossed Saint-Joseph Street. Abuzz on a normal day with all the hustle and bustle of the hotels, restaurants, shops and cabarets, it was now deserted. The few passersby were window shoppers chatting through their protective masks of cloth. He paused at the corner to stare up at Salle Frontenac alongside Place Jacques-Cartier, the place where he had first met Rose.

The building housed a covered market below with a cultural centre on the upper floor. Local youths gathered upstairs to play card games and checkers. The Brault twins were the undisputed champions of the five hundred game until Thomas left for the war. Paul having lost his partner, his good buddy Gilles suggested he team up with Rose, who had joined the card group that week. When Paul glanced up from his hand to wait for his new partner's bid, his heart skipped a beat. He forgot all about the intricate strategies he had planned for the cards he held. Rose placed her card trick on the table and stared up at him. He fumbled and laid down his cards before his opponent had a chance to bid. He had just lost the game *and* his reputation as a card shark, but he had won her heart.

They met up every evening after she came back from her nursing training until he left for his first logging camp in the late fall. Rose's Aunt Lea, who lived in the Irish district of Saint-Roch, made a habit of holding on to Paul's letters. Rose had to finish washing the supper dishes and tuck in her two young cousins in the bed she shared with them before Aunt Lea handed over her mail. Three years later, Paul had managed to save enough money to buy a proper ring and a wedding dress for Rose. On the day they married and moved in with Paul's parents, the lilacs were in full bloom in the wealthy gardens of upper Quebec City.

Salle Frontenac triggered conflicting emotions for him. A slow ache tugged at his heart for the many happy hours spent here playing cards with Thomas before the war, and... after he was gone... that floating, light-hearted sensation of meeting up with Rose during their courting years. Overshadowing these tender feelings was the painful memory of last spring's Easter riots that had taken place here. The fighting had added unneeded fuel to the already rocky relationship between the English and the French.

Canadian troops had opened fire on anti-conscription protesters with Lewis guns—the very same machine guns used to kill Germans on the battlefields. Soldiers gunned down four innocent bystanders that Easter Sunday. One of them, a fourteen-year-old crossing Place Jacques-Cartier on his way home from church. Paul's good friend, Gilles, was one of the seventy wounded in the shootings. He died two days later from the infection caused by the explosive bullets used by the soldiers. Paul had stood transfixed by all the chunks of human flesh clinging to the wire fence alongside Place Jacques-Cartier the next morning. His stomach clenched, wondering if they belonged to his childhood friend. He glared at the soldiers armed with rifles patrolling the streets. War had come to Canada after all. Quebec, under martial law, was a land occupied by soldiers from its own country—and remained so until the Great War ended in November of that year.

He continued down the narrow streets towards the tanneries and shoe factories in the industrial district. His parents lived not far from there, within walking distance of the old shipyards where most of the Irish immigrant families had settled years earlier. The burnt ash smell of coal smoke and toxic fumes from the factories accosted him—more noxious to him now after leaving the sweet smell of the pristine northern woods.

After four years working in the bush, Paul was confident he wasn't always going to be a lumberjack. The job was demanding but didn't rob him of his soul—not like his earlier years spent working in the shoe factory. He wanted to learn all there was to know about operating a lumber camp. One day he'd be the one in charge of the outfit and he'd treat the loggers much better than they were now. Going back to a robotic job breathing the noxious fumes of the factories was out of the question for him. He loved being outside in the fresh woodland air infused with the sweet smell of cut wood.

The woodsmen, living so close together in the shanty from late autumn to the spring thaw, soon became family. The loggers arrived with the first signs of snow in the fall and started building their shelter and outdoor toilets. Next they cleared the rugged roads needed to haul in the equipment and supplies and to haul the logs to the rivers and streams in the spring. They'd only start felling trees after all these installations were built.

Their living area didn't allow the men much room to move around, but their camaraderie sustained a doggedness to stick it out no matter what. The foreman had his makeshift spruce desk tucked in a corner. Bucksaws hung from protruding nails in the top section of the wall near the stove. The men stood their axes against the wall below the saws at the end of the day. The cooking area had a long, roughly built wooden table for meals, and large barrels of melted snow for wash water. Cold wind blowing through the crevasses in the walls and ceiling forced everybody to sleep with their clothes on. Lice and ticks shared their straw bunk beds and mice scurried through the bags of provisions. The cook didn't have a large variety of food to serve them. Beans, porridge and bread for breakfast; beans, salt pork with turnips for lunch; and fish with potatoes for supper. On the rare occasions when the cook received a letter from home, there'd be apple pie or cake to go with their tea.

Paul sometimes lay awake nights imagining how the loggers' lives might be improved. On stormy days, when blowing snow made it impossible to cut trees, he'd sometimes help with the paperwork. This allowed his foreman to join the other guys howling with laughter as the cards scraped across the rough table. Paul took care of all the forms and calculations needed to run the outfit. He discovered the tricks of balancing books, the cost of provisions and equipment, and the names of the logging companies who hired teams of men to cut trees in specified areas of the Canadian forests. His most valuable lesson from all this was that food and housing for the loggers didn't have to be cut for the contractors to make a profit.

The thought of seeing how much Bébé Janette had grown since he had left in mid-October made him quicken his steps. Rose had written that the baby's first front teeth were now showing. Paul's heart almost exploded when she added that 'Papa' was the first word Janette had uttered—loud and clear. She was the most beautiful baby Paul had ever set eyes upon. Big brown eyes, and a thick head of black curls like her mother's.

He'd have to remember to wash his hands before picking the baby up. Rose had been strict about that since the second wave of the Spanish flu scare had started up again earlier in the fall. Hearses were so hard to get that streetcars were used to transport the closed coffins as near as possible to the cemetery. Calgary had run out of coffins and his outfit had obtained another urgent order for pine planks. When Paul first started at the camps, loggers were felling trees for the British shipyards. Now each tree that fell would become someone's casket.

More people were dying from this flu than the tens of thousands of soldiers killed by mustard gas or bullets in the Great War. Paul's breath caught in his chest at the possibility that anyone in his family might fall victim to this killer disease. So far there had been the sad story of his two young cousins placed in the same pine box because of lack of money, and their mother's own coffin nailed shut the next day.

He couldn't wait to tell Rose his good news. Sharing the flat with his parents hadn't been easy for her and the baby. He had almost enough money saved up now to afford the furniture they needed to get their own flat. She'd have time to shop around the stores when he returned to the bush camp in two weeks and they'd buy what they needed when he came back in the spring. He'd have plenty of construction work during the summer months to keep a salary coming in until the logging camps started up again next fall.

Light snow had fallen earlier. Paul's work boots left a trail of wide prints behind him on the sidewalk along the row of ill-lit three-storey tenements. Several other large footprints crisscrossed the sheet of snow on the front porch of his parents' first-storey flat. He climbed the steps two at a time and came to an abrupt stop in front of the front door.

Someone had left it ajar. That never happened in this house during the cold weather. The flat was so drafty that his mother had to tuck old blankets at the base of each door and window to block the cold air from entering. Anybody who didn't make sure to push the blanket back into place after entering got an earful from her.

Something was definitely wrong.

His hand trembled as he nudged the door open. The strong smell of disinfectant and camphor made his stomach contract. He reached back to close the door and kicked the old blanket back with his heel.

"Leave it open a crack, son. We have to clear the air in here." Anne stood in the doorway of the kitchen at the end of the darkened hallway. A thick wool sweater buttoned up to her neck and a rosary dangling from her fingers. She didn't come to greet him as she usually did but huddled her small frame against the wall, clutching her rosary to her chest.

"A real tragedy, my son!" She lowered her head and made the sign of the cross. "It happened... so fast. The priest got here just in time to—"

"The priest? What are you trying to say, Maman?" His heart pounded hard and his breath came out in gasps. A rosary hung from the doorknob at the entrance to the bedroom he shared with Rose and the baby.

"No... not Bébé Janette." He bolted down the hall, shoved the door open and looked around in a panic. The smell of disinfectant was stronger here than in the hallway. The baby's crib was missing. He screamed out his daughter's name. "Where is she, Maman? Is she at the hospital?"

"Please... for the love of God... don't touch anything, Paul." Anne stood behind him in the doorway, tears running down her cheeks. Her words came out in spurts, laden with pain. "She came home from work yesterday morning. The poor girl... so very tired... she... told me to stay away... and... to take the baby to the emergency nursery."

"The nursery? That's only for—" He stared at the open window. A wave of cold sweat surged from his shoulders down to his lower back. "No... not that, sweet Jesus... not our Rose" The bed was down to the bare mattress. No sheets, blankets or pillows. He spun back to face her. "Where did they take her, Maman?"

Anne pressed her rosary to her chest. "A real tragedy... she didn't... last 24 hours, son. The priest came just in time for the Last Rites. They... took her right away... that poor girl... not even a church funeral. Your father's gone with them to... bring her to the ceme—"

He didn't wait for his mother to finish and hurtled out the front door towards the church grounds. By the time he reached the corner of the cemetery reserved for flu victims, the priest and the caretaker were leaving. Roger stood, shoulders slumped, staring down at the wooden cross planted in the soft ground where they had just buried Rose's pine box. For the first time since Paul was a toddler, Roger wrapped his arms around him, letting his son's tears soak into the fur collar of his Sunday tweed coat.

He went back to his refuge in the sanctity of the pine forests of northern Quebec. Rose often visited his dreams, standing proud among the tall evergreens of her youth, always with her gentle smile and dark, sad eyes. He'd reach out to touch her and he'd jolt awake to find himself in the darkened cabin among his snoring fellow lumberjacks. It came to him one day that if he wanted her near, he'd have to remain living among the trees that she had loved so much.

CHAPTER 21

Montreal
October 1970

Denis looked up from the front section of the *Gazette* on his lap. The rest of the newspaper sections lay scattered on both sides of him on the sofa. Janette stretched her neck from her armchair by the front window to stare down at the street.

"The elections are on today." He lowered his gaze to read more. "The papers are claiming Jean Drapeau will win by a landslide."

"You go on ahead without me." She glanced at the empty coffee mug and full ashtray on the end table beside him, hoping to have time to clean up before they arrived. "I won't bother. The only candidate worth voting for has been arrested along with all the others suspected of being sympathizers."

His head shot up. "Well, he won't get many votes behind bars. He should watch what he says in public."

"You mean express the will of the people? Heaven forbid." She looked away, raising her eyebrows. "Isn't that what a good politician is supposed to do?"

"Not when we're under martial law." He went back to his newspaper.

She gazed out the window again. This wasn't a good time to get him talking about the FLQ, nor about the French daring to speak up for their rights. His Irish Catholic ancestors had been treated like dirt by the British back in their own homeland. Yet he wasn't able to link that to what was happening at home in Quebec. It was almost as if he denied her true identity, ignoring the humiliation her parents, her grandparents, and those that came before them had also suffered at the hands of the British. "Aren't you going to be late for work?"

"I'm managing the breakfast shift starting tomorrow morning." He swung the newspaper down beside him and stretched out his arms. "The partnership at this restaurant gives me more freedom than when we had our own bakery. You and I only had Monday together. And Nadine and Philip took up all your free time."

"Yes." Janette smiled. "Those were happy days."

He hesitated, then his face lit up. "Maybe after—that's if you feel like it—we can start that new puzzle."

She tightened her grip on the arm of the chair. She had scheduled this visit when she knew he'd be out. She needed this time alone to get to know Nadine again. Denis was sure to get huffy about her coming over—we were doing OK without her, he'd say. It'd be better if she told him after the visit was over. "Why not visit your mother? It's been a while since you've seen her and the nurse at the residence says she isn't doing so well."

"Sure, why not? We'll go together. The visit goes by faster with you there. She never has anything to say to me."

"Don't be silly. She'll be glad to have you all to herself." She stood up and leaned sideways to look down the street.

What if he's still home when they get here? He'll be peeved that I hid something from him.

"What's so damn interesting out there? You've been staring out that window for the last half hour." He peered at her through his cigarette smoke. "And what's with the swanky dress?" He raked his fingers through his hair. "You're expecting someone, aren't you? Is that why you want me to go out?"

She turned to face him. "Don't get yourself into a snit. I should've told you before this." She walked to the sofa, shoved the newspaper aside and sat down beside him. "Papa's on his way here. He's—"

"Your father? Since when do you dress up when he comes over? That's not it. You're hiding something from me again."

She sat up straight. "Again? What do you mean? When have I ever kept anything secret from you?"

He blew out his cigarette smoke towards the ceiling and shook his head. "Sorry about that, Janette. Forget I ever said that." He leaned his elbows on his knees. "Sometimes… secrets are better left buried." He took another drag. "Take my brother John. If he hadn't found out about Nadine not being his, he and Claire might be alive today. He didn't have to know."

"John and Claire? What do they have to do—" Her thoughts faltered a moment, wondering what he was getting at. She got up and marched back to her chair. Thirty years of marriage and he'd waited till now to admit he knew about Joe. Not once had he questioned being Philip's father and had been a good parent to him every day of the boy's life. Why wasn't he man enough to come out with it? All that time letting it fester inside of him. Confronting the truth might've forced him to take a different path in life. His own brother had stabbed his wife to death when he found out her secret. Did Denis fear the same violence within himself? "Is there something bothering you Denis—something we should be talking about?"

"No… forget what I said. I just thought you were… waiting for someone… and you didn't want me to know. That's all it was. And that blue dress you've got on… that'd make any man want a closer look. You're as beautiful as—no, more beautiful—than the day we met. I'd be a goner without you, Janette. I let my imagination take over, that's all. Sorry about that. If you want me to go out, I'll go right now."

She went to say something, but chewed her bottom lip instead. He was protesting too much. It was time for her to clear the air. Right here and now. Remind him of that day back in 1946. More and more soldiers were coming home, some crippled like Denis, others with vacant eyes, lifelong victims of the horrors of war.

Joe had pushed the door open to their bakery on a sunny April afternoon. Denis sat at the corner table working on the accounts with baby Philip beside him in the playpen. Joe, tall and strong as a mountain, stood there staring at her with a look of want in his dark eyes. Her knees gave out and she gripped the side of the countertop. A wave of warmth radiated throughout her body. He had survived the war.

Philip started wailing. Loud enough to get Joe's attention. Did the baby hear the frantic drumming of her heart? Did Denis? Joe stared, head tilted, at the baby's thick black hair and smooth olive skin, so like his own. Denis glanced up at him, his prosthetic leg stiff and awkward under the table. The two men studied each other in silence. Denis' face went ashen, his eyes darting up and down the man's body, comparing—judging himself. Joe squared his shoulders, muscles tight and straining through his summer shirt, and without even a backward look at her, was out the door.

Denis hadn't said a word, looking back down at his accounts book as if no one had entered the shop. She had marched back to the kitchen, glad to have another batch of dough that needed pounding out.

"Don't bother yourself about this, Janette." He pushed himself up and grabbed his jacket from the arm of the sofa. "I'll walk over to the tavern and have a pint with the guys so you can have some space."

"It was you, Denis." She leaned her head back against the armchair. "It's you I chose."

He stooped to gather the newspaper together and wavered, grabbing on to the arm of the sofa to catch his balance. "We've had some good years you and me."

She closed her eyes and pressed her lips together. Maybe he was right. Some things are better left unsaid. "Papa found her."

"Who?" He leaned down to place the paper in the magazine rack, knowing she always worked on the *Gazette*'s crossword puzzle while he watched the news.

Her voice rose, excited. "Nadine. Can you believe this? He's bringing her over."

"Nadine?" His jaw dropped.

"That's why I wanted some alone time. I didn't want you getting all mad and making me lose her all over again. It hurts bad to know we'll never see our Philip again. But now I have a chance to be a mother again, Denis. I can feel alive again."

"After all the pain she's caused you. Not a word from her in twenty years and out of the blue, she pops up. Did she find out about the will? Is that it?" He limped to the window and gazed at the cars driving by. "Well, she's not welcome here. I won't let her hurt you all over again."

"Not that damn will again. Your father left her the money, so you and your brother better accept it. And who said she even knows anything about it? She just wants to see me. Is that so hard to believe?"

"I'm sure your father told her. If she had wanted to see you that bad, she's had twenty years to do so." He turned away from the window and put his jacket on. "You better call him right now and tell him to leave her exactly where he found her."

A knock at the door. Their eyes met.

Janette went to get up but he waved her down. "I'll get this."

"You better not be mean to that girl, Denis Pritchart." She stood up straight and headed after him. "I mean it. Don't force me to choose again."

He stopped in his tracks and took a long breath before opening the door.

Paul stood smiling in the doorway, his broad shoulders almost hiding the slim woman behind him. Janette clenched her fists to stop her hands from shaking. Her father hadn't brought back the sixteen-year-old who had disappeared so many years ago, but a full-grown woman with stories and a life of her own. Had the closeness they had then survived, or had Nadine strayed too far and too long for them to reconnect?

Paul nodded at Denis, reached back to take Nadine's arm, and stepped in. "Look who I discovered at the meeting last Friday." He came to a stop in front of Janette and hugged her. "This isn't a time for tears. Our little Nadine is back." He moved sideways to stand beside Denis, leaving the two women to face each other.

Nadine held Janette's gaze, her arms limp by her side. Janette wiped her tears on the sleeve of her sweater, and without a word, threw her arms around Nadine. The two clung to each other, their eyes closed, oblivious to the two men watching beside them. Paul held back his own tears, while Denis stood rigid, his face impassive. Paul went out the door, glancing over his shoulder at Denis. "Don't lock up. I have to move the pickup. I'm parked a block down on the wrong side of the street."

Denis continued to stare at the two women.

Nadine stepped back after a few moments, swallowed hard, and looked at Denis. "Uncle Denis. It's been a long time."

He hesitated a moment, glancing at his wife before facing Nadine. "It sure has. We had given up on you."

Janette grabbed Nadine's arm and guided her towards the sofa. "Don't you listen to him. I always knew we'd see you again. Now make yourself comfortable. I'll go make tea and we can catch up." She paused to stare at Denis before stepping out of the room.

He lifted his chin up. "Don't worry, I'm going. I'm waiting for Paul to come back."

Janette frowned and stepped out of view into the kitchen area.

Nadine dug into her handbag for Kleenex to dry her eyes. More tears were sure to flow with all they had to say to each other. Her intention had been to tell Aunt Jan everything that had happened during their long separation. But seeing her after all these years, certain things might be better off left out for now. Twenty years had taken their toll on Aunt Jan. The slow, halting way she had made her way to the kitchen reminded Nadine of what Papi had said about her health problems.

She owed all to this generous, kind-hearted woman, who had never thought twice about welcoming her—a sad child mourning her parents' violent deaths—into her home. Aunt Jan had been a loving parent to her longer than her real mother had. She had a right to know why she had stayed away so long. But sharing her whole story with her might leave her with unwarranted feelings of guilt. She didn't want Aunt Jan to feel responsible for what had happened. The right time to tell her would come, but not today. There were so many other things they had to catch up on. First, the happy news. Her child—her own flesh and blood, had come back to her.

Denis edged closer to the sofa where Nadine sat. "I assume Paul told you about my father's will. Why else would you show up out of the blue like this?" He glanced towards the kitchen and continued, his tone lower, harsher. "Had I known, I would've made sure this visit never happened. In her condition, Janette can't handle another heartbreak. I won't allow you to hurt her all over again." He reached into the inside pocket of his jacket, pulled out a business card, and flipped it in her direction. It landed inside her opened handbag. "Call my lawyer. He'll take care of everything. There's no need for you to ever come here again."

She stared up at him, not sure how to answer him. Her intention had been to let him know she didn't want to claim the inheritance. She hadn't anticipated such a hostile confrontation within minutes of her arrival. It was obvious he was doing this without Aunt Jan's knowledge. That he'd think the money was the sole reason for her visit wasn't surprising, but she wasn't prepared for the look of hatred in his eyes.

"Look, Uncle Denis, I'm sorry for never giving any news. I had a lot of problems to deal with. I came here to try to mend any suffering I caused—not to aggravate Aunt Jan's heart condition. I didn't know Grandpa Pritchart died till Papi told me last Friday. I don't want any part of that inheritance. It's for you and Uncle Peter. I was going to tell you as soon as Aunt Jan and I got settled."

"You expect me to believe that? I don't know how you got my father to leave you anything, but we'll see how this stands up in court." His face and neck burned, his voice shook.

Nadine's heart sank. He was too angry to listen to reason. Convincing him how little she cared about the inheritance was next to impossible. No amount of money could make up for past wrongs. It had taken her a long time to realize she wasn't responsible for what happened. Aunt Jan and Grandma Stella would only blame themselves if she told them everything. She had hurt them enough. Her secret had to remain with her. She had to fix this now, or he'd make it impossible for her to see Aunt Jan again. She fished in her bag, pulled out a pen and small notebook, and scribbled down her address. "Here." She handed him the note. "Get your lawyer to mail me an agreement stating I'm refusing any inheritance. I'll sign it and mail it back as soon as I get it."

He raised an eyebrow at her, scanned the paper and tucked it into his back pocket. Paul strode in from outside and came to a stop when he saw the hard look on Denis' face. His eyes darted towards Nadine who, face ashen and head lowered, pretended a desperate search of her purse. He was about to ask what was going on when Janette poked her head in the kitchen archway. "Come in here, Nadine. It'll save me from carrying the tea things all the way there."

Denis turned to his wife. "Don't you go overdoing things again."

Janette rolled her eyes at him and smiled at Paul. "Denis was just about to walk to the tavern before you arrived. Looks like you could use a beer too."

Paul grinned at Denis. "This must be our cue to leave."

Denis pushed his shoulders back and, with a slight limp, marched out the front door.

Denis sat down at a round table in the ill-lit tavern and signalled to the barman wiping down the large jars of pickled eggs beside the cash register. "Bring us two large Molsons, please."

Paul pulled out the worn pine chair across from him and made eye contact with the barman before sitting. "And make that a *tablette* for me, please."

The barman reached on the shelf for the beer glasses. "Right away, Boss."

"*Tablette*?" Denis made a face. "May as well order a bottle of piss. If it's not ice cold, I won't touch it."

"All you square-heads like your beer cold. Thing is, by the time you get down to the dregs of your 22-ounce bottle, it'll be as warm as my *tablette*. So we'll drink piss together."

Denis glanced around the room. Most of the tables were full with the usual crowd of workers stopping in after work for a few quiet beers before going home to the wife and kids. The rowdy crowd—

students and the unemployed with their loud politics and social grievances—usually dropped in later in the evening to rant.

"Better watch who you call a square-head in this place, Paul. This is an English watering hole. We don't see many Frenchies come in here. When they do, they don't rock the boat. There's been quite a few tables and chairs thrown around lately. The guys are pretty antsy about that FLQ thing and the army hanging out around town doesn't help."

Paul laughed. "I've got nothing against swinging a few chairs myself. You're not scared of a bit of action, are you now?"

Denis tapped his artificial leg. "Not fast enough to avoid the punches with this thing. But I was in plenty of brawls before the war. My brother Peter and I always had to jump in to get John out of scraps. That boy was smart but he never kept his mouth shut. Especially if it had anything to do with Frenchies. No offense, Paul. The Frenchies and the English were always duking it out where I grew up." He shoved the salt shaker and ashtray aside to make room for the two quart beer bottles and glasses the barman was about to place on the table. "And the bugger went and married one. Figure that one out."

"Seems to me you did too. Did you expect Janette to lose her identity when she married you?" Paul raised his glass. "But it proves there's a bit of sense lurking in that thick square-head of yours. Two out of three brothers marrying *Canadiennes*. That must've made your old man foam at the mouth."

Denis made a face and salted his beer. "The old man couldn't stand Claire—loud and vulgar as a two-bit hooker, he'd say. It got his goat that she spoke only French to John and Nadine when they came for Sunday dinner. That's how come Nadine came to us after the incident. Peter and his wife wanted to take her but my old man figured the kid was better off with someone who spoke her language." He gulped down his beer and wiped his mouth on his sleeve. "He worked the trains across Canada all his life and he'd brag he never once had to speak a word of French. He had more respect for Janette. She hardly spoke to him, but when she did, her English was pretty good. After all this time with me, you can't tell she has an accent anymore."

Paul leaned back in his chair. "She must've learned the language helping my mother do laundry for those rich English ladies back home. She'd climb up the hill to Quebec City three times a week with a rucksack of their clean laundry and come back with more of their shitty clothes. She needed to know a bit of English to get served in the department stores uptown—the sales clerks refused to speak French, even if they knew how. I learned it working for English bosses. Our money was good, but God forbid they serve us in French. And you square-heads wonder what the FLQ is all about. Language, man. It's what holds us together. If we lose it, we'll disappear, just like you Irish in the huge English sea."

"Let's change the subject, Paul. People are looking our way."

Paul refilled his glass and glanced around with a smile. "Nothing I can't handle. But Janette will get upset at me if I bring you home on a stretcher. Warmed my heart to see her so happy today. Did her a world of good to have our Nadine back."

Denis lit a cigarette and blew the smoke out from the corner of his mouth. He stared down at the table and reached out to bring the ashtray closer.

Paul sipped his beer and studied his son-in-law. He had proved to be a good husband for Janette after all. When she'd announced her intention to marry him weeks before Denis left for the war, Paul had tried to talk her out of it. A dinner invitation at the Pritchart home a week before the wedding told Paul all he needed to know. Denis' father appeared to be a strict disciplinarian who ruled over his wife and sons. Janette had grown up under his mother's care to be independent and resourceful. When she left Saint-Roch for Montreal to find work at eighteen, she wasn't about to have anybody lord over her. Paul had worried about the possible clashes if Denis followed his father's tyrannical ways. But Janette had taken it all in stride, going about her business without giving Denis' family much thought.

Paul had suggested they postpone the wedding until Denis came back from the war. Janette refused to budge. Timothy Pritchart insisted on an Irish Catholic ceremony at his local church. Janette put her foot down and they got married back in her Saint-Roch parish with Paul's family. The Pritcharts didn't attend. When Denis came back from the war, his left leg amputated below the knee, Nadine was already ten years old.

"This has to be a first, Denis. Together like this. We never get a chance to talk man-to-man. You always find a reason to leave the house when I visit."

Denis cleared his throat and rubbed the back of his neck. "No offence, Paul. You and her always speak French together, and I can't understand half of what you're saying. Janette doesn't mind. She hardly sees you, so she likes to have you all to herself."

Paul looked away, pensive. "You're right about me not seeing her often enough. She grew up too fast for me to catch up with her." He reached for his beer. "When you get to my age—especially after downing a few beers—you think about things you could've done or said better. Before the effect of this beer wears off"—he grinned—"I wanted to tell you that you haven't been too bad of a husband to my daughter. Not half as bad as I thought you'd be. You've always treated her with respect and she's never been without."

"Appreciate that coming from you, Paul. I couldn't have done it without her after the war. She kept the bakery going by herself while I was in the trenches—and she had Nadine to take care of too. When I stepped off that boat I was too weak and depressed to do anything except handle the accounts. She handled everything else until I got my shit together."

"If I remember right… that's when you switched her back to the kitchen—away from the customers."

"Yeah, well… it gave her more time to be upstairs with Nadine and Philip."

Paul threw his head back and laughed. "And out of the public eye. My daughter's a beautiful woman. I remember how you'd rush out of your chair each time a male customer came in."

Denis gestured towards Paul's unfinished beer bottle. "I'll finish that up if you're not drinking it." He filled his glass and waited to drink some more before commenting. "You know, Paul. Between you and me. I've never said this to Janette… but… I'm pretty sure she wouldn't be with me if it wasn't for my leg."

Paul hesitated. "That's something to discuss between you and your wife—when you're sober, that is. Beer makes demons appear a hell of a lot bigger."

Denis stared down at his hands. "Better not. We probably couldn't… go on… if it was out in the open."

"It's not something I can decide for you. Not knowing works for a while, but the truth has a way of sneaking up on you." Paul glanced at his watch. He hadn't meant to stay this long. Denis was starting to slur his words. He'd drive Nadine home and head on back to Saint-Roch. "You didn't look too happy about seeing Nadine. Is something up between you two?"

Denis butted his cigarette and straightened in his chair. "What makes you say that?"

"The expression on your face when I came back from parking the truck. Like you were ready to blow a gasket."

Denis raised a shoulder and looked away. "I don't want her hurting Janette again."

"What makes you think she will?"

"She disappeared on her twenty years ago, three months after Philip died. What do you think that did to Janette, eh?"

"She was a sixteen-year-old kid with big problems."

"The only reason she came back is because you went and told her about the will."

"She doesn't want the damn money."

"We'll see."

"What do you mean by that?"

"She's supposed to sign a release from my lawyer saying she's refusing the inheritance. I'll believe it when I see it."

"Sounds like extortion to me. She hands over the money and she gets to see Janette. Then you'll decide she's taking too much of Janette's time away from you. Same as when she was kid. She spent more time with your parents than she did at your place."

"Mother loved having her around. Janette had no energy left for me after seeing to Nadine and Philip." He lit another cigarette. "Janette and I have been doing OK these past few years. She had started slowly getting over the loss of Philip and hadn't mentioned Nadine in a long time. What do you know? Out of the blue, Nadine shows up. Who's going to pick up the pieces when Nadine takes off again?"

"You better get something in that thick head of yours, Denis Pritchart." Paul pushed his chair back and stood up. "If I hear a word of you stopping Janette and Nadine from seeing each other, it's going to be your pieces you'll have to pick up. I've waited a long time to see Janette's eyes shine like they did before, and I intend to keep them that way. I couldn't do much for her when she was growing up with me working up north a good part of the year. But now that I'm thinking of retiring for good, you're going to see a hell of a lot more of me around here—a hell of a lot more than you'd like."

"I've got something that belongs to you, Aunt Jan."

"Really? What can that be?" The two women were on their second cup of tea and had been talking nonstop at the kitchen table since Paul and Denis left an hour ago. The reason why Nadine had stayed away for so long didn't come up. Nadine was grateful for Aunt Jan's hesitancy to pry and resolved to wait for the right time to tell her. Aunt Jan sure had the right to know, but it didn't have to be on their first reunion.

Nadine held her breath before reaching into her handbag. Good thing Denis wasn't there to witness this. Another weapon in his arsenal against her. His coldness towards her earlier had made one thing clear—he didn't want Nadine back in Aunt Jan's life. He never had. Thinking back, he hadn't been any warmer with his son Philip. He had never mistreated him. But the only time Nadine had seen him show any tenderness towards him was during the boy's last days at the hospital before he died.

She pulled out a man's black leather wallet from her bag and placed it on the table.

Janette stared at it a moment, puzzled. "My God. You still have that old thing." She looked up, beaming. "That belonged to your mother. I gave it to you... remember? You must've been around twelve at the time. I figured you were old enough to hear the story about your mother hitchhiking to Montreal from back east. That was the only thing I managed to salvage that belonged to her. Her story and her wallet. Grandpa Pritchart threw all her things in the trash before Grandma Stella and I had a chance to sort them."

Nadine shrugged. "The Pritcharts blamed her."

Janette stretched across the table and squeezed her hand. "Not everybody. I adored her. She was so beautiful and fun-loving. She didn't deserve to die like that. Grandma Stella will never admit it, but I always thought she mourned Claire as much as she did her son."

"Do you remember, Aunt Jan, that nightmare I used to get where I'm all covered with blood, and I've got a salty, metallic taste in my mouth and my lips feel sticky? Something heavy is pressing down on my chest and I can't breathe. When I manage to wipe the blood from my eyes with the back of my hand, I see a woman lying on top of me. There's blood spurting from her eyes and mouth and I start screaming. It's weird, but I still get it every once in a while."

"How can I forget? It was a terrible thing for any young child to live through. You didn't speak a single word for two months after you got out of the hospital. You wouldn't let anybody touch you except for the times I slept beside you after one of those nightmares. Denis was overseas then, so it was just you and me. When he came back, you were doing so much better. Philip came along not long after... the poor child was always sick. My insides went dead when we lost him. And when you left a few months later and never came back... I saw no good reason to live after I lost both of you." She reached for Nadine's hand again and squeezed it. "No matter what everybody said, I always believed you'd come back to me. Just like your own daughter did. We'll get together when she feels better. She has a lot of adjusting to do. It's difficult for a child who hasn't known love to accept that she deserves to be cherished." She got up and headed to the counter. "Now put that old wallet away and I'll bring out my *pouding au chômeur.* When Papa called with the news, I made sure to have your favourite dessert ready for you."

"Wait, Aunt Jan. I have to give this back to you now or I'll lose my courage. It's one of the reasons why I stayed away. I was so scared you'd stop loving me because of this."

Janette retraced her steps and sat down. "You don't ever have to worry about that. You're in my heart for good. You don't have to tell me why you never came back. I'm so happy you're sitting here in front of me. It doesn't mean I don't want to know. When you're ready to talk, I'll be here for you."

Nadine unfolded the wallet and paused. The shame she had felt had stopped her from setting things right with Aunt Jan after she left. The thought of writing to her had crossed her mind through the years, but Aunt Jan deserved better than that. She vowed to find the courage one day to tell her in person. The time had come. "I always envied the love you had with Papi. Sometimes I imagined I was his daughter and he loved me as much as he did you."

"Oh, Nadine. You're the granddaughter he always wanted."

Nadine pressed her lips together. "Being his adopted grandchild wasn't the same as being his blood family. If I was his flesh and blood, I could do no wrong. He'd love me no matter what. When Philip was born, I was a little jealous of him. But I got to love him so much. I understood why everybody made such a fuss over him. He was the real thing, not a pretend daughter like me."

"Pretend?" Janette straightened in her chair. "I hope I never made you feel—"

"No, Aunt Jan. You and Papi were always so kind and loving to me. I knew you cared. I wouldn't have come today if I wasn't sure of that." She unsnapped the coin section of the wallet and pulled the contents out, gripping them with her closed fist. "I remember you not wanting to make Papi sad when I was a kid. Nobody was allowed to mention your mother's name when he came around. His love for her became sacred to me and I used to daydream of someone loving me like that too."

Janette nodded, pensive. "They had a special love, all right." She raised her head to gaze out the kitchen window. "That doesn't happen often… and when you have it, you've got to hang on to it, no matter what."

"The day Papi decided to give you your mother's wedding ring, it made me want to dance. I figured the ring would protect me from everybody who didn't love me. The kids at school used to call me *assassin* behind my back because of what happened to *maman*. I got to thinking I was responsible for her death—that if it wasn't for me, she'd still be alive. I knew you kept the ring with your grocery money in that old tobacco can in your closet. So when you went out, I'd slip it on and imagine it protected me from anything that hurt."

Aunt Jan reached for her hand. "I know what you're about to tell me, and—"

"I stole it, Aunt Jan. You were so kind to me and I stole from you." Nadine opened her fist and a ring, along with a tiny plastic bracelet, rolled onto the table. "I was so scared, all I could think of was the baby. I thought I'd feel less alone if I had the ring. I was going to put it back after. But when I realized I wasn't ever coming back, I put it away in my mother's wallet, swearing I'd find a way to get it back to you someday. I was so ashamed of stealing from you and afraid you'd hate me for it."

Janette reached for the ring and examined it. "It took me quite a while to even notice it was gone. When I did, I knew you had taken it. It brought me a bit of comfort to know my mother's ring might ease a bit of your suffering. Even if you pawned it to buy food, it served a good cause. I had no use for it. It came to me through my mother and now it should go to you." She took Nadine's hand and placed the ring in her palm. "Put it on your finger and wear it without shame. I'm more interested in this plastic bracelet here."

Nadine wiped her tears with the back of her hand. "It's time, Aunt Jan. I've rehearsed this so many times. But I've forgotten the words I wanted to say. What if I start and if something's not clear, ask and I'll tell you whatever you want to know."

CHAPTER 22

Paul pulled his truck over in front of Nadine's apartment building. "Janette and I will be driving back from Saint-Roch on Wednesday afternoon. But I won't have time to stop by to see you. I have a few sites to visit north of here. The union has received a few complaints about the logging practices over there. They want a detailed report, so it'll take me a good couple of weeks. Stop worrying about that daughter of yours and get a proper night's sleep."

Nadine turned to her aunt on the seat beside her and hugged her hard before stepping out. "I'm so happy I finally got to see you. Thank you Papi for that. Hope I didn't cause any trouble between you and Uncle Denis."

Janette closed the door of the truck and waved at her through the open window. "Leave Denis to me. He'll come round. You have bigger things on your mind. I'll see you when I come back."

Paul drove out of town and took the highway heading east towards Quebec City. Although glad to have his daughter on the seat beside him, he wondered at her sudden decision to come along.

He remembered Denis keeping a slow pace behind him when they left the tavern earlier. He wasn't clear whether Denis had been too tipsy to keep up or was brooding about how their conversation had ended. Had he been too harsh with him, or had Janette and Denis squabbled?

His son-in-law was too protective of Janette, even when it concerned her own father. She was more than capable of making her own decisions and didn't need anyone coddling her. Whenever Denis left the room, Paul noticed a slight catch in her breath, as if someone had flung a window wide open. Denis had never received him with open arms, but that might well be a family thing. Timothy Pritchart hadn't been any more welcoming on the two occasions they'd met. The first, at the Pritchart home for Denis and Janette's engagement supper; the second, at young Philip's funeral. Denis had never learned to share Janette or to respect her need for independence.

He smiled at her. "You're as beautiful as your mother, both inside and out. No wonder Denis keeps a close watch on you."

She folded her arms across her chest. "I suppose you lassoed my mother in too."

"Lasso my Rose?" His eyes softened. "Never in a million years. She was like a majestic bird soaring over the highest trees. That she even landed to stay with me for a while was the greatest gift a man could ever wish for." He glanced at her. "You're upset with Denis, aren't you? You've never asked to come stay with me before. I understand you want to visit my mother's grave, but springing it on Denis at the last moment isn't like you. You were out the door before he knew it. I'm more than happy to have you, but is something going on?"

She dug into her purse and pulled out a pack of cigarettes. "Nadine told me about him signing those adoption papers. He had no right. She and the baby would've been safe with us until she got back on her feet. Think of all the suffering his signature caused. He separated me from my daughter and Nadine from hers. And he never once said a word to me about it."

Paul frowned. "She was underage and I guess he worried about the neighbours. Think back twenty years. People weren't very tolerant when it came to unwed mothers."

"I never cared much what neighbours thought. Having a baby around to care for while she went out to work... would've been good for us... after we lost our Philip."

"Yes, all that was possible. But a lot of water has run under the bridge since. Are you going to hate Denis for something he did twenty years ago?"

She took a long drag of her cigarette and butted it out in the ashtray. "Wait till he discovers I took his pack. He hates to see me smoke." She leaned her head back on the seat. "Of course, I don't hate him, Papa. But all the suffering that poor girl went through pining away for her child. And there was me worried sick night and day about what happened to her. Had Denis been in the house when she told me this, I would've taken a swing at him. He needs to be out of my arm's reach for a couple of days. I'll be OK once I've had time to think things over. If Stella still lived at home, I'd go stay with her for a few days. You're the only one I've got to turn to now. But you haven't changed, Papa. Always gone off somewhere for work."

He reached sideways and placed his hand over hers. "I'm sorry I haven't always been there for you. It must've been tough while you were growing up. But I'm thinking it's time to retire now. I hope I can catch up on a bit of lost time."

"I've never blamed you, Papa. I missed you a lot, but you had to put bread on the table. I had a pretty good childhood with Grand-maman. She was like a mother to me, although she never let me forget who my real mother was. I was only six years old when Grand-papa died, so I don't remember much of him. We always had to be extra quiet when he was home, so Grand-maman would let me stay outside later with my friends."

Paul laughed. "He was a grump all right. Times were hard before the Great War. No one had money except the English families who lived uptown. The only thing Papa had on his mind was getting enough food on the table to feed his family. We ate meat once a week on Sundays, but only when we could afford it. There was no time for talking about feelings or taking his boys out fishing."

"You had a twin brother, right? Grand-maman kept a picture of him on her bedroom wall with a rosary hanging alongside it."

He swallowed hard and took a moment before answering. "Thomas and I started life together sharing our mother's blood and listening to the drumming of her heart. We were born in different bodies but we shared the same soul. When he died in that damn war, a large part of me went with him. He was only sixteen when they shipped him overseas. He most likely got shot by a German kid the same age as him. They weren't old enough to vote, but they

213

gave them a free license to kill. I vowed on my mother's head that no one would force me to kill someone who had done me no harm."

"This is the most I've heard about your brother. Guess it's a family thing. Don't talk about the dead. All I know was that Grandmaman hated that he didn't have his own space in the cemetery that she could visit."

He turned off the highway and followed the signs leading to the nearest restaurant and gas station. "Talking about Thomas brings him back home to me. You're the closest link I have to him. Just as courageous and independent as he was. My mother never mentioned him, but maybe she should've. Memories are what make us who we are. Without them, we have no sense of self. She took the news of his death pretty hard. We all did. But Thomas has a right to live on. It's by talking about him that he'll stay with us. There's a good snack bar in the next village where we can talk. They have great coffee and it's halfway to Saint-Roch."

CHAPTER 23

Saint-Roch, Quebec
1914-1918

Paul and his brother Thomas were thirteen when they started as shoe buffers in the factory. Twelve hours a day, six days a week, sanding leather soles.

Their father snipped heavy leather hides into shoe parts in the cutting room on the first floor. He'd only let go of his scissors long enough to share his lunch with his boys when the dinner bell rang. The woody residue of tannic acid used to transform animal hides into leather, embedded into his skin and lungs, gave him the ruddy look of an outdoorsman. Yet his constant scratchy hacking in the dark of night shook everyone awake in the Brault household. A promotion to foreman seemed fitting after thirty-five loyal years of inhaling the acidic fumes and leather dust. He knew his way around every assembly line in the factory and it weighed on him that he was never considered.

Bilingual workers in most factories had a better chance of moving up. Except for the odd foreigner, low-level workers were usually French-Canadian. English was the language of money and power. An executive position offered to a foreman with a French family name was uncommon. French-Canadians who operated successful businesses in Saint-Roch moved their family up the hill to Quebec City. That's where all the English upper class lived among the tree-lined wide avenues and well-kept parks.

Like most working-class French-Canadian boys, Roger had started putting in long hours in factories at twelve years old. No time for him to learn a second language, and no need either. English was never heard at the local Sunday Mass gatherings. Nor at the pool halls and bowling alleys where the youth met on Saturday evenings. Nor in the drafty classrooms and grimy playgrounds of poor districts like Saint-Roch. But it dominated in the large department stores, at movie theatres, at fancy restaurants and at bars. At all the big businesses of upper-town Quebec City. Getting served in French at those places was a pipe dream to some, but a thorn in the heart of many.

Fumes from the glue and the shoe polish in the factory permeated the workers' hair and clothes. Dust from the sanding stuck in their throats and made their eyes water. Combined with the smell of unwashed bodies and tobacco smoke, the hot days of summer were unbearable. The foreman locked the doors during the day so employees didn't waste time going out for a breath of fresh air.

The pay was low but it covered the rent, and the children's contribution helped put meat on the table a bit more often. Paul kissed his mother on the cheek, slipping his first week's pay into her apron pocket. She leaned forward at the kitchen table where she was peeling potatoes and sobbed. Thomas, who was never far behind his brother, ruffled her hair and pressed his pay into her closed fist. She pulled out her handkerchief from inside the sleeve of her sweater and wiped her eyes before reaching for her paring knife. They had chicken stew and dumplings for dinner that week after Sunday Mass.

In the summer of 1914, the Brault brothers had been working three years at the factory when the army recruiters came to town. Prime Minister Borden called for volunteers and promised Canadians never to impose conscription. Rumours that it was going to be a short war—over before Christmas—inspired some to enlist right from the start.

Colourful recruiting posters appeared everywhere. On billboards. On electric tramways. On the sides of tall buildings, telephone poles and restaurant walls. Thomas didn't need to know what the slogans on the English posters were about. The images of courage mesmerized him. The brave soldier in full army attire holding a rifle over his shoulder caught his eye each time he passed by. The huge Union

Jack in the background didn't bother him. He didn't feel the call to fight for a country whose imperial army had lorded over his people for centuries. But the lure of heroism was another story.

The poster that finally won him over was in French. Two soldiers stood with an arm resting on each other's shoulder. A Canadian infantry soldier in his smart khaki regalia, and a French soldier in his dapper blue jacket and bright red pants—two close friends standing their rifles on the ground as if they were baseball bats. A fitting reminder of Montcalm, the French military hero killed in the 1759 battle to defend Quebec against British attackers. Though France had since then completely forgotten that Quebec existed, bringing the forgotten French hero out of obscurity served the recruiters well. The thought of foreigners invading the country of his ancestors prompted Thomas to step up to the recruiting desk. He would escape the slave labour of factory work.

He towered over the other men queued up to enlist, so the doctor checked the arches of his feet and his strong white teeth and declared him fit for battle. The recruiters turned a blind eye to his peach fuzz and the large infantile way he signed his name on his enlistment papers. They needed fresh soldiers to make up for all the losses in the trenches. All the military forms were in English. The recruiters pointed at the blank spaces, told him what to write, and he was good to go. He felt a twinge of guilt when he lied about his age, but hadn't Montcalm also started his military career as a boy soldier?

His parents weren't alone in their stand against fighting in a British war. Besides the unemployed, most of the English lining up to enlist at the start of the war were British-born and nurturing a heartfelt allegiance to their motherland. Most people in Quebec felt neither closeness with France nor any loyalty to King George V. Anti-war sentiment was shared by farmers across Canada who needed their sons to help with the farm work and by religious groups who refused to take up arms.

Thomas kept his plans secret and continued to work in the factory beside his brother. Paul woke up one morning to see the grey wool blanket already tucked under the mattress of his brother's narrow bed. Placed on top of Thomas' side of the rickety dresser separating their two cots was his most prized possession: his 1911 Imperial Tobacco hockey card of Eddie Oatman with the Quebec Bulldogs. He had penciled over the player's hockey stick to make it look like a rifle.

Paul's throat tightened. He'd never see his twin brother again. His knees buckled, and gasping for breath, he lowered himself back down on the edge of the bed. Hatred for those who had sent to slaughter the only one whose heart drummed in unison with his spread throughout his body. He swore never to take part in a war that relied on the spilling of blood to win. If conscription ever became law, he'd rather hang from the imperial gallows than join the ranks of mass murderers.

In October 1914, Thomas was part of the First Canadian Contingent arriving in Britain. The news that his son had boarded a warship sailing for England enraged Roger. Paul had waited until the ship left port before saying anything. He knew Thomas well enough. There was no stopping him. He would've found a way no matter what.

"*Les maudits anglais.*" Roger paced up and down the kitchen. "We already have our own war to fight here. Ontario won't let our kids study in French. And they expect us to fight a war we don't believe in." He paused in front of the stove and stared at Paul, who sat drinking tea at the table. "For the love of God... Thomas is only sixteen. He still forgets to tie his damn shoelaces. How can they expect him to point a gun? Why didn't you try to stop him?"

Paul averted his gaze. "By the time I figured it out, he was already heading to the training camp in Valcartier." He looked up, a pained look in his eyes. "You know how damn pig-headed he can be. Nothing can stop him when his mind's made up. He'd find another recruiting office the very next day. He wanted to be a hero like the ones on all those stupid war posters."

"He's always been the stubborn one of you two." Roger sat on the chair across from Paul, his shoulders slumped, his head lowered. He was silent for a long moment before pushing his chair back and standing up straight. "Canadians aren't ready to fight a damn war.

Our boys are being sent off with those useless Ross rifles—damn things are always jamming and they're too damn heavy and long for the trenches. And the army does everything in English. How is Thomas going to understand what he's supposed to do? They'll yell for him to duck and he'll stay standing and get shot."

"Don't worry so much, Papa. He'll have to copy what the others are doing and hope for the best. I hear a few French-Canadian infantry battalions have formed, so maybe he can ask for a transfer."

Roger slammed his fist on the table. "That's not how it works, son. When the French-Canadian battalions get there, they'll break them up and place them on the front lines of the English ones." He pushed his chair back from the table and continued pacing.

"He's gone, Papa. Nothing we do or say will change anything."

Roger turned to face him. "Swear on your mother's head you won't be foolish enough to enlist. They haven't imposed conscription on us so far, but it doesn't mean Borden won't turn around and force it on us when our dead boys block up their trenches."

Paul grasped his teacup and leaned back in his chair. "Don't worry about that. The only time I'll swing a rifle onto my back is to hunt for my supper. And if Borden does go back on his word, they can't go after me until 1918, when I turn twenty. The war will be over and forgotten by that time. The recruiters will have to get up real early to find me in the woods. They'll soon see I'm no coward when it comes to defending my right not to kill someone who's never done me or my family any harm."

Roger sighed and sat back down at the table. "Thank God. That's one less son I have to worry about. This war is so wrong."

"Not for everybody, Papa. Britain and France need this war if they want to survive. And if people here want to jump on the war wagon, that's their choice—but nobody better come tell me I have to kill innocent people. Our Thomas got caught in that war-hero dream. He's got to live it out. I ache for him every day, and I... hope... he comes back to us, but that's all I can do... that's all anybody can do."

Roger leaned forward, folding his arms on the table. "I tell you, this war is all wrong for us. They call us cowards for not enlisting.

Did you hear about Henri Bourassa's article in this week's *Le Devoir?* He accuses the Prussians of Ontario of being French Canada's real enemy, not Germany."

"Bourassa might be right, Papa. The more they try to stop us from speaking French, the less we want to fight their war. If they'd stop treating us like slaves, we might try to see things their way. We do all their dirty jobs in the mills and shops so they can afford big houses and shiny cars while we struggle to put bread on the table. *Merde* on them and their war. I don't care what they call me as long as they don't force me to kill."

"You'll see. They'll find out Thomas is just a boy and send him home." Roger looked hopefully at his son. Receiving no reply, he placed his two palms flat on the table and pushed himself up. "Now I have to figure out how to tell your mother about all this when she gets back from church."

Anne clutched her heart and did the sign of the cross when Roger told her why her son had disappeared. She vowed to the Holy Virgin Mary never to eat meat again until her Thomas returned. During spare moments between her outside laundry jobs and her housework, she'd pull her rosary out of her apron pocket to recite her Hail Mary. She continued to set the table for four and prepared her absent son's favourite meal every other day. When Paul asked her why she never made shepherd's pie anymore, she replied that Thomas wasn't too fond of it. He liked his mashed potatoes, meat and corn kept separate on the plate. But layered on top of each other was less appetizing to him. Roger and Paul glanced at each other in silence while she served herself a plateful of peas and potatoes.

Paul had always worked alongside his brother. He couldn't get used to having a stranger share the same cloud of brown leather dust at the sanding station. When the cold and snow hardened the ground in November he joined the local lumberjacks travelling to the logging camps of northern Quebec. Robust and hard-working like the Brault men before him, he was a welcome addition to the rugged group of axemen. He'd swing his axe like a man possessed, stripping the bark from the heavy logs and squaring them to make them easier to transport. Each tree he cut down brought him closer to Thomas. Pine caskets for the soldiers murdered and buried overseas. The pay at the camp wasn't any better than factory work. But the air was fresh, a luxury compared to the noxious fumes of the factories. With these woodsmen who spoke his language and shared his background, he found a sense of freedom and camaraderie for the first time in his life.

Thomas was already buried in French soil the day his postcard arrived, six months after he sailed. The picture showed him smiling knee-deep in mud on the training fields of Salisbury Plain in Northern England. Anne emptied out her cracked cup filled with coins from her laundry jobs. She asked the priest to hold a Mass for her dead son, thanking Jesus that Thomas was at least resting in the land of their ancestors. She pinned his postcard on the wall beside her bed along with a rosary blessed by the priest from the Basilica of Sainte-Anne-de-Beaupré. Healed pilgrims left their crutches and braces there as proof that miracles occurred. Not that Anne expected her Thomas to rise up from his shallow grave. But his spirit would stop his surviving twin from joining the senseless carnage overseas.

Paul's young age had saved him from being enlisted until the spring of 1918. Borden's Military Service Act of the year before had cancelled all previous exemptions to the draft. The army was desperate for new recruits after suffering heavy losses on the battlefields. Volunteers were few. Married men and the sons of farmers now had to register for the selection process. Certificates of Exemption were given for special cases, although only certain religious pacifists were able to claim them. Spotters, or federal agents, hunted out and arrested any male they came across who couldn't produce exemption papers.

There was a certain look about spotters. The determined way they strolled down the street, shoulders rigid, eyes darting from one side of the street to the other, ready to chase any suspicious male. Paul, like most eligible recruits, learned to duck into alleyways and slink into dark corners.

CHAPTER 24

Nadine stepped out of the second-floor elevator accompanied by Mrs. White. Grandma Stella's arduous breathing, a rasping, as if she were trying to claw her way out of a dark narrow tunnel, hit her as she entered the room. Nadine shuffled back a step, a heavy feeling in her stomach. "I... didn't realize...."

"We're doing all we can for her. It's been four days since she's been down with pneumonia. She had been coughing quite a bit for a while so we had the doctor examine her. The antibiotics haven't worked—the immune system is pretty weak at her age. She hasn't eaten a mouthful and we have trouble getting her to take any liquids. The family has requested she stay in her familiar environment rather than transport her to the hospital. The doctor prescribed something that will keep her as comfortable as possible. She hasn't spoken in days so don't expect too much from her." She patted Nadine's arm and left the room.

Aunt Jan had warned her that Grandma wasn't well. She had expected to see a much older woman, but not as pale and frail as the one she saw in front of her. She pulled up a metal chair and sat down by the side of the bed, a deep ache in her chest. She should've tried to see her long before now. Her stubborn resolve to shun the Pritcharts had struck right into the heart of this gentle soul who had always treated her with love and respect. Aunt Jan and Papi had been kind enough to forgive her neglect but it was too late for Grandma. A high price to pay for her pride. She had wanted to punish Grandpa Pritchart, but in the end, the wrong people had suffered.

Soft Gregorian chants filled the room. She searched to see where it was coming from and noticed the eight-track tape player on top of the dresser. Aunt Jan had called this morning reminding her to make sure the tape was kept on. The staff didn't always remember to push the play button when they came to check in on her. It was Grandma's balm, her way of blocking out the fears that had plagued her all her life. On her nervous days, she hadn't been strong enough to face the Sunday Mass crowd, so Nadine stayed home with her and crawled under her heavy woollen quilt. Arms wrapped around each other, they'd listen to the Gregorian chants playing on the small record player she kept in her bedroom. Listen to my heart, my little Nadine, she'd whisper, it's rising as high as the melodies.

Nadine reached for her hand, a little cool to the touch, but as silky as she remembered.

Do you know who I am, Grandma?

Can you hear my breathing?

It was a game they used to play, blindfolded, when they'd try to locate each other by listening to their breathing. Grandma always claimed she heard the drumming of Nadine's heart from across the room.

"Grandma. It's your Nadine. Listen to my heart beat. It's thumping so hard my ribs hurt. Listen, Grandma. It's your Nadine come back to you."

She leaned her head on the bed and closed her eyes. There would be no response. The only thing left to do was to stay by her side while her soul rose and fell with the laments of the melodies. This was her final journey back to the mystical green land of her ancestors she had talked so much about. "I'm right here, Grandma. You're not alone. Don't be scared."

Nadine woke up not long after with a stiffness in the back of her neck. The small room was still, illuminated by a ray of sunshine. She felt a hand brush her hair and her head shot up. Grandma gazed down at her, a soft glimmer in her eyes. Nadine's heart skipped a beat and she straightened in her chair. But before she had a chance to say anything, Grandma had closed her eyes again.

A nurse rolled her cart into the room, her assistant close behind. "Please wait in the hallway while we take care of Mrs. Pritchart. This won't take long."

Nadine got to her feet and went downstairs to the lounge in search of a coffee machine. A nursing assistant serving the afternoon snacks told her they had no vending machines and offered her tea from the kitchen. Nadine thanked her but declined, knowing the tea served to the residents would be weak and tepid. She climbed back upstairs and came face-to-face with the nurse and her assistant coming out of Grandma's room. They both stopped in their tracks when they saw her and glanced at each other.

The nurse stared at Nadine a moment before speaking. "The doctor is with Mrs. Pritchart."

Nadine's heart skipped a beat. "Is something wrong?"

"The doctor will answer any questions you might have." The nurse gave her a quick nod and continued down the hall, her assistant at her heels.

Nadine bolted into the room. The doctor, completing a form on his clipboard, paused to look at her. "Are you a family member?"

She rushed to the bedside. "She's my grandmother. What's going on?"

The doctor slid his pen into the top pocket of his lab coat. "Pulmonary complications. I'm sorry for your loss, Madame." He turned and walked out the door to continue his rounds.

Nadine swallowed the burning lump in her throat and leaned down to press her lips on her forehead. Grandma had left her world behind, but not without first saying farewell, pausing in her journey to offer a moment of comfort, as she always had. She had detected Nadine's anguish, heard the drumbeat of her heart. The loving touch of Grandma's fingers through her hair would stay with her forever.

She stepped towards the dresser, pressed the play button on the tape machine and said goodbye to the caregivers waiting in the hallway. Grandma had shed her cloud of fear and loneliness to embark on her new journey. She wouldn't have wanted anyone feeling sad. She took a deep breath and resolved to focus on her goals for the day and not to allow the pain of Grandma's departure to overwhelm her. First, she had to call Aunt Jan and then, most pressing of all, have a serious talk with Lisette. Gregorian chants accompanied her all the way to the elevators.

Nadine came home to find Lisette curled up in a blanket on the sofa listening to CKLM radio. They were rebroadcasting their program on Barbara Cross. The kidnapped British diplomat's wife was reading aloud a letter she had written him. Her voice posh-sounding, but wavering and faint at times.

—It is now… more than a week since I heard from you. You are constantly in my thoughts… and you must know how I long for your safe return—

Nadine pulled off her shoes and switched on the overhead lights. "A bit dark in here. Have you had supper?"

Lisette pulled the blanket over her head. "That's too bright. It hurts my eyes."

Nadine switched the ceiling lights back off and turned on the softer table lamp instead. Were the overhead lights that strong, or was it a sign of vision problems? It was time to have a serious talk.

—It has been a great consolation to me to have been able to read your letters and to have some idea… of what your thoughts have been at this time of separation—

"At least the woman gets letters from him." Lisette sat up as Nadine walked past her. "I don't even know if Serge is hiding out… or if he's locked up. They make new arrests every day. Prisoners aren't allowed to see a lawyer, never mind call anybody. And I can't risk asking if they've picked him up. They'll bring me in for questioning for associating with a terrorist."

Nadine considered telling her the bad news about Grandma Stella but decided to wait for her to calm down. The girl was right about avoiding any contact with him. The cops were desperate to find the kidnappers and they'd jump on any chance to get information leading to their capture. She had to stay away from him no matter how worried she was about him. Under war measures, aiding a member of the FLQ in any way got you up to five years in jail.

She sat down in the armchair across from her daughter "It's only been a short while, Lisette. Worrying about it won't bring him back any faster."

Lisette put her elbows on her knees and rested her head in her hands. "My child will grow up without a father... without a real family."

Nadine let out a soft sigh and looked away. The girl was so obsessed about forming a proper family—something Nadine hadn't been able to give her. No magical words or formulas could ease her anguish. Maybe if she had been stronger when Lisette was born and found a way to resist, to hold on to her baby. The child might've grown up knowing that family is all in the heart, that it didn't always follow an established pattern. If Serge wasn't around to parent the child, some other capable person could. Family was formed with love and loyalty, not by legal status. But Lisette wasn't ready to hear any of this.

—Your letters have moved me to hope that we will soon be together again. I do hope the FLQ will... continue to allow you to write to me—

Lisette straightened. "That's it." Her face lit up. "He'll write me. The cops can't trace his letters."

—To those holding my husband, I express the hope that... as a victim of circumstances... he will be well treated. I beg you to free him without any more delay—

Lisette reached out and switched the radio off. "She can't be serious. They can't release him—not before their demands are met."

"Give her a break, Lisette. The woman sounds like she's scared her husband will end up like Laporte. You'd feel the same way if your Serge had been the one kidnapped. She doesn't know what's happening to him just like you don't know what's happening with Serge. As far as she knows, he might be dead. The FLQ have sent a few communiqués since Laporte's death but the cops won't allow the radio stations to broadcast them anymore."

Lisette shot her a dark look. "Thanks for your encouragement. The possibility of Serge's death will sure help me sleep better tonight."

"Sorry, I didn't mean to upset you. I was just comparing your situation with the woman's. You're both living the same kind of frustration."

Lisette turned her back to stroke Peaches dozing on top of the sofa beside her.

Nadine rubbed the back of her neck and leaned forward in her chair. "I went to see Grandma Stella earlier... I've got some bad news to—"

"Can it wait till the morning?" Lisette scratched Peaches behind the ears, triggering loud purring. "I've had enough dark thoughts for today."

"There's never a good time for bad news. It will be just as hard to take tomorrow as it will be now." She swallowed hard, pushing down the ball of heat in her throat. "She'd been sick for a while, and... this afternoon... while I was visiting her... she left us."

"I'm so sorry." Lisette sat up straight, letting go of Peaches, who sprang off the couch. "She was a nice lady. I wanted to go back to visit her but they locked me out."

Nadine pressed a fist against her chest. "Pretty sad thing to say, but she was my best friend—my only friend—when I was growing up. I did her wrong neglecting her all these years, so any pain I feel now is well deserved." She paused to wipe the back of her hand over her eyes. "I'll have to call Aunt Jan later to find out about the funeral arrangements." She stood up slowly. "But life goes on no matter how much pain you're in. I'll make coffee and fix us a light supper. We have other things to talk about."

Lisette gave her a puzzled look, and got up to fold her blanket.

Nadine opened the fridge and pulled out the loaf of bread, left-over chicken and the jar of mayonnaise.

Lisette sat at the kitchen table and watched her prepare the sandwiches. "I tried to find Serge this morning. I needed to know he was OK."

Nadine stopped her knife mid-way through a sandwich. "So, did you?"

"I knew you wouldn't approve, but what the heck. It's my life." She leaned back in her chair and crossed her arms. "I took the bus to Sylvie and Pit's place but nobody answered the bell. No curtains in the windows—I guess they've moved. So I stopped by Serge's taxi stand." She straightened and brushed her fingers through her hair. "He must be wondering how I'm doing after all this time. I just wanted to let him know everything was OK. His boss—a real asshole—told me he wasn't working there anymore, but if I left a note he'd pass it on to someone who knew him. The way the creep looked at me—like I was some pregnant bimbo trying to pin Serge down—I knew he wasn't going to tell me whether the cops picked him up or not."

Nadine placed the sandwiches and mugs on the table. "Let's just finish our meal. I'm sure Serge is laying low till the fuss has died down. According to the papers, the Civil Rights Union has set up a separate committee to check on the treatment of the detainees. Serge is only a sympathizer. If they have him, they can't keep him forever. Focus on you and the baby. That and working on your term papers will keep your mind off other things."

Lisette picked up her sandwich and put it down again without biting into it. "There's something I should make clear. A sympathizer is someone like me. I've participated in a few protests and gone to rallies and meetings. But Serge is a bit more involved than that."

"How implicated?" Nadine slid her plate closer, ready to start eating. "Didn't you say he was a fundraiser for the FLQ?"

"Where do you think he gets the damn funds?" She held Nadine's gaze. "Banks, taverns, grocery stores, drugstores, nightclubs. Any place that keeps a pile of cash on hand."

Nadine's eyes widened and her stomach turned over. "Armed robbery? Is that what you're saying?" She leaned back against the back of her chair. It was a silly question, but she needed to get her mind around this.

"Don't look so shocked." She grimaced, pushing her sandwich to the side. "It's not as if he keeps any of the money. It all goes to help the cell with explosives and whatever else the group needs to carry out their activities. Pit holds the gun and Serge fills the knapsack. But the gun's only for show. They've never hurt anyone." She clutched a handful of her hair and twisted it around her fingers. "Now you know why I'm going out of my mind about this and why Serge can't contact me right now. Though I wish he'd call me to let me know he's OK. I guess he can't risk it."

"He's got that right." The thought of her daughter handcuffed and locked behind bars left a sour taste in Nadine's mouth. "Look at you. Your hands are trembling and you're all sweaty. Promise me you won't try to see him again."

Lisette remained silent. Nadine saw the lone tear flow down her cheek and she controlled her urge to put her arms around her. Having her flinch when she touched her was hard to take. Lisette just wasn't ready to accept her mother's love and sympathy. She had been deprived too long to recognize the healing aspect of this balm. *Not yet.*

She had no idea what to do to ease her daughter's heart. All Lisette wanted was to give her child a loving family. She had chosen a man with a different dream. She slid Lisette's plate back in front of her. "You have to eat. You might not be hungry but your child is." The percolator stopped brewing and she got up from her chair. "I'll get the coffee."

Nadine switched off the stove and walked back with the percolator. Lisette had started on her sandwich. She stared at her daughter's unkempt hair and the dark rings under her eyes. The last weeks of pregnancy had taken their toll. Nadine reached for her sandwich and they ate in silence. Her daughter was smart enough, but how was it she wasn't able to see she was stuck with a man who lived only for his cause? He'd never be able to be there for her when she needed him.

Nadine wasn't about to risk rocking the boat by speaking her mind. All she wanted was to share a meal and have a quiet conversation with her daughter. Nothing else mattered right now.

Lisette glanced up from her plate. "I know you don't think much of Serge. But don't worry. He's the most honest, dedicated man I know. Right now, I have to be strong and accept coming second place in his life. He's got to give his all to what he believes in. He's got this big poster in his room with a quote from Louis Riel that sums it all up: 'I have nothing but my heart and I gave it away long ago to my country.' I know when this FLQ thing has fizzled out—it has to, it's too small to continue much longer—he'll be back." She placed her hand on her belly. "This child and I, we'll be his country—his family."

Nadine went to touch her hand, but stopped before Lisette noticed. "Go drink your coffee and relax in front of the TV. I'll call Aunt Jan from the office. I guess Uncle Denis must've broken the news about Grandma to her by now." She paused, a pained look in her eyes. "This isn't going to be an easy call. Aunt Jan and Grandma were pretty close."

Lisette pushed her chair back. "Didn't you say you had something else you wanted to talk about?"

Nadine hesitated a moment. "That can wait. You have enough on your plate right now. We'll set aside some time soon when things are calmer."

CHAPTER 25

The sun's weak morning rays filtered through Nadine's bedroom drapes. She woke gasping from the same suffocating dream that had plagued her from early childhood.

She's lying flat on her back in the yard, wet blades of grass plastered to the side of her neck. Her nightie, cold and sticky, clings to her skin. Someone, heavy and motionless—Maman?—is on top of her, pinning her down, blocking her breathing. She tries to tug her arms out from under the body but each movement brings a fresh spurt of blood. Where is it coming from? Blood trickles across her face, making her eyes sting. A thick salty taste in her mouth. Spasms of pain surge from her neck down to her legs. She stretches her mouth wide to scream—no sound.

She threw off her blanket and slipped out of her sweat-soaked nightshirt. Damp strands of hair clung to her neck and face. That same dream—no less disturbing than the last time—continued to revisit her. If dreams were supposed to carry messages, what did this one intend to tell her? To remind her of her mother's murder? If so, it's job was done. Encrypted in her heart and mind, the horror of that day occupied a permanent slot in her psyche.

He must've grabbed the longest blade in the kitchen drawer, though if Claire was as delicate as Aunt Jan claimed, a pen knife would've done her just as much harm. She imagined him taking two steps at a time, stumbling down the stairs after her. His fast, deep breaths. The sharp smell of whiskey in the air as he got ready to pounce. Her heart drumming through her chest. The muscles of her legs straining as she sprinted, clutching a heavy, crying five-year-old against her chest. Her eyes fixed on the wooden gate leading to the back alley and to freedom. And then falling, plunging face down into the wet night grass. The first thrust of his knife slicing into her mother's lower back.

Nadine stared down at the narrow horizontal scar on her thigh—a gruesome childhood keepsake. What was he thinking? Did he mean to stab me too, like those big toothpicks they use to skewer a club sandwich together? The blade pierced right through my mother's organs and into my upper thigh, missing by a hair the big artery that leads to my heart. He would've noticed the twitch in Claire's eye or a slight movement in one of her fingers. He yanked the knife out—dripping with a blend of my mother's blood with mine—and thrust it right back in again. Higher, nearer to her heart. Deeper, until the tip of the blade sliced through her body to the soft tissue beneath my collar bone.

She got out of bed and brushed a shaky hand through her hair. Why did she dwell on something she had buried so long ago? A dark cloud of pain that had anchored deep in her consciousness. She had learned to block these thoughts during her waking hours but had no control of them while she slept. If dreams were nature's way of guiding people, she would need more clues to understand. She had lost contact with the child who had lived through that ordeal, yet the hurt lingered.

She was five years old when it happened. She could still hear her mother's sharp breathing as she tore down the back steps and across the lawn, clasping her daughter in her arms. Had she not been hampered with a child, she might have escaped her husband's brutal attack. The evening window shoppers had been a mere block away. Was that what the dream was about? To point out that her mother might still be alive today if it weren't for her? But Claire hadn't hesitated, her heart pounding into her daughter's chest, determined to reach the safety of the downtown crowd. It never came to mind to leave her daughter behind, even at the risk of her own life.

Nadine ran her finger along the velvety smoothness of the scar on her thigh. It had taken on the shape of a malicious eye when she was a kid. She'd imagine a horrid creature lurking beneath the whitish membrane, keeping watch on her, inflicting punishment for every wrong move or rebellious thought. Never had she spoken of that horrible day to anyone. The policeman who had come to question her at the hospital had only gotten a nod or a head shake out of her. It had taken her two long months before uttering a single word after Aunt Jan came to fetch her. She had guarded the memory of that day like a talisman, and as a child would curl up in bed with her hand over her scar. It was a pain that linked her to her mother, shared by no one but them.

Footfalls along the hallway. Lisette was up early. Sleep was difficult in the last month of pregnancy and her worries about Serge didn't help matters. Nadine wished for a magic wand that would swish all her daughter's troubles away.

A sudden thought surfaced. She sat up straight.

The memory of her mother's murder had to be set free.

Claire had been a fun-loving woman who probably wouldn't have wanted her daughter to remember her as a victim. Had she survived, she would've shrugged off what happened and continued revelling in and dancing to the music she so loved. Keeping the horrific event secret only served to feed her pain, allowing the blood dream to return. Same as her silence about Grandpa Pritchart—better to have screamed it to the heavens and let the pieces fall where they may.

She had blocked out her past self, thinking the hurt would disappear along with the memory. A new name. A new life. No connections with her past. But the pain had lived on, ploughing into her dreams or usurping a quiet, tender moment. By locking the pain inside of her, she had made it an integral part of her being. The time had come. Open wide the windows. Release those hurtful memories and strip them of their control over her.

She got up and reached for her housecoat. She'd begin with her daughter. You owe me, Lisette had told her when they first met. The girl was right. Whatever pain Lisette had experienced growing up was because of her. Making up for all those lost years Lisette had grown up unwanted and unloved wasn't possible, but she'd start by opening up and being honest no matter what.

Lisette was in the kitchen flipping pancakes. The percolator was brewing and the table set for two.

"You're up bright and early." Nadine sat down at the table.

Lisette glanced at her over her shoulder. "Couldn't sleep. Thought I may as well start on my paper."

"Don't forget the new health insurance plan comes into effect today. You'll have to register with them to get your health card." Nadine's stomach tensed.

Stop avoiding the subject. Say it now or you'll put it off again.

"Thanks for preparing all this"—she looked up at the clock—"but I never eat anything this early. Coffee is my big breakfast item."

"Not a problem." Lisette switched the burner off, brought the platter of steaming pancakes to the table, and slid a few onto her plate. "These are still good cold with jam or peanut butter."

Nadine went to the kitchen to pour two mugs of coffee and came back to the table. She waited until Lisette had finished eating and had reached for her coffee before speaking. "I've been meaning to tell you something. We've been so busy getting things organized here, and then there was the funeral… it never seemed to be the right moment."

"That's the same tone of voice social workers would use when they moved me to a new home." She shot Nadine a questioning look. "They always found something I had to work on to make things easier for everybody. So what did I do wrong this time?"

"Nothing." She shifted in her chair. "You've done nothing wrong. Remember when you asked me if I knew anyone on my mother's side who had eye problems?" She wrapped her hands around her mug. "I've never met my mother's family, so I wasn't sure."

"No big deal." Lisette elbowed her plate aside and poured milk in her coffee. "My eye doctor wanted to make sure before he operated."

"I should've told you this before. But… you being so close to giving birth, I didn't want you worrying. Still, you have a right to know."

Lisette pulled her eyeglasses off and wiped them with the hem of her nightie. "These stupid things are always dirty no matter how often I clean them. Sometimes I see blotches and I'm never sure if it's my eyes or my glasses." She glanced up. "You were saying?"

"Well... Papi tells me that Grandpa Pritchart died of a rare kidney disorder which affected... his eyesight and... his hearing." She paused a moment to consider her words. "He was practically deaf and blind before he died. It's some kind of genetic thing that only female children can inherit."

Lisette yawned. "That's too bad for the old guy. Good thing we're not related—Hey! What's that face for? It's not as if it's a great revelation. Grandma Stella did tell me John Pritchart wasn't your real father. So, what's the big deal?"

Nadine looked down at her feet. "Did she say that? Uncle Denis said something along those lines at the funeral. I never did feel I was part of the family but I never knew for sure. Nobody ever spoke about it—not to me."

Relax. Breathe in.

She'll hate me. But she needs to know.

It's now or never.

"It's a small consolation, in a way, knowing it wasn't my own father who killed my mother." She squared her shoulders. "Not that it makes her murder less morbid."

An ache in the back of her throat made her pause. She was about to rip her insides apart to reveal a secret that had been lodged inside her so long it defined who she was. A splinter embedded deep under her skin that only pain could dislodge. "I understand that you'd rather not hear anything negative right now, but bear with me on this."

"Wait a minute." Lisette raised her palm and pushed her chair back. "If I have to hear something depressing, I better get a refill." She headed to the stove and came back with the percolator. She topped up their mugs and sat back down. "OK. I'm ready for your doom and gloom."

"I always figured I'd hurt too many people if I said anything about this—" She stopped and stared down at her mug. "Now that I have you back in my life, I don't want to risk losing you by keeping this from you." She clenched her coffee mug to steady the slight tremor in her hands. "Uncle Denis often sent me to stay with his mother when I was a kid. Grandpa Pritchart was away a lot working the trains. Grandma stayed in bed often because of her heart condition and she'd always been too nervous to stay by herself. I'd take the bus straight from school on Friday afternoons and spend the weekend with her. When Grandpa wasn't around, she'd let me eat all the cake I wanted for breakfast and we'd sometimes hop on the tramway to go eat a Pogo at Eaton's basement restaurant. Grandpa was always a little scary to me—tall and wide-shouldered with hard fingers that left red marks on my back when he hugged me."

She paused to sip her coffee. Lisette's eyes were glued on her, waiting for her to go on.

"One Sunday afternoon when I was fifteen, he came back reeking of alcohol from a double Toronto-Montreal run. I was in Grandma's room reading to her. He handed Grandma her sedatives, though she wasn't due to take them till much later. Then he grabbed the book from me. 'I got you a nice dress from Toronto,' he told me. 'Show me what it looks like on you.' I remember thinking I had just enough time to try it on before catching the next tramway home. The dress was too clingy and low-cut for my liking and I yanked it off. I was standing in my underwear ready to put my clothes back on when he threw open my bedroom door. The way he stood staring made me want to run. I yelled at him, 'Wait, Grandpa, I'm changing.' But he stepped forward instead and closed the door behind him."

Lisette's mouth fell open. "The slimy old prick. I hope you kicked him where it counts."

"I remember grabbing my sweater to cover myself and shouting at him to get out. He put his hand over my mouth. 'French whore,' he kept repeating, 'just like your bitch of a mother.' He shoved me onto the bed, and… after he—" She looked away. "After he zipped his pants back up, he turned to me and said, 'If you don't want to kill off your grandmother, you better keep your slutty mouth shut.'"

Nadine sprang up and bolted to the sink, a crippling wave of nausea surging through her. She leaned her head down, splashing cold water on her face.

Lisette hadn't touched her coffee the whole time Nadine had spoken. She fumbled with her mug, brought it to her lips, then put it down without drinking. "You never told anyone?"

Nadine shook her head and straightened, staring out the window. "I knew he'd deny it all. And he was right about Grandma. It would've been the end of her. He was her rock."

"Not even a word to Aunt Jan?" She reached for her mug again, hesitated, and pushed it away. "It must've eaten you up. Especially if you had to face the old prick."

"I swore he'd never touch me again. I invented a whole bunch of excuses to avoid seeing him—and I didn't, not once, after that afternoon. That meant not seeing Grandma either, but that was the price I had to pay. By the time December came along, Aunt Jan figured out the reason for my sudden weight gain. She didn't argue when I refused to go to Grandma's Christmas dinner. Come January, Uncle Denis drove me to the maternity home. I never saw any of them again till after that chance meeting with Papi." She stopped to think. "I take that back. That isn't quite true. I came across Uncle Peter about a year or so after I left."

"The old bastard got you pregnant?" Lisette leaned back in her chair and folded her arms across her belly, incredulous. "I see now why you'd drop his family name." She thought a moment, studying Nadine. "Getting an abortion those days must've been pretty risky."

"Never. It never once crossed my mind. I stayed nine months at the maternity home."

"But you were carrying your rapist's child." Lisette straightened in her chair. "Hey. Wait a minute. That means—"

Nadine turned to face her. "Yes. That old bastard was your father."

Lisette pushed her chair away from the table and stood up, a pained look in her eyes. "But you said—" She gripped the back of her chair. "He had—" She ripped her glasses off and slammed them on the table. "I've got the same thing he had, right?" She reached up and touched her eyes. "I'm going to be deaf and blind, same as him. And the baby, what about my baby?"

"You can't be sure." Nadine stared down at her feet. "If they know what to look for, maybe they can—" Her head shot up at the sound of her daughter's erratic breathing. She stepped towards her, a heaviness in her chest and arms. A hot rage surged through her at the power Grandpa Pritchart still held to inflict pain on her, and now, on her daughter. She reached out to wrap her arms around her, but Lisette shoved her away and stomped towards her room, slamming the door behind her.

Nadine lowered herself back down in her chair and fumbled with her coffee mug. Her throat burned and her knees felt weak. The horrible secret that had festered inside her and defined her existence for the past twenty years was finally out. She felt a lightness in her chest, but at the same time, saddened at the pain it had inflicted on her daughter. Had she been right to tell her? Would the ugly truth destroy the closeness she had so longed for? Lisette's anguish was understandable. Her dream of having a normal family life was crumbling day by day. A lover who prioritized his political ideals before her needs. The possibility that she and her child might have inherited a crippling disease. Her daughter needed someone to support her and she was ready to climb mountains to do so.

She reached out for the tepid mugs of coffee and shuffled to the sink. She had to get ready for work. Lisette would have time to wrap her mind around all this while Nadine was gone. Monday wasn't a busy day at the office. She'd catch up on her paperwork and leave a little earlier to come home in time to have supper with her.

She reached into the back of the closet and pulled out a brown leather skirt she had bought on a whim a few months back. It had looked OK on her at the store, but when she tried it on at home she noticed how it inched up higher on her lap when she sat down, exposing the scar on her thigh. To avoid questions, she had always worn clothes that hid both scars. The reflection she now saw in the mirror made her appear elegant—a woman ready to face the world. She took a deep breath and rooted in the closet for one of the more feminine blouses she reserved for home.

CHAPTER 26

Nadine had started giving Aunt Jan a quick call on her lunch break since Grandma Stella's funeral. Her aunt mourned the loss not only of a beloved mother-in-law, but also a close friend and confidant. Her health had taken a bad turn, leaving her without an appetite and drained of energy. Her heart condition made her doctor reluctant to prescribe more drugs, advising complete rest instead. Nadine called every day to encourage her to heat up whatever meal Uncle Denis had prepared for her before he left for work.

The day's busy schedule had only allowed Nadine to phone Aunt Jan at the end of the afternoon. Papi's voice on the other end took her by surprise.

"My inspections at the camps didn't take as long as I thought. I don't deal much with workers' conditions anymore. It's more about checking the kind of mess left behind by their heavy machinery. On a more cheerful note, how's my granddaughter doing?"

"Besides worrying about her boyfriend and stressing over her schoolwork, I'd say she's slowly getting used to me. I still can't get over having her living with me. I missed you at the funeral on Saturday."

"My pickup broke down on the way. I was lucky it happened not far from a mechanic friend of mine who got it working again. I finally made it here last night."

"Are you in town for long?"

"Well… I've decided to move closer to my family. I'll be apartment hunting near here. Janette insists I stay with them until I find something. That daughter of mine had me worried, but she's looking a little better today. She's having a hard time letting go. She was the same when my mother died. Even when we know a loved one is reaching the end, it doesn't make the loss any easier."

"It'll be great to have you close. Why don't you all come for supper tomorrow? Aunt Jan and Lisette already met at the funeral, but it'd be nice for you to meet her too."

"Janette's resting right now. But I doubt I'll have to twist her arm about the invitation. It'll do her good to get out."

"And how is Uncle Denis doing? He's never home when I call." She didn't mention that her calls to Aunt Jan were planned for the times when she knew he'd be out.

"He won't let her do anything for herself. It gets on Janette's nerves, so she'd rather he go to work. We all have our own way of dealing with grief."

"He wasn't too happy to see me at the funeral. But I hope he decides to come tomorrow."

"We have to give him time to adjust."

Nadine drew her breath, remembering how Uncle Denis had made a point of avoiding her at the funeral parlour, heading off towards other mourners whenever she approached him.

Nadine left Lisette talking with Aunt Jan and headed down the stairs of the funeral parlour to the restrooms. She noticed Uncle Denis at the coffee counter and crossed the room, relieved to see nobody else was around.

"Uncle Denis." Her voice low, her knees weak.

He slid the coffee pot back into the machine, his face hardening when he saw her.

"I'm so sorry about your mother. She was the kindest grandmother."

He glared at her. "But she wasn't, was she?"

"What do you mean?" She gave him a puzzled look. "Not kind, or not my grandmother?"

He reached for the milk. "She was never unkind."

Nadine clenched a fist behind her back. He might make it hard for her and Aunt Jan to see each other, but he'd never remove Grandma Stella from her heart.

"She's the only grandmother I ever knew. I adored her."

"You sure made that clear. Not a word. Not even a phone call in twenty years."

He took his coffee and went to sit at a table near the stairs. She swallowed hard and followed, sitting across from him and staring down at her lap. He was right. Neglect, foolish pride or cruel indifference—guilty on all counts—she could've set it aside once in a while and called. She knew that now. It had taken a chance meeting with Papi to figure out that trying to escape her past was a lost cause—that it had made her who she was. Denying painful memories only made you tighten your grip on them and blocked you from moving forward.

"All that worrying about you wore Janette down. The loss of our son almost killed her, but when you disappeared too, her health went downhill."

"I'm sorry about that."

"A bit late for that." He slid his coffee aside and walked towards the stairs, pausing before going up. "By the way, my lawyer is still waiting for that release form he sent you."

"I've been meaning to take care of that. I've been busy trying to help my daughter—"

"It only takes a second to sign a form." He gripped the handrail. "I don't want to hear anything about that bastard kid of yours. Janette's already calling her our grandchild. I won't have it. She's nothing to me and never will be." His voice, menacing. "You said you'd sign that release but I should've known it was all lies. Peter and I have been trying to settle this for close to twenty years. If you want to see Janette again, you better move on it." He stormed up the stairs before she had a chance to reply.

Too shaken to go back into the funeral parlour to say goodbye to Aunt Jan, she had spotted Lisette standing by herself near the doorway and had steered her outside towards the bus stop.

"No problem, Papi. I'll understand if Uncle Denis doesn't come. But I hope that won't stop you from showing up. You'll just love

Lisette. She might be a little blunt at times, but her heart is in the right place." She didn't expect Uncle Denis to show up. But she'd be as polite and as pleasant as it took for Aunt Jan's sake if he did decide to come.

"You can count on us being there. Looking forward to meeting her."

Uncle Denis hadn't been wrong about that release form. She had left it on her desk at home after opening her mail. With the flurry of having Lisette with her, she hadn't gotten around to taking care of it. She'd have to search through her paperwork, sign it and mail it back right away. Anything to make Aunt Jan's life a little easier. She wanted no part of that inheritance. It felt too much like guilt money. Why else would he make her the sole beneficiary of his bank account? She didn't blame his two sons for appealing the will—they were the rightful beneficiaries, not her. If refusing the inheritance meant she'd be free to visit Aunt Jan, it was well worth it.

Nadine walked out of her office with a light step. How could she have survived all those years without the support of the people she loved? Now that she had them back, she'd never let anything come between them again. Let Uncle Denis and Uncle Peter grab hold of all the money they wanted; she had her family now.

The acrid odour of scorched meat hit her when she opened the door to her building. She hurried up the stairs. No smoke, but the smell was stronger as she approached the door to her apartment. She fumbled in her bag for her keys and had just grabbed them when the door flew open.

Lisette stood in the doorway holding a plastic garbage bag in her hand, a stunned look on her face. "Didn't expect you home so soon."

"What's that smell?" Nadine pushed past her.

"This is kind of embarrassing. I thought I'd cook supper." She glanced down at her bag. "But now I've got to run it down to the outside garbage can."

Nadine rushed into the kitchen. Peaches meowed from her perch on top of the refrigerator—her escape whenever something disturbed her. A roasting pan with blackened potatoes stuck to the bottom sat in the sink. She filled it with water and threw open the back door to let out the smell. She was sliding the windows open in the living room open when Lisette walked back in. "The whole building smells of my cooking."

"What happened? Did you fall asleep with the oven on?"

"I forgot to set the timer." She raised both palms in the air. "I was so busy clearing your desk, I forgot to check on the roast. Then I remembered to change the cat litter. I left the door ajar when I brought the old litter down to the garbage.... What's that look for? I only stepped out for a minute and when I came back upstairs I saw Peaches fly by me. I chased him all the way downstairs. Good thing the outside door is always kept closed. I tried to grab him a few times, but he'd take off as soon as I got near him. I finally cornered him in the laundry room and when I got back, the fire alarm went off. By the time I'd switched off the oven, shoved the burnt roast in a garbage bag, and shut off the alarm, you appeared." She flopped down at the dining room table. "Don't worry. I'll replace the meat tomorrow."

"No need." Nadine reached up to pull the cat off the top of the refrigerator and carried him back to the table with her. "These things happen."

Although a little put out about ruining the meal, Lisette didn't show any sign she was still upset about their conversation about Grandpa Pritchart. Nadine had expected her to be moody and bitter, and had resigned herself to being forever blamed for all her daughter's woes. The hard facts of her medical history couldn't be easy for her daughter to come to terms with, but she must've thought it over—she seemed to be back to normal, whatever her normal was.

"In any case, after my day at the office, I'm not hungry for a big meal." Peaches jumped off Nadine's lap and bolted out the room. "No harm done. There's enough bread and cheese for us both. I'll be going grocery shopping tomorrow after work. Papi, Aunt Jan... and maybe Uncle Denis are coming for supper. I could sure use a coffee right now." She got up to fill the percolator and paused to look back over her shoulder. "Did you say you cleaned up my desk? I planned to do that this evening."

"I had no choice. I didn't have enough room for my notebook. Everything's in three neat piles now, so you probably won't be able to find anything." She sprang up from her chair— "Right. I almost forgot. Be right back"—and headed towards the office. "I found something that didn't fit in any of the piles I made."

Nadine had just sat down at the table when Lisette reappeared with a sheet of paper in her hand. "This has nothing to do with your work, isn't a bill, and isn't junk mail. I didn't know which pile to throw it on." She slid it across the table and flopped down on her chair.

"That's where it went." Nadine smiled up at Lisette. "Thanks. I need to take care of this. Don't worry about sorting things out. Just push them aside and I'll get to it later."

"What's it about?"

"Nothing that matters. Not to me in any case." She folded the paper and tucked it into the pocket of her cardigan. "It's something I promised to do for Uncle Denis." She slid her chair back and walked to the stove. "I better check on that coffee."

"What did you promise him?"

Nadine reached in the cupboard and brought down two mugs. Her daughter was being a little too pushy. The form had been among a slew of other documents on the desk and she would have had to read it before deciding in which pile to place it. Why bring it up if she already knew what it was about? Why not start a fourth pile instead of making such a fuss? "It has to do with Grandpa Pritchart's will."

"The old prick left you a bunch of dough, right?"

"That form wasn't meant for your eyes. It concerns Uncle Denis and me." She'd have to be careful about what she left hanging around now that she had someone living with her. Although she had decided not to keep any secrets from her, Uncle Denis might want to keep this private.

"No big deal." Lisette squared her shoulders, a sullen look on her face. "Anyhow, I already knew all about it."

Nadine brought the coffee mugs to the table and sat back down. "What to do you mean? I only found out about the inheritance a short while ago."

"Serge found your name on this Unclaimed Accounts list while I was first searching for you. It's where people have bank accounts or insurance money in their name without them ever knowing about it. When the money remains dormant for so many years the Canadian government claims it. I was trying to encourage Serge to find a safer way of raising money. So he checked the list for the fun of it. Him and I weren't on it, but you—"

"Hold on." Nadine straightened in her chair. "He'd have to know my name to do that. Social Services wouldn't have disclosed it without my permission."

Lisette lifted a palm up and shrugged. "He had that all figured out. I pretended to have a big coughing fit and the woman stepped out of the office to get me some water. That's when he opened your file and found your name. The woman didn't have a clue."

Nadine crossed her legs, uncrossed them, and crossed them again. That Serge thought nothing of stealing her private information sent a wave of cold sweat down her back. And that Lisette was a willing participant was even more disturbing. "I had no idea that list existed." She looked hard into her daughter's eyes. "Why would you care if I was on it? You consider the invasion of my privacy to be a joke?"

Lisette put her mug down. "Hey. I never approved of him looking into your file. He never said anything to me before going into that office. He figured if I connected with you, I had almost given up on that idea until Social Services called me, that you'd help me. Now that I think about it, I guess he already knew way back then that Pit and Sylvie wanted me out. Getting together with you was the perfect solution to him. He's the one that encouraged me to call you back after I didn't show up that time. He has more faith in you as a person than you have in him."

Nadine didn't know how to take this. Was Lisette saying Serge had orchestrated their reunion, and that she herself had never cared less about it? Was her inheritance the only reason she agreed to meet? She tilted her head and stared down at her hands. "The solution to what exactly?"

"He was just looking out for everyone. Keeping me safe and maybe get funding that didn't require a lot of risks. Is that a crime?"

Nadine's shoulders stiffened. "Are you saying he wanted you to get money from me to finance his terrorist activities? I suppose he figured you could manipulate me because I was so happy to have you around. Is that why you agreed to see me?"

A flush crept across Lisette's face. "I started searching for you before Serge found out about your name being on that list. I needed to find out about my medical history—which, by the way, you took your sweet time to warn me about. Serge figured I'd be safe with you while this crazy manhunt was on. We joked about someone leaving us a windfall, but no one said anything about extorting money from you. People do make donations for causes they believe in, you know. That was a pretty stupid thing to accuse him of."

"So why the interest in this release form?" Nadine held her daughter's gaze.

She's being defensive about Serge. Can't blame her—nobody wants to see their lover's faults. So change the subject. Let things ride. Is it worth alienating her over this? I dreamed about and longed for this child from the minute I first felt her move inside of me. Does she feel that primal urge to reconnect with me, or is she here to harvest whatever she can out of me?

"Just curious, that's all. What's the big deal? As your daughter, I should know what's going on in your life."

Nadine yanked the form out of her pocket and slapped it on the table. "You know exactly what's on this paper. I'm refusing any claim of being the beneficiary of Grandpa Pritchart's bank account." A wave of nausea surged through her and she pushed her coffee mug aside. "I won't let him pay me off. No amount of money can erase what he did. My uncles are contesting the will. Let them have it all. Not once did Grandpa bring his family out to a restaurant. Grandma always had to skimp on her grocery money if she needed to buy a new pair of shoes. Whatever money he left goes to his two sons. I'm more than OK with that. All I want is to be able to visit Aunt Jan whenever I want to."

Lisette massaged her lower back before pushing herself up. "A grand gesture on your part. But aren't you also trying to buy your way back into their good graces? You mention his two sons. What about his daughter? Don't I also have a say in the matter?"

Nadine's heart went out to this tall beautiful woman, her face flushed, her eyes flaring with the injustice of the situation. "Oh, Lisette, you can forget about that. The Pritcharts never even accepted me as being part of their family."

Lisette's features hardened. "They can't deny me when I tell them I'm their little sister."

"You think they'll care?" Nadine slumped forward, placing her elbows on the table and clasping her hands together. "They wouldn't have believed me twenty years ago and they sure won't buy your story now. The man is long dead. His boys aren't responsible for what he did. Leave them whatever tolerable memory they have of him."

"I don't want to join their damn clan. And anyway, there's tests that can prove we're related." She flopped back down on her chair and rested a hand on her belly. "All I want is what I'm owed. You might not want or need the damn money. It's not like I'm going to give this kid away and move on with my life. I want a home of my own with a room and a backyard for my child. Serge will move in and we'll have a real family." She straightened in her chair. "I'll accept a payoff anytime. The old prick owes me big-time for what he passed on to me. He owes my kid too."

"You don't get it, do you?" Lisette's hurtful comment about not giving her child away had taken her breath away. No matter how she explained the adoption, her daughter still held it against her. "The money's not mine to give. I haven't claimed it."

Nadine tried to avoid the anger in her daughter's eyes. She didn't want to argue—her mind was set. She had just reunited with Aunt Jan and had no intention of letting her go. At the same time, she understood where her daughter was coming from. Having never had a family of her own, the money could make it easier for her to live out her dream. And there was her dogged determination to get back with Serge. She'd be more than willing to help him out with his funding needs just to have him near her.

"Please try to understand. I can't do this to Aunt Jan. Uncle Denis won't let me back to see her if I don't sign this release."

Lisette stood up, a hard look on her face. "Fine. Hand your money over to your stupid uncle. See how wide he opens the door to you once he's got his hands on it. You figure you can keep me here just because I'm pregnant and homeless? Think again, lady. I'll be out of here by tomorrow. And don't even try to contact me." She turned on her heel and stomped out of the room.

Nadine scrambled to make sense of her daughter's reaction and tried to protest, but the door to Lisette's bedroom slammed closed before she could even get a word out.

The ebony sky had already started to wane when Nadine flung off her blanket. Except for the five- or ten-minute periods when she had managed to doze off, sleep hadn't claimed her. Visions of her pregnant daughter disappearing into a thick wall of fog had plagued her all night. After finally reuniting with her daughter, she was about to lose her again. Over what? Her stubborn resolve to avenge an injustice done to her as a young girl? Her only means of reclaiming her dignity back then had been to cut off all contact with her family and create a new identity. But in doing that, she had hurt the few people who had cared for her. Was she about to repeat the same mistake by choosing pride over her daughter?

She might not be able to undo past wrongs, but she could try to deviate the karmic path of Grandpa's intent. He had thought to make amends by naming her as beneficiary in his will. If she claimed the inheritance she'd be condoning Grandpa's actions and the Pritcharts might hold Aunt Jan hostage. Her aunt's deteriorating health made it harder for her to oppose Uncle Denis. But she still had a mind of her own, and her husband would have a battle on his hands. It had never occurred to Nadine that he might renege on his agreement once he received the money.

By accepting the inheritance she'd get Lisette. But maybe not. Might she disappear once she got what she wanted? All these speculations were weighing down on her chest. Her daughter was right— she was trying to buy her way into people's lives.

She ran a hand through her hair. Her head pounded from lack of sleep. Why did she have to reach a decision about this? Either way, she stood to lose both Aunt Jan and Lisette.

Stay on the sidelines, Nadine.

Don't take a stand. Let the uncles claim the inheritance once the deadline expires.

But the ball was in her court. Papi had told her about the inheritance. Serge had discovered her name on that list. And Lisette was pressuring her to decide. Hiding her head in the sand wasn't possible anymore. Whatever she decided, she'd be accused of doing the wrong thing. It was up to her to act.

If she handed the inheritance money over to Lisette, a good part of it was going to end up helping Serge with his terrorist activities. Didn't that also make Lisette guilty of buying into Serge's life? Don't we all, at some point, bargain to belong? With our possessions, our sexuality, our loyalty, even our dignity—whatever means necessary to get what we want.

Grandpa Pritchart would turn over in his grave knowing his hard-earned money was being used to fund the FLQ. Claire's worst fault, in his eyes, hadn't been her stringy, overdone roasts or her pie crusts as hard as cement. He just couldn't tolerate her being a Frenchie who butchered the Queen's English. Speak white, little girl. Speak white. He'd rap Nadine's knuckles each time he detected a French accent. Even buried six feet under, he still kept an iron grip on her emotions.

She reached for her housecoat and paused to listen. Footfalls. Lisette was up. Nadine headed for the kitchen. A bulging knapsack lay by the front door. Lisette sat on a chair at the kitchen table, her body hunched over her belly, struggling to reach her shoe laces.

"Where are you off to at this hour?" Her heart in her stomach, she leaned back against the kitchen counter. Had she dozed off earlier, the girl would've been long gone before she had even hauled herself out of bed. She might never have heard from her again.

Lisette secured the knot on one shoe and stretched over to the other side for the next one. "First thing, I'll hand in my term paper and grab a quick breakfast. Straight after that, I'm off to the welfare office before the line-ups. I'm sure I can find a cheap place somewhere near the university."

"Don't... go, Lisette." Nadine steadied her breathing before continuing. "This is your home for as long as you want it. I've made up my mind. I won't be signing that release. I'll make arrangements with the trust company that's holding the money. When it goes through, we'll get it transferred to your name."

Her decision was sure to shake things up between her and the Pritcharts, yet she didn't want to lose her daughter over this. Maybe Uncle Denis' concern for Aunt Jan's health would make him reconsider his threat of barring Nadine from seeing her. He'd always been attentive to his wife's needs and might one day understand her wish to be with her daughter. Telling him about her change in plans wasn't going to be easy. She expected a harsh reaction, but her relationship with Lisette was too important.

Her head shot up and she straightened in her chair. "Is this some kind of dumb joke?"

"No, Lisette. I spent the whole night thinking this over. I'm dead serious."

"So what's the catch? No offence, but nothing comes for free. Even life has a price tag."

Nadine lowered herself into a chair. "Pretty bleak coming from someone so young."

"I don't think I've ever been young."

"Believe me, there's no catch. It's yours. If you don't take it, my uncles will."

"What about the thing with Aunt Jan?"

"I'll have to deal with that one day at a time. Papi might help me out with that."

Lisette removed her jacket. "Well... if you've thought it over. But I'll believe it when it's in my bank account." She hesitated. "It's supposed to be... a big amount. You don't have to hand it all to me."

"I don't want any part of it. You were right. He owes you. It belongs to you."

Lisette stretched her legs out and pried her shoes off with her feet, a half-grin at the corner of her mouth. "My ankles are too swollen for shoes these days and it's a bit too cold for sandals." She glanced back at Nadine, uncertainty in her eyes. "You're not just saying that, are you? It's pretty cool and all that, but if you change your mind, it'd be a real letdown."

"Don't worry. My decision is final. I wish he hadn't left me anything." Nadine brought the percolator to the sink.

"So you could hate him good?"

Nadine shrugged. "I guess that's one way of looking at it. But then again, he'd twist full circle in his grave if he knew where that money might end up." She switched the stove on and reached in the cupboard for the loaf of bread. "That kid of yours must be getting hungry by now."

Lisette smiled. "So am I. We did miss supper last night." She watched Nadine take the dishes out of the cupboard. "I didn't sleep much last night. I kept thinking you would have been better off ending the pregnancy. All I was then, and all I still am, is a hassle for everybody involved."

Nadine looked back at her over her shoulder, incredulous. "Are you kidding? I was a scared sixteen-year-old surrounded by good Catholics. It never crossed my mind. It wasn't safe or legal. In any case, I loved you from the moment your tiny feet danced inside my womb."

Lisette stared down at her hands and focused on her fingernails until the toast popped up.

Nadine turned back in time to see her wiping her eyes on the sleeve of her sweater. "You want peanut butter or jam on your toast?"

"Both." Lisette slid her chair closer to the table. "Butter, too."

Nadine switched on the radio and they listened to the news while sipping their coffee. The broadcaster announced a $150,000 reward offered by both the Canadian and Quebec governments for any information leading to the arrest of James Cross's kidnappers. Lisette's face fell. Jail terms of up to five years still applied for members of the outlawed FLQ and for those aiding the kidnappers. The two women fixed their eyes on each other in silence for a moment. It was clear to them both that if Serge was still out there helping with the funding, the promise of the hefty reward would soon cut his activities short.

CHAPTER 27

The sidewalk in front of her apartment building was strewn with autumn leaves, wet and clinging from night rain. Nadine glanced up at the dark clouds before stepping into the back of the taxi cab.

Lisette slid in beside her with as much grace as her round belly allowed. Her doctor expected her to give birth any day, advising her to rest as much as possible. She had ignored Nadine's earlier suggestion that they postpone the money transfer until after the baby was born. The Trust Company, located on the second floor of the bank building, was a mere half-hour walk from the apartment. They opted to take a cab so as not to overexert Lisette.

She looked on as her daughter fidgeted to find a comfortable position on the hard vinyl seat. Dark shadows under her eyes. Swollen ankles and feet. After struggling to force on her runners, she had tucked the laces into the inside of the shoes rather than tie them up. Nadine bit her lip, grateful that the doctor insisted on strict weekly visits. "What's the sad face for? I thought you were happy about doing this."

Lisette leaned back against the headrest. "Sure, I am. I'll be able to afford my own place at last. Serge will move in with me and the baby... that is"—she looked at the driver and lowered her voice—"after all this business is finally over." She turned to gaze out the window. "It's a pretty good day for me, but it won't be for Serge. If I told him my good news it would help make his day too."

Nadine dug her fingers into her purse. "You've heard from him?" She had hoped he'd stay away longer. They were just starting to settle into a comfortable mother-daughter relationship.

Lisette shook her head. "I guess he still can't call me. Today's the anniversary of Louis Riel's hanging. Wherever he is—unless he's locked up—he'll be burning a candle to commemorate."

Nadine relaxed the grip on her purse, relieved to hear Serge hadn't yet made any effort to contact her. The longer he stayed away, the faster Lisette would figure out she could manage without him. "No need to go on about something that happened nearly a hundred years ago. And you don't have to look for a place right away. Not till you get your strength back after the baby is born. It might be a while before it's OK for Serge to show up."

"Maybe you're right." Lisette rubbed the back of her neck. "I don't have the energy to go apartment hunting right now. This big tummy won't let me sleep for very long. I'm always twisting and turning to find the right way to lay down. It's like I'm scared I'll squish the baby." She glanced at the myriad of people strolling along both sides of the street. "Hope the toilets are close to that office. I've got to pee almost every five minutes these days."

"This is lunch-hour traffic, but we're almost there. Only four more traffic lights." She listened to the soft rustle of Lisette massaging her belly through her blouse, wishing she could reach out and feel the life stirring within her daughter's womb. But Lisette hadn't encouraged such closeness and Nadine didn't feel she had the right to impose herself.

"My doctor says he doesn't want to do any testing before the baby comes."

"Makes sense." The traffic had started to slow down. Nadine checked for signs of flashing police lights ahead. An accident could bring traffic to a standstill. "Worrying about this won't help. The baby might not inherit the problem. Sometimes these things skip a generation—not that it would make it any easier on future grand-children. Let's take it one day at a time."

"Still. I'd sure like to know what I'm up against."

"They have newer treatments now."

"They only treat the symptoms. It isn't a cure." She crossed her arms and stared outside. "It won't stop my kid from ending up deaf and blind. That old pervert should've had his prick sliced off."

"I second that... but—"

Lisette turned to face her. "Don't tell me you're sticking up for the creep."

"Never... but I'm still thankful to have you. The first time you started kicking inside of me I stopped focusing on what he had done. The love I felt for the life growing inside of me overpowered the hatred I felt for him. You became my reason to get up in the morning. When they took you away, the only thing that kept me going was knowing we'd meet up one day." She reached out to touch Lisette's shoulder but stopped in mid-air when she saw her arm flinch. She'd have to be patient. Her daughter wasn't ready—or willing—to accept her affection. "Try to relax and think of the good things in your life."

"You mean like being close to nine months pregnant, kicked out on the street and dumped by the baby's father? Have I missed any other wonderful things happening to me?"

"For starters, you're young and healthy. Grandpa's inheritance will take care of your money problems for now. Once the baby is old enough, you can go back to school. The rest will take care of itself."

"You forgot about Serge."

"Did I?" Nadine hesitated. "He'll be back in your life as soon as he can. So relax and enjoy the free time before the baby comes."

"You might have a point." Lisette leaned back and closed her eyes.

Nadine gazed at her. If only she had the courage to tell her she'd be better off without Serge—that she'd always come second to any cause he might give his heart to.

Apart from Grandma Stella's funeral, the past two weeks had gone by without a hitch. Her supper with Aunt Jan and Papi had been a success. Lisette, as well as Peaches, had enjoyed being the centre of attention all evening. For the first time in her life, Nadine felt she was part of a real family.

Lisette had decided to take a break from school and Nadine opted to skip her lunch hours, leaving work earlier to be with her. Besides being nervous about giving birth, Lisette was much less moody. At odd times, Nadine witnessed a considerate, gentle side of her daughter that hadn't been evident when they first met.

She suspected her daughter's lack of sleep wasn't all due to her pregnancy. Lisette often stared into space or scanned the daily paper for any mention of new arrests. The justice minister had insisted the FLQ remained a threat and requested that the army stay in Quebec for a longer period. The coroner's inquest into the death of Pierre Laporte, as well as the testimony of arrested members, made the front pages of the daily newspapers. A few members had made headlines when they avoided arrest by hiding behind a false wall in their closet during a police raid. The police and the army intensified their search. A letter received at a local radio station was proof that James Cross was still alive. Negotiations with the kidnappers continued. Lisette read every word written in the newspapers and stayed glued to all radio and television broadcasts.

"You won't forget to deliver that note?"

"How can I?" Nadine grinned. "You remind me every single day." She pointed at her purse between them on the seat. "I've got it ready in my bag. As soon as the doctor tells me the baby's on the way, I'll make sure it's delivered to Serge's boss at the taxi stand."

Lisette straightened, stretching her shoulders back. "He wants to be there when the time comes."

"Don't worry." Nadine noted that the traffic had slowed to a crawl and frowned. "If he gets the message, I'm sure he'll drop everything to be with you." Lisette was convinced Serge would soon come stay with her once the baby was born. But the FLQ crisis was far from over. The manhunt was still in full force. The kidnappers demanded all political prisoners be set free without penalty, safe passage to Cuba and a sizeable gold ransom. James Cross wasn't about to be released.

"I wish he was here with us to sign those papers. He's the one who convinced me to contact you after his roomies kicked me out. He made everything happen."

"I suppose." Nadine paused, pensive. "He also encouraged you to ask for the inheritance money." She pulled at her sweater, uncrossed her legs and crossed them again. The thought of Serge doing a search on her still made her blood boil. He had used her personal information to manipulate both her and her daughter. If the inheritance had come from another source, it would've been less complicated. Handing everything over to her wouldn't have happened. The money she was about to transfer was going to benefit a man who thought little of her daughter's welfare. If Serge wasn't arrested, he was about to be. A man on the run wasn't what she wanted for her daughter. But she knew it was that or nothing. When this political crisis was over, he'd find another thing to fight for. Saying anything against him would just alienate Lisette. She'd have to stick by her daughter and help her pick up the pieces as they fell.

Lisette looked daggers at her. "You make it sound like I put a gun to your head."

"Sorry. That didn't come out right. I was just thinking about how angry Uncle Denis was after I told him I had changed my mind about accepting the inheritance." She stared down at her folded hands.

"That money has always been yours. If you don't want it, it has to come to me. Peter and Denis can get lost. Aunt Jan will figure out a way to see you."

"I'm not too sure about that. Papi tells me her last checkup didn't go well. The doctor told Uncle Denis to make sure she doesn't stress too much."

"Seeing you can't upset her."

"No, but he'll take it out on her if we visit each other. Not in a physical sense, but sometimes making a fuss or constant nitpicking can do a lot of harm." She let out an impatient sigh. "This money business is putting a strain on her. I wish I could've found a way to make my decision a little easier on her."

The traffic came to a halt just as they passed the corner of Stanley Street, a few buildings away from the trust company. Lisette fidgeted in the seat. "Let's get out here and walk the rest of the way. It looks like the road is under construction up ahead. Why stay stuck here when we're only a short block away?"

Nadine stretched her neck to see beyond the stopped cars and noticed a city employee holding up a stop sign. Lisette was right. She reached in her purse for her mother's black wallet. She had opted not to place it back into her wooden box but to give it a new life. It had kept her secrets long enough.

Lisette reached down for her purse. "I need to stretch my legs before they start cramping again." The cab driver put the car into park. Lisette swung the door open and stepped onto the street. "I'll go to the other side and wait for you in front of the building."

"Watch yourself crossing Sherbrooke Street. The traffic might start up again and you'll be smack in the middle of these crazy Montreal drivers."

"Don't worry." She laughed. "Nobody's going to ram into a mother carrying her child across the street. And by the way, we're on Ste-Catherine Street. They're not as crazy here."

Her words made Nadine's heart skip a beat. Why had she said Sherbrooke Street to her? She handed the driver his fare and her head shot up. Lisette was weaving her way through the idling cars towards the Trust building, a protective hand over her belly, hair dancing in the autumn breeze.

No, Lisette. Come back.

The impatient whir of car motors. The noxious smell of gasoline. A chill surged from the back of Nadine's neck down to her knees.

Isa bolts through traffic clutching her newborn in her arms.

The nuns chase her across Sherbrooke Street, their black gowns billowing behind them.

Nadine sucked in her breath.

Get a hold of yourself.

This is Lisette.

She'll be fine. No one's chasing her.

She pushed the door open, rushed around the back of the cab and charged across the two lanes of idling cars, her stomach in turmoil.

Lisette paused on the sidewalk to massage her lower back and continued walking.

A compelling urge to touch her daughter took over Nadine. She wasn't dreaming. Lisette was safe, but she needed to be sure. She sped up, her heart drumming through her chest.

The traffic started to pick up. Lisette approached the front of the building and stopped.

Nadine stretched out her hand to touch her daughter's arm—

An alarm bell sounded from inside the building.

Pedestrians stopped to gawk from the sidewalk on both sides of the street. The door to the bank on the ground floor burst open. Two masked men dashed out, charging towards the alleyway between the buildings. The first one carried a bulging duffle bag, the second one waved a gun.

Lisette hesitated a moment. Her face fell. "That's Serge! Serge! Over here!"

Nadine grabbed her arm. "Let's get out of here."

Lisette brushed her off. "Serge! Wait! It's me!"

Serge glanced at her over his shoulder. He lost momentum for a split second, then picked up speed again.

"Wait." Lisette stumbled forward. "You don't have to do this."

Goosebumps ran down Nadine's arms. "Don't Lisette! They've got a gun."

Please! Don't take my daughter away.

The first man disappeared into the alley. Serge stopped to tear off his mask beside the mailbox in front of the building, a frantic look on his face. He made a wild gesture for Lisette to go back. "Stop Lise! You'll get hurt."

She continued towards him, tears streaming down her cheeks. "Please don't do this, Serge."

He fumbled turning towards the alley, dropped the gun and sprang to pick it up.

Nadine charged through the onlookers who had gathered to watch.

Don't take my daughter.

Not again. Please.

The mailbox blew up like fireworks, shooting slivers of red metal and bits of burnt paper into the air. The bank's glass walls and upstairs windows burst out into a thousand glistening shards.

Lisette!

Nadine rushed to her daughter's side. She lay in a pool of blood among the debris of glass and charred metal, her arms stretched towards Serge's limp body.

The acrid smell of sulphur.

The taste of lead in the air.

Sirens.

The surgeon nodded to her, turned and headed back towards the operating room. Through a blur of tears, Nadine watched him disappear. A painful tightness in her throat and a numbness in her chest immobilized her in the plastic chair in the waiting room.

He's made a terrible mistake. Lisette's strong. She just needs to come home with me. I can take care of her.

Snippets of the surgeon's words echoed in her mind:

… metal fragments from the explosion penetrated the heart area… declared dead on arrival… emergency Caesarean… able to save the child… healthy boy….

She leaned forward, resting her head in her open palms. She'd wait. The surgeon would come back and say Lisette was weak, but that she had made it out alive.

The smell of sulphur still lingered in her sweater and the noise of the explosion reverberated in her head.

A hand touched her arm.

"Papi. You came."

He took her hand. "I had just walked through the door at Janette's when you phoned."

"I hope the news didn't upset her too much." She brushed her fingers through her hair. "I didn't know who to call."

"She had to know. I made sure she was resting before I left her."

"I'm still not sure what happened. I remember Lisette running, and that loud noise before the ambulance took her away."

"I overheard the cops talking with the surgeon earlier. It was another one of those FLQ bombs. They planned the robbery during the lunch hour rush to make it harder for the cops to get there. The explosion would've given them more time to escape but one of them bumped against the mailbox and the bomb blew up too soon. One guy got away and the other one died in the blast."

She rested her head against the wall and closed her eyes. "He was the father, Papi."

"Who was?"

"The one who died. He was the father of Lisette's baby."

He stared at her a moment and frowned. "I heard the cop say that a few witnesses thought Lisette knew the robbers. He wanted to question you but the surgeon told him you were still in shock." He helped her up. "It's time to take you home now."

She shook her head and stumbled back a step. "Lisette needs me."

"She doesn't need anybody now." He put his arms around her and pulled her close. "Let her go. Nobody can hurt her now."

Nadine dug her face into his chest and let the tears fall. Papi was right. Her beautiful daughter was gone. This time there would be no return. She looked up after a few moments, pushing wet strands of hair away from her face. "The child… we can't let them take her child."

Papi reached down to grab her purse from the chair and took her arm. "The baby will have to stay here until he's been seen to. It'll be up to Social Services to do their work. I can't see them refusing your request to be his legal guardian—you are the boy's grandmother after all. And I still remember how to change a diaper. Holding a baby in my arms again will put a bit of spring in my step. Let's go see that handsome grandson of yours. We're from strong blood, you and I. We can beat this."

Nadine smoothed the wrinkles in her skirt and pulled his arm close. A faint ray of sunshine pushed its way through the heaviness in her chest.

AUTHOR'S NOTE

Although the references to historical names and events are real, this story remains, first and foremost, a work of fiction. October of 1970 was a tumultuous time for the people of Quebec. Emotions ran high, ideals soared and plummeted, yet they emerged from this with a clearer, more confident vision of themselves as a society. I made a creative effort to anchor my novel within the confines of the actual events—but in the end, my characters dictated the ebb and flow of the story.

ALSO AVAILABLE FROM BARAKA BOOKS

21 DAYS IN OCTOBER
A novel by Magali Favre
(translated by Arielle Aaronson)

TRUDEAU'S DARKEST HOUR
War Measures in Time of Peace, October 1970
Guy Bouthillier and Édouard Cloutier

A PEOPLE'S HISTORY OF QUEBEC
Jacques Lacoursière and Robin Philpot

YASMEEN HADDAD LOVES JOANASI MAQAITTIK
A Novel by Carolyn Marie Souaid

GREAT QUEBEC FICTION FROM QC FICTION*

2018 GILLER FINALIST
SONGS FOR THE COLD OF HEART
Eric Dupont
(translated by Peter McCambridge)

LIFE IN THE COURT OF MATANE
Eric Dupont
(translated by Peter McCambridge)

LISTENING FOR JUPITER
Pierre-Luc Landry
(translated by Arielle Aaronson and Madeleine Stratford)

EXPLOSIONS: MICHAEL BAY AND THE
PYROTECHNICS OF THE IMAGINATION
by Mathieu Poulin
(translated by Aleshia Jensen)

* *QC Fiction is an imprint of Baraka Books*

MIX
Paper from
responsible sources
FSC® C100212
www.fsc.org

Printed by Imprimerie Gauvin
Gatineau, Québec